ALSO BY NATALIE BARELLI

Until I Met Her (*The Emma Fern Series Book 1*)

After He Killed Me (*The Emma Fern Series Book 2*)

Missing Molly

The Loyal Wife

The Accident

The Housekeeper

Unfaithful

www.nataliebarelli.com

THE HOUSEKEEPER

A TWISTED PSYCHOLOGICAL THRILLER

NATALIE BARELLI

Furphies Press
NSW Australia
Paperback ISBN: 978-0-6482259-7-3
Large Print ISBN: 978-0-6482259-9-7
eBook ISBN: 978-0-6482259-8-0
2.1

Cover design by coverquill.com

ONE

I am sitting in a large leather armchair, a reading chair. It is so comfortable that I never want to leave it. It's square, like a hollowed-out cube, and when I rub my hands slowly along the top of the thick arms, I find it's even softer than it looks. The leather is made to look old—distressed, they'd call it. It's not really my style, but it is, without a doubt, the most comfortable chair I've ever sat in. It's also north of two thousand dollars, so you'd want it to be.

I am waiting for the guy who is going to interview me. This is his store: BHive Furniture. I don't really want to be here—except for the chair—so I am going to get it over and done with and then I am going home.

He walks in and frowns at me. I get flustered at how much I've been enjoying his furniture and stand up immediately, feeling the blush creep up my neck, and shake his hand.

"Hello, I'm Jack. What's your name again?"

"Claire."

He does a little flick of the head—just a tiny one—and smiles, like he's waiting for a punchline.

"That's my name!" I chirp in the light, singsong voice I use when I want people to like me. But I bet he thinks the name is a bad match. I know I do. It's such a pretty name, and completely wasted on me. Claires are tall and elegant. They are kind, sunny individuals with open faces and good intentions.

I am none of those things. I am about as un-Claire as you can get. I am overweight and lazy, I have bad skin, my hair is always limp no matter how many products I rub in it. Everything about me is washed out, beige. I should be called Charolais or something. Or Bovinia. Although April says I'm not overweight, just a little behind in my gym routine.

Jack releases my hand and wipes it quickly on his jacket pocket.

"Okay, well, it's this way."

Sometimes, when I take the time to think about it, which admittedly isn't often, I do think I'm strange. I didn't used to be, but circumstances have tipped me over that invisible edge. Now, everyone else seems normal and well adjusted. They have friends and go to book clubs, they live in the suburbs and watch their kids play sports on Sundays and have barbecues afterwards. They throw dinner parties and drink crisp Chardonnays out of tall stemmed glasses and laugh at each other's jokes, then remember a shared anecdote and argue about who remembered it better and the whole thing will look like an old episode of *Friends*. Meanwhile I sit in my room and eat Doritos dipped in salsa while binging on old *Revenge* seasons.

I have one friend: April. I met her through Craigslist

when I was looking for a place to live. *Large 1BR in 2BR apt SOHO All Inclusive!*

My room is nothing flashy—and I did think calling it "Large" was a stretch, no pun intended—but it's big enough for my double bed, wedged as it is between the wall and a dresser, and it has a closet with a tall mirror on the front that I've covered up with a strip of wallpaper. The window looks onto the back courtyard, which I'm not crazy about. I'd prefer the street, but at least it's quiet—unless it's winter, which is when the oil heater under my window starts to go nuts, making noises like someone has taken a sledgehammer to it, and I wake up with my heart somersaulting in my chest.

April works hard—she's an HR lawyer, or something to do with employment, and she's constantly busy. She was able to get herself a mortgage, which, to some extent, I am paying off. Sometimes she'll even accept goods instead of money, like the St. Laurent bag I stole from a store once but pretended was gifted to me in exchange for posting a pretty picture of it on social media. She didn't seem concerned by the tear where the security tag had been.

"You're an influencer?" she had asked, wide-eyed. Sometimes I worry about April. It would be too easy to take advantage of her, which seems kind of weird if her job is to make sure others are not taken advantage of. She only asked because of my social media habit, and maybe because I lie occasionally. One day when she asked me what I was doing all the time on my screen, I showed her other people's glamour shots and pretended they were mine.

The truth is, I only work two mornings a week, and on other days I spend an average of six to eight hours scrolling on my phone and trolling people on Instagram. Is that strange? I don't know. Sometimes I tell myself that I don't live in a dark basement eating mold off the walls, so I'm okay. I'm not crazy, just a little obsessive.

My addiction to Instagram started like everyone else's addiction to social media: I wanted to see what all the people I once knew were doing now. These were girls I just about grew up with. Girls who shared the same luxurious lifestyle as I had, whose parents frequented the same exclusive clubs, who even used the same shopping assistants, the same stylists, as my parents. Girls who vacationed in the same locations as we did: Telluride in winter, St. Barts in summer, the Hamptons or Cape Cod on weekends. I didn't know anyone outside that world until I got shut out of it.

After a while, stalking my old friends became more than a hobby. These women were living my life, essentially. I imagined myself in their photos, my face cut out and stuck over theirs. I imagined being married to their husbands or engaged to some hot guy who'd gone to an Ivy League university and was now running his father's hedge fund. Like them, I would have small children by now, as well as an incredibly important and glamorous job. Like them, I would be incredibly busy, what with juggling my perfect life and my perfect career and my perfect kids! But I'm not busy—unless you count my two mornings a week of dubious employment at Dr. Lowe's office—which is why I have time to stalk.

It goes without saying that my profile has nothing to do with me. Who wants a sad, pathetic twenty-four-year-old loser in their timeline? No. My fifty-five followers think that I am a "freelance publicist/eternal optimist." My posts are collages of stock photos, me-not-me in exotic places, my fake office with its *fabulous* vision board, my hot boyfriend (the back of his head anyway) in bed, crumpled sheets down his back. It's incredible how easy it is, really, and I'm not even trying, I'm only interested in stalking my old "friends."

So no, I'm not an influencer. That goes without saying. But I gave April the St. Laurent bag in exchange for a whole month's rent, so that was good.

Now I am only at this job interview because of her. I would never have bothered otherwise, but she has this thing, this *faith* in me, I call it. She insists on trying to pull me out of my misery. She's like a missionary sent to promote the power of positive thinking in a foreign country, with me being the foreign country.

"I don't want to be pulled out of it, April. I like my misery. It's taken a lot of effort to be this miserable. Why would I throw it all away?"

"You're so melodramatic. I really don't know why you put yourself down all the time. You're very pretty—just, you know, take care of your skin, put some makeup on. Go out for a walk every day, and you'll lose a few pounds in no time. You won't recognize yourself."

"You'd make an excellent motivational speaker, you know that? Or a cult leader."

"You don't know what you're missing, that's all. Get a job. Go out more. Make some friends, you'll find out."

"Whatever. Any more Doritos in the bag?"

The owner of BHive Furniture is a good friend of April's. He mentioned to her in passing that they were looking for a new admin person, someone who could check inventory, issue invoices, and—this was the clincher for her —*someone who could manage their social media marketing.* She recommended me.

"It's perfect for you. You're just the person they need."

But back to April, who had this fixation about me applying for this position.

"I already have a job, April."

"Answering the phone two mornings a week isn't exactly a career. Even if it is well paid, for what it is."

April often wonders out loud how I manage to pay $1,320 in rent on two mornings' work a week at a small medical office in midtown. Like most people, if I could not work at all, I wouldn't. But whatever money my family ever had is long gone, so when I dropped in to see my doctor for my antidepressants prescription, and his part-time receptionist had just quit because a patient had puked on her open-toe shoes, and the office had descended into total chaos, I said, "I'll tell you what, Dr. Lowe, I'll work the phones for you today and you don't charge me for the next five visits. How about it?" By the end of the day he'd offered me the job. I was the receptionist two mornings a week from eight a.m. until noon for a measly eleven dollars an hour, whereupon Sally, the other receptionist, would take over.

In my second week, I arrived twenty minutes early and walked in on him enjoying some "me" time with some big tits fetish website.

"You can feel mine if you like. One hundred bucks," I said.

I have big breasts, and they're not being used right now. I figured I may as well put them to work. That worked out fine, so much so that for a weekly hand job and a boob feel, my salary went up two hundred and fifty dollars. Like I said. I'm lazy.

Needless to say, April doesn't know that part, and when she says, "Every job has its dignity, no matter how menial," she means even answering phones.

"But you're capable of so much more, Claire! Don't you want a career? Build a life?"

"No, I don't. And I don't have any experience. Not *real* experience, not like a marketing person."

"It's not a marketing job, Claire. It's an admin position. With plenty of scope. That's the beauty of it, don't you see? You *could* become a marketing person, because you would be so good at this!"

"Well, I don't have anything to wear for a job interview anyway, so that settles it."

She gave a small shake of the head. "You always exaggerate." And before I could stop her, she was in my bedroom, pulling out clothes from my wardrobe and throwing them over her shoulder and onto the unmade bed.

"You have all these beautiful clothes, Claire. Why don't you wear any of them?"

"Because they don't fit me. I don't even know why I keep them." I took the silver evening dress from her grasp and returned it to its rightful place, balled up at the back of the closet.

In the end, she settled on a tailored blazer and matching flare pants in a small black-and-white-check pattern.

"This is mine?" I asked, taking the coat hanger from her. I didn't even recognize it. I wondered if I'd stolen that, too. "Forget it. I'll look ridiculous."

"No, you won't. You'll look great. Professional but also edgy. Influential."

Lazy people can be pretty stubborn, and I'm no exception. But no one could withstand April when she set her mind on something. In the end, it was easier to give in, even though I knew full well I had virtually no hope of getting this job.

But now that I'm here chatting with Jack and his business partner Kate, something shifts. It takes a moment to figure out what, but then it clicks. I'm having a good time. I begin to think that maybe, just maybe, I could do this.

"Tell us about yourself, Claire."

I'm hardly going to tell them the truth. But this is an admin job, and I can operate a computer and answer calls. I also have a talent for acting, which is something I've realized over the years and have used to my advantage many times. Anyway, April must have said lots of nice things about me, because Jack and Kate want to know if I have any thoughts about marketing the brand on social media. As it happens, I do. They listen, they like my ideas, they take notes and ask questions, they thank me for my suggestions, they laugh at my jokes, which always makes me bolder, and by the time I leave thirty minutes later, I am thinking that this job could be fun. Jack and Kate seem really nice, and now I wish I'd worn something else. This outfit I have on belongs on someone tall and slim, someone who oozes confidence. A proper Claire. Then, yes, sure, it screams cool, edgy. On me, it says... I don't know. Clown.

I step out of the building just as a woman walks past with her dog on a leash, some small black stocky thing that immediately barks at me, saliva dripping from its exposed fangs.

"Coco! Enough!" she shouts. Then she looks at me apologetically. "Sorry, I'm so sorry. Coco!" But she's barely strong enough to restrain that thing, and as she pulls at the leash with both hands, her pretty pink Kate Spade handbag somehow slides off her arm and onto the sidewalk. There's a split second where I consider grabbing it and making a run for it, but, notwithstanding the barking beast, I'm in a good mood.

"Don't worry about it!" I say, waving my hand. And let's face it, this is Manhattan, the Upper East Side. You can't walk five feet without getting entangled with some Italian leather leash with hand-sewn edges, a Dior-clad socialite at one end and a Tibetan mastiff at the other.

She gives me a small smile, picks up both the purse and the dog, and walks away briskly on heels so thin and sharp she could play darts with them. I reach for my cell to call April.

"How did it go?" she yells into the phone.

"Yeah, good. Where are you?"

"Subway, Delancey—one sec."

I turn onto Park Avenue, wedge the phone in the crook of my neck and fish around my bag for my MetroCard.

It's hot and sticky, the kind of day that sends everyone in and out of stores in search of air conditioning, and I'm sweating. It's also lunchtime, and therefore seriously busy. Avoiding people takes some skill.

A waft of perfume makes me look up. Something about the scent triggers a distant memory that I can't quite catch. Or maybe it's the familiar smell of money that makes my nostrils twitch.

I am right next to Alex Moreno's Salon, where everyone in this neighborhood gets their hair done. An elegant woman, midforties maybe, dressed in a light metallic ensemble and now sporting a perfectly layered shoulder-length cut, has just walked out. She's probably called Claire. I glance briefly inside without thinking, and there's a split second when the whole world stands still.

It's her.

TWO

I stop so abruptly that someone behind me knocks my shoulder, sending me stumbling forward. I turn around to glare at the young man. He takes out one earbud and makes a frustrated clicking sound with his tongue. I hiss at him, bared teeth, and he jumps back before giving me a wide berth. I retrace the last couple steps so that I am again standing in front of the salon.

"Did you hear what I said?" April's voice in my ear. I forgot I still held the phone, and yet I am clutching it so hard against my ear it hurts the cartilage.

"You're breaking up, April. I'll see you at home." I hang up.

She's here, in New York, in Alex Moreno's Salon. I'd say I couldn't believe my eyes, but I know I'm right. It's not so much that I recognize her, it's that I *feel* her. Like the sight of her brought back memories that slice right through the barely healed scars.

The door has closed again, and I don't want to go inside in case she spots me. Would she recognize me? I doubt it. Most days I don't recognize myself. I am nothing like the slim, confident girl from all those years ago. Back then I had porcelain skin and long, wavy blond hair that cascaded down my back. Now it's dull and limp. If my mother could see me now, after all the money she spent on my education and appearance, I swear she would die. But then she's already dead, so…

It should have been me, in there, getting my hair styled by Alex Moreno, stylist to the stars, and she should've been at home, wherever that was, her head hanging over a small, chipped bathroom sink, her hair sticky with Clairol Nice 'N Easy in Medium Caramel Brown, with cold rivulets of water running down her neck and wetting the back of her T-shirt.

I get close to the glass, but the frosted pattern makes it almost impossible to see inside. I move to a spot with more glass, less frost, both hands cupped around my face.

There she is. I stare at her in the large wall mirror, what is left of my heart breaking into a thousand shards. She's flicking through a magazine, eyes cast down. She's prettier than I remembered, more … woman, self-assured. Something in the way she runs one long finger over her eyebrow. Behind her a guy with a short stubble is waving a hairdryer around her head, and there's a moment when her hair flies out in all directions and she looks like Medusa.

And then she looks up. At me. Her eyes meet mine, and I stand back and hold my breath. But I'm wearing a pair of knockoff Burberry sunglasses, the large wide-framed type, and as I said, I don't look anything like the happy, naive thirteen-year-old I was then. Proving my point, she goes right back to staring at herself while her hair gets pulled and styled and straightened. She has no idea who I am.

There's an Italian bakery on the corner with a single wrought-iron chair and a small round table outside. I sprint over to it, feeling the sweat trickle under my armpits, and I don't think it's just because of the temperature. I settle myself on the chair and drop my bag on the table, scouring the contents for a crumpled Kleenex, then pat the beads of sweat off my neck. Then I put the phone back to my ear and pretend to listen, but my eyes are trained on the front door of the salon.

What is she doing in New York? She lives somewhere out in the sticks, doesn't she? Somewhere cold and wild where they cut a circle in the ice, drop a fishing line and call it lunch? She must be rolling in money if she can afford to get her hair styled at Alex Moreno's. Isn't she scared someone might recognize her? I am biting the skin around my thumbnail so hard I draw blood. Small specks of it, pearling on the edges. I'm still holding my cell against my ear when a heavyset woman with tight black curls and a white apron comes out of the bakery with both hands on her waist and her head tilted at an angry angle. "Can I help you?" she snaps.

No, you can't. Get lost.

I'm not looking at the hair salon anymore. I point at the phone as if that explains everything, because I'm not going to waste five bucks on an overrated espresso. Not even if it's made with Icelandic glacial water and then filtered again for extra purity. I'm about to tell the woman that my fiancé has been in a car accident and I'm trying to find out which hospital they took him to, when *she* walks right past me.

She doesn't notice me, doesn't even throw a sideways glance in my direction. She readjusts the strap of her

Chanel monogrammed bag on her shoulder, and I catch the diamond-and-platinum wedding band on her finger.

"No, thank you," I say.

I throw my phone back into my bag and follow her.

I don't know where we're going or how long it's going to take, but I am right behind her anyway. I keep back a few paces, enough to keep track of her but not so much that I'd fall over her if she stopped abruptly. She looks so pretty, so confident, with her summer skirt flowing left and right in time with her brisk step. She's wearing a light denim jacket that on her manages to look elegant and cool, with her wavy brown hair down to her shoulders and parted in the center. Like her skirt, her hair bounces prettily with every step while I am biting down on my own teeth and digging nails into my palms.

She crosses to the other side of Madison Avenue and stops abruptly outside Ralph Lauren, and I feel exposed. If she turned around right now, she'd see me sticking out like a living statue on the street corner. I fish around my bag for my cell, pull it out and pretend to check the screen, but all the time I have my eye on her. She pushes her sunglasses— real brand ones, I bet, not some knockoff pair she found on the bus—to the top of her head.

As it happened, there is a text. From April. *Everything ok?* it reads. But she's on the move again. She flicks her wrist, and I figure she must be running late because she takes off faster. I sure hope she doesn't hail a cab, but if she does, I am ready, with my cell in hand, to snap the license plate so that later I could call in and spin a story that would hand over the destination.

There's a French pâtisserie on the next corner. I know

it well, and normally I'd stop and get myself a macaron because eating is what I do, but not this time. My stomach is clenched shut.

Now we are walking along Central Park, and I am sweating profusely. I knew I should have worn a skirt in this weather, but I'm not a skirt person, not with *this* body, and now the fabric is chafing my skin on the inside of my thighs.

She turns onto East Sixty-Third and I cross to the other side before doing the same, as if going places of my own. She stops outside one of the nicest townhouses on this block, a brick brownstone, more red ocher than its neighbors, with a large terrace on the top floor. Then, abruptly, the front door opens and swallows her inside.

I used to live two blocks from here. Everything around here is familiar to me because it is part of my childhood, which is why I never, ever come here if I can help it. I have not been above Thirty-Fourth Street for years.

I wait a few minutes in case she comes out again, and then I cross the street and scan the front door. There's no plaque, nothing to indicate who she's seeing inside. I press my palm against the stone, its granite texture digging into the soft pads of my hand. I keep pushing until it hurts.

"Are you all right?" a voice asks behind me. I turn around.

"Yes, thank you," I say to the elderly woman in my sweetest voice. She nods briskly and walks on.

I had a life once, a life nicer than most. The kind of life you have when you live in a brownstone just like this one.

Then Hannah Wilson showed up and took it away from me.

. . .

I think of Hannah Wilson just about every day. Some days I try really hard *not* to think about her, which just makes it worse. Hannah Wilson is like a scab on my heart. I pick at the events of ten years ago, usually without thinking. It's just how things are. Sometimes I imagine a different outcome, one where we find out what she's really like before it's too late. In that fantasy, the whole world finds out how evil she is, how wronged our family was. The world feels sorry for us, and she goes to jail. But it just makes me more angry, and within minutes into the fantasy, my chest is throbbing with indignation anyway.

April is already there when I get home that night. She's never home before seven. "Is it that late already?" I ask, fake-surprised like a spouse who promised to be home in time for dinner but instead has spent the last hour at the bar having just one more for the road.

"You got the job," she says, ignoring my question. She's standing at the sink, her back to me, turning faucets on and off again and dropping this morning's breakfast dishes in the rack.

"How do you know?"

"They couldn't reach you, so they called me. Where were you all day?"

"Huh, I got the job. Wow." I pull out a chair and sit down heavily. I'm surprised. And flattered, too. I think that if I hadn't seen Hannah, I might have taken it. Strange to think about that, considering all the time I've spent actively avoiding getting a real job.

She turns around. "Are you pleased?"

"I'm not going to take it, April."

"Why the hell not?"

15

Because there's no way I can go to work, move on with my life. Not now that she's back.

"It's not for me. Sorry." I try to smile, but she shakes her head and turns back to the sink. I fill the void by telling her how sorry I am and that I appreciate what she's trying to do.

"You're a good person, April. And a good friend."

"Next time, wash your own dishes. I'm not your maid." We don't speak after that. She does what she always does—changes into her tracksuit pants and T-shirt, slips on her bed socks and drops herself on the couch to watch TV. At some point she'll get up and heat up a bowl of noodles or one of those low-fat meals she keeps in the freezer. I retreat to my room, where my stash of chips and candy bars awaits, then stay up half the night looking for Hannah on social media.

There are lots of Hannah Wilsons in the world, but the one I'm after doesn't like social media, which is not surprising, considering. But a few years ago, I found out she part-owned a flower store in Canada called 99 Petals. It was a public page, and there was a photo of her and another woman standing outside the storefront. Her name was in the caption, but I would have recognized her immediately anyway. It made me bite the inside of my cheek so hard it hurt to eat after that. She looked happy, which was the worst part.

At first I assumed she worked there, but after reading the post—something about celebrating one year of the store—I realized she part-owned it with the other woman in the photo. Just knowing that she'd moved on like that, that she had a good life, made me want to bite someone.

I called the store and ordered thousands of dollars' worth of flowers. I was very convincing; it was for a celebration at a megachurch nearby, I'd said. Our usual florist was unable to oblige. I gave the real name and address, and even paid a hundred-dollar deposit. Then I waited until the day itself, when I figured they would have prepared all the arrangements, and I reported my credit card stolen. I told my bank I hadn't ordered flowers from Toronto, why would I? I don't know anyone there. Then I added, "It's funny, though, because a friend of mine got their card charged without their knowledge, for thousands of dollars' worth of flowers. I'm pretty sure it was the same place. Maybe you should get your fraud department onto them. Sounds like a front for a shady business."

I don't know if they lost thousands of dollars' worth of flowers in the end, or if the bank investigated their business for fraud, but I like to think both are true.

Anyway, I didn't find her last night. Nothing on Facebook or Twitter. I pored over Instagram, but I found nothing recent. Just a couple of shots from long ago on that flower store account.

After that, I tried to sleep but only managed snatches of moments with my eyes closed and the start of dreams of falling.

THREE

This morning, April has left already without saying good-bye. I make myself some breakfast, then I call Alex Moreno's and tell them I am calling on behalf of Hannah Wilson.

"Who?" they say.

"Hannah—" I stop myself. She's not Wilson anymore. I saw the wedding ring, and the engagement ring with a stone the size of a small planet. "Hannah. She was there yesterday, late morning?"

"Oh, you mean Mrs. Carter?"

Mrs. Carter. Okay, there are lots of Carters out there, but that's a start.

"Sorry, we're old friends," I say, gagging inside. "I've known her for so long under her maiden name, Wilson, I always forget to call her by her married name!" I laugh, and she does too, because she has excellent customer service skills.

"I'm calling on the off chance you found her glasses case? It's pearl-colored, with a gold rim. She thought she might have left it there."

She'll check immediately, she says, if I could hold? Of course. Thank you. There's a bit of noise and talking, but muffled, as if she has her hand over the phone. Then she comes back and she is very sorry but no such case has been found. Does Mrs. Carter believe she left it at the salon?

"She's not sure, it was just a thought. Oh well, if you happen to find it, could you have it delivered back to Mrs. Carter?"

There's a tiny intake of breath, understandably. After all, what's stopping Mrs. Carter from coming back to pick it up herself? And if it's not there now, why would it turn up later? But again, top-notch customer service skills. I'm going to leave a review on Yelp as soon as I hang up.

"Of course. We'd be happy to," she says.

"You have the address?"

"One moment." I hear fingers on keyboard and fear she's going to ask me to spell it out. I'm thinking of ending the call—*Oops, sorry, going through a tunnel, can't hear you*—when she reels off the exact address and asks, "Is that right?" But my heart drops and I hang up abruptly after all. It's the same building I saw her walk into. That address, it has to be one of the most expensive properties in Manhattan. And she *lives* there? I bite on my index finger until I almost bleed, leaving small purple teeth marks in a crescent shape. Then I bang my fist on the kitchen table, almost knocking the mug over. I pick it up and throw it hard in the general direction of the sink, but it doesn't even break.

An hour later I am walking slowly past the building, glancing at the heavy oak door before continuing to the end of the block. I scout out both sides of the street, then turn the corner and lean back against an iron fence. I don't even have a plan, because I am stupid. I can't keep walking up and down the street; I'd get arrested before I had the time to say *Hannah Wilson, remember her?* But there is no café, no park, nowhere for me to sit idly and wait.

What there is, however, is a bar. Right across the road. It's one of those exclusive establishments, furnished with leather and mahogany and where you might sip a single-malt in the afternoon. Not my usual haunt, but it will be open for lunch and it has a large window made up of little squares of glass bordered by a timber frame. I still have two hours to kill before it opens, so I walk over to Central Park—which is literally right there—and find an empty bench. If Hannah lives in that building, then I am in no rush.

I pull out my cell phone and open Instagram. Then, my chest heavy with apprehension, I search for Mrs. Hannah Carter, and boom—her face jumps out at me, beautiful and happy, and it hurts so much that I have to put the phone facedown on my lap for a moment. But I have to know, so I look again, my stomach clenching a little more with every exquisite photo.

Hannah Carter getting married at the Church of the Heavenly Rest, flowers everywhere. Mrs. Carter, a vision in white tulle and small pink buds. Mrs. Carter standing outside the church with confetti in her hair, laughing at something her husband had said. Mr. Carter with one arm encircling his wife's waist and the other lifting a glass of champagne, on a terrace at dusk. Then Mrs. Carter on her honeymoon in a picturesque small town in Provence, taking a selfie with green vineyards behind. Another one with the two of them, on a terrace overlooking the Eiffel Tower. In every picture, he looks like he can't believe his luck, and she beams at the camera. I bite my knuckle again so hard I know it will leave a bruise.

Fuck you, Mrs. Carter. How did she do it? How did she ensnare him? She can afford a wedding in Manhattan and a honeymoon in France while I have to flash my boobs just to make the rent? I've been hustling a living since my folks died, stealing cash from relatives and wiping tables. No one was offering to marry me at two hundred bucks a head for a hundred-person guest list, linen and decorations not included.

I lean forward, press the heel of my hand against my forehead and will myself to calm down. I tell myself that now that I've found her again, maybe I can do something about it. It would be like a project. It would distract me. Within minutes, my pulse has returned to a manageable rate and I am breathing normally again.

I take another look at the screen. He's not what I expected, Mr. Harvey Carter, which means he's exactly what I expected. He's not particularly good looking, certainly nothing like her. He must be in his late forties, early fifties. He wears thick-rimmed glasses, and his head is bald on top. He has a round face, and in every photo he is smiling. He reminds me of my father. My pulse again gets away from me, and I look up to take a breath—and there she is, walking right past me, only a few feet away. She must have just turned off her street.

I shove my cell back in my bag and follow her down Fifth Avenue. She stops at a building two blocks away, and I wait until she's gone inside to check the copper plaque beside the door. *Dr. Malone. MD, Psychiatrist.* That cheers me up. Could the marriage already be on the rocks? Has life turned out to be harder than she thought? I take a photo on my cell and upload it to my fake Instagram account.

#somepeopleareevil #somepeoplearesick #somepeopleareboth

I get a handful of comments immediately, mostly because it's so cryptic and I never post stuff like that.

#allwillberevealed.

I grab a bagel with cream cheese from a deli across the street and eat it on the walk back, without waiting for her. I kill time, an hour or so, by going in and out of fashion stores and trying things on I have no hope of buying. Then I go to the bar, where I settle by the window and order a cup of coffee. Hannah returns and goes back inside, but not much happens after that, and by the third cup, the pretty waitress asks me if I'm waiting for someone. She feels sorry for me, I can tell. She thinks I've been stood up, but that I just can't see it, like I can't give up and I'm going to wait as long as it takes because I know, deep down, that he's coming for me.

"No, it's just me," I tell her, crushing her little fantasy into a pile of dust.

"Oh," she says, her pretty mouth shaping like a perfect circle, like she's about to blow a ring of smoke. She gives me a quick smile and leaves. At dusk, the lights come on in Hannah's house. The French doors upstairs are open onto the stone terrace, and I see a glimpse of an enormous glass chandelier.

The next day, I take my place again at the window and notice the staff exchange glances. It's a different waiter, a young man with a cowlick and very thin fingers.

"Will someone be joining you?" he asks.

I smile. "No." But I'm ready for this question. "You

don't mind, do you? I'm writing a screenplay—" I brandish a notepad and a pen.

One side of his mouth rises in the beginning of a smile. "Really? For a movie?"

"Not quite."

I catch a sliver of condescension in the way he raises his chin. I've just confirmed to him that I am a nobody, one of a million in this city who thinks she's going to send her screenplay to Martin Scorsese and win an Oscar.

"It's for Netflix," I say. "A series. We've only sold the first season at this stage, but we're hopeful." I smile.

Now he's interested, and we are back on track, me with my pen and a friendly waiter.

"Really? Can I ask what it's about?"

It's about a horrible person who gets her comeuppance.

"It's a true crime story," I reply sweetly. "About a woman who cons married men and kills them. But it's impossible to work at home, you know, with all the noise. We're doing renovations, all five bathrooms. Nightmare. Anyway, the network has given me a strict deadline, and since I'm also scouting for filming locations... this place is nice, by the way. I'll bring it up at the next production meeting—you never know."

"Wow, that'd be awesome." He hurries back to the bar, where his colleagues are drying glasses, and the three of them huddle in whispers, throwing the occasional side glance in my direction. They leave me alone after that because, you know, I have to work. But then Hannah's door opens and she comes out with a stroller, and I'm so shocked that I knock the coffee cup over. I throw some coins on the table and follow her to the park, where she sits on a bench and pulls out a book. Then she changes her mind, taking a swaddled baby out and into her arms, but I can't bear to watch and go home early.

I spend the next few days in the bar, at my window, as I've come to think of it, on high alert, my neck stretched, my eyes trained on the street, which is completely unlike me. I'm usually more sloth than meerkat. I never eat lunch there because, well, prices, but I still have consumed endless cups of tea or coffee, and I don't have any money to spare. Which means I'm going to be late on my rent this month and April won't be pleased, considering I've turned down the job. And yet, I feel energized. Elated. I have a purpose. At Dr. Lowe's office, people comment on how much happier I look. Dr. Lowe says my hand jobs are even more enthusiastic than usual, and he adds fifty bucks onto my usual fee because of it. And Mrs. Usher, who comes every other day for her allergies—and other imaginary ailments, because Dr. Lowe always tells her she's perfectly healthy and yet she returns, undeterred—comments on it.

"There's something different about you," she says, frowning.

"There is? I don't know what you're talking about."

"You have a boyfriend, that's what it is."

I laugh, and I swear Dr. Lowe's head snaps so fast I think it might do a full rotation.

And so, over the next ten days, whenever I am not manning the phones for Dr. Lowe, I am at the bar. I don't even take off my coat in case she leaves her house and I have to run outside. It kind of helps in a way; the staff think I must be an artist because I'm eccentric.

One time I followed her to Bergdorf Goodman, where I pretended to browse while watching her try on a pair of Jimmy Choo shoes. Then she took a Valentino dress that the saleswoman had pushed on to her into the changing rooms, and I considered trying on a Donna Karan silk shirt, just so I could join her—*Excuse me, can I get your opinion? Does it make me look fat?*

In the end, she bought a very ordinary black lacy number off the rack. Not even from the designer section. I was understandably confused, but then I understood. It's her husband's money—she's pretending to be *reluctant*, like she didn't marry him because of it. Like she really *loves* him. He'll think that's so sweet, and when he trusts her completely with *his* money, she'll pounce and take him to the cleaners.

Slow clap, Mrs. Carter. Well played.

Then some days I don't see her at all. I only saw her husband once because he usually takes the car, a Bentley no less—they have a single-car garage on the lower level—and I recognized his face.

Other than obvious deliveries and couriers, there's only one other person who comes and goes. A woman, older than Hannah, in her forties, maybe. She's very thin, very straight-backed like she trained in the Army. I suspect she's part of the staff—something about the way she moves, the way she hurries whenever she walks in or out. Especially out.

Sometimes Hannah takes a cab. She has a habit of walking to Park Avenue to catch one, so I'd follow her for nothing and then come back to the bar. I told the waiter once it's because we're shooting around here and it's important to have a photo; it helps me complete the scene. It all sounds so farfetched I keep waiting for one of them to call the authorities or the psych ward. *You guys missing anyone?* But this is Manhattan, so anything goes, I guess.

So far, she's gone back to her shrink twice. I wonder why, so I call to make an appointment for myself.

"Dr. Malone has an opening on the fifth of December at ten thirty."

"December? But that's months away."

"We're very busy, yes."

She says this smugly, the receptionist. Like it's a good thing. I want to point out that being busy, for a psychiatrist, means she's not very good. I almost ask if they are repeat customers, those people hogging the calendar for months on end. Do you have a ten-visit discount pack? What does that say about your success rate, then? Asking for myself; I'm pretty fucked up too.

"Would you like to take the appointment?"

"Yes, please."

"The first session is two hundred and seventy dollars," the smug receptionist says. I let out a snort, then pretend to cough. "Is that all right with you?" she adds.

"Yes, that's fine."

"There's a fifty percent fee if you cancel less than seven days before your appointment."

I have no intention of keeping it. Not at that price. I swap two digits in my Visa card number and give a fake cell number.

FOUR

It was Olivia Cortez who first brought up with my mother the possibility of Hannah working for us. Our regular nanny, whose name I can't remember, was leaving to get married and my mother hadn't as of yet found a replacement.

In some kind of twisted irony, that summer was one of the best of my life. My best friend, Philippa, and I spent that month at a horseback-riding camp together. My horse was called Button, a gorgeous creature, almost white, with a brown diamond shape above her nose. I can still remember the feel of her damp, cold nose against my cheek, how she would lift her head up when she'd see me and nuzzle me when I'd get close.

I'd only been there for a few days when someone called out to me. Your mother's on the phone, they said. After ten minutes of catching up on news, she said, "And we found a nanny for John, did I tell you?"

"You did? That's nice," I said, biting into a red apple, turning to gaze out the window, my mind already disconnecting from the conversation. My mother, who could talk incessantly in those days, proceeded to tell me a convoluted story whereby her friend Olivia Cortez had a cousin in Canada who was married to someone or other, and at the end of that human chain was "a young Canadian woman who wants to come to New York for the summer. She's looking for a position as a nanny. I'm told she's charming and great with children. Olivia said she wants to study art and that's why she wants to come to New York."

I think of this conversation sometimes, about how innocuous it was on the surface. And yet this was the moment that began the sequence of events that would end with the death of both my parents. It still eats me up at night that I didn't recognize it. I imagine myself back there, that day on the phone—"But what do you know about this girl, Mom? Has she done this work before? Does she have references? Can you even trust her?"

My mother was the brightest light of my life. She was beautiful, caring, smart. She wanted me to become anything I set my mind to. She said I could be the first female president of the United States if I wanted to. Not because of my grades, which were okay, but because *girls* can do anything. *Anything you want!* she'd say. I was sent to Groton School in Massachusetts, and I loved every minute of it. I'd just finished my freshman year by the time Hannah came into our lives.

In the end, my mother said yes to Olivia Cortez because if my mother could help someone, she did. She was generous like that, and it's what killed her. But she was looking for a nanny, and this young woman who wanted to come and spend a summer in New York was finding it diffi-cult to find a position. In her mind she was confident that Hannah Wilson would do a fine job. But more than that. You said something to my mother like *wants to better herself, would love to spend time at MoMA* or whatever, and my mother was all over it. So she welcomed Hannah Wilson into our home and into our lives, and we all lived bitterly ever after.

I saw Olivia Cortez once, years later, in a shopping mall of all places. I spat in her face. She had no idea who I was.

It's now in the middle of the second week, and the novelty is starting to wear off. It's all very well following her around the place, watching her push a stroller or eat a Greek salad at Bel Ami, but it's not like I'm *achieving* anything. I have a bunch of photos, but the best I got was her picking her nose, so I only uploaded that one. *#gross*. I'm drinking so much tea and coffee, I'm beginning to vibrate. And I'm peeing all day. On top of that, I canceled work once because I was afraid she might go somewhere significant, and I'd miss out on finding out something about her. I suffer from Hannah Carter FOMO.

"I'm sick," I told Dr. Lowe, without a hint of irony. "I've got the flu, I think." I coughed a few times.

He sighed into the phone. "You'll come in on Monday?"

"Yes," I replied. Because I have superpowers and I know exactly when I'll be well again.

In the end, I didn't find anything out on that day. And now, finally, something happens. That same woman, the straight-backed one, walks out of Hannah's building, but this time she stops and rummages through a large black handbag hanging on her arm. She pulls out … what is it? A tissue, I think. It takes me a moment to realize that … she's crying?

I sprint to the top step outside the bar, but I'm not fast

enough and there's a man talking to her. He has one hand on her shoulder, like he's consoling her. I squint at them from my side of the street and wrap my coat tighter around me.

"Ms. Petersen?"

I turn around. "Yes?"

Bill, the bartender, holds out a takeout paper cup. "Your espresso. You only just ordered it, I thought…"

"Oh, thank you, that's great."

I take it from him and turn back. The man is still talking to her, one hand on her elbow. I want to run across the street and insert myself between them, but instead I act cool, distracted, as I pull out my cell and pretend to read something on my screen, my head down, like everyone else in this town. By the time I get to the other side, I am so involved in what I'm reading that I quote, accidentally, end quote, bump into the back of her, spilling some of my coffee onto the sleeve of her coat.

"Oh God. I'm sorry! I didn't see you—"

The guy glares at me, which is fine. I'm good at glaring. I glare back.

"Here, let me," I say, taking a tissue from her and dabbing it gently at the sleeve. "I'm really sorry."

"That's all right," she says with a slight lisp on the *s*. "No harm done."

I pat her on the part of her arm that doesn't have any coffee dripping from it. "I'll pay for the cleaning, of course," I say.

The man wants to leave, I can sense it, but he's also concerned about her. I narrow my eyes at him. "Do we know you?" I ask, my tone dripping with suspicion. I make it sound like *he's* the interloper.

He recoils in surprise and shakes his head. "No. Sorry."

"Well, then, I'll take it from here," I say, and I'm pleased that he doesn't need to be told twice.

I turn back to the woman and put my hand on her arm. "You're sure you're okay? I didn't hurt you, did I?" She starts to say something, but then her face collapses and she bursts into tears.

"What happened?" I ask softly. "What's made you so upset?"

She opens her mouth, distorting her face, but still doesn't reply.

"Which way are you going?" I ask gently.

She shakes her head. "I—I don't know." I feel my shoulders drop. I'm beginning to think that she's not the staff, she's an elderly relative with a memory problem.

She reminds me of a woman I met once, waiting for my parents outside the Lincoln Center. She must have been at least seventy, beautifully dressed, her fingers nervously clutching at large pearls on her neck. She came up to me because she needed my help. Or so she said.

"Of course," I replied. I was normal then. Kind, even. She held out a page torn out of those old desk calendars. On it, scribbled in pencil, was a date and a time.

"Do you know what this is?" she asked.

"Hum, no, sorry."

She looked on the verge of tears. "It's just that … I don't remember," she said.

I figured she had some kind of memory lapse, and I pointed to the phone number scribbled under the date and time. "Maybe you should call this number. They might be able to tell you something."

That seemed to confuse her again, so I handed over my

cell—a black flip phone that back then was the coolest thing ever. "Try it, call them now. See what they say." I even punched the numbers in for her. She grabbed it and took off across the Plaza with my cell phone still in her dried-up, bony fingers.

I stood there frozen, then shook myself awake and took off after her. "Excuse me? You've got my phone!" But she'd already turned the corner onto Amsterdam Avenue, and next thing I knew she was getting onto the M11. When the bus drove past me, I raised my arms to get her attention, but she looked straight ahead. I couldn't work out whether she was crazy, or whether this was some elaborate scam to steal my phone. But I saw her again once, months later. I guess she had a thing for the performing arts, because my mother and I were standing outside the Belasco Theatre on Broadway when she approached us, still with her scribbled torn-off piece of paper. She asked my mother for help, and I tugged at my mother's sleeve. "Don't," I said. Then I positioned myself in front of the woman and extended my hand. "Can I have my phone back?"

I could tell from the angry look in her eyes that she knew she'd been caught out. But my mother said my name, in a shocked voice.

"Claire! What's gotten into you?"

I told her I'd explain later, but when I turned back the woman had disappeared through the crowd. Then my mother scolded me for being rude and scaring *that poor woman away*.

"No, Mom. She was about to steal your Blackberry. Remember how I told you an old woman stole my phone?"

"Don't be ridiculous, Claire. That had nothing to do with this."

In my mother's mind, the old woman who had taken my phone was poor and homeless and desperate, and probably suffering from dementia. She certainly didn't wear a string of pearls and a nice tailored jacket.

I take another look now at the woman in front of me, but it's definitely not the same woman, not even remotely. And the other one would have to be eighty or ninety years old by now, surely, whereas this woman is in her fifties. Still, this is New York. You can't be too careful.

"She fired me," she says at last, an astonished look on her face, like she can't quite believe it herself.

That makes my pulse bounce with the possibilities. "Can I take you somewhere?" I ask, which makes no sense since I don't have a car and I sure can't afford cab fare anywhere.

Her chin wobbles. "I have nowhere to go," she says. "Nowhere at all."

"Okay, well, let me think." And for a crazy moment I consider bringing her home with me; then I run through the various scenarios that would entail. Would she end up sleeping on the couch? Would she turn into that dreaded New York curse: the guest that wouldn't leave? Would I have to pay extra rent for her?

"Let me take you for a drink. My treat. Then you can decide what to do."

FIVE

I didn't want to take her to my stake-out establishment, so we walk together quickly to the bar at the Plaza Hotel two blocks away, me holding her firmly by the elbow, just in case she changes her mind.

"They make the best martinis," I say, as if I went there all the time. Inside, I maneuver her toward the big red velvet armchairs and press a menu into her hands. She selects a Taittinger Champagne & Domaine de Canton Liqueur, while I desperately scan the page for the cheapest drink, then throw caution to the wind and get a martini.

"This is so nice," she says, taking her phone out and setting it down on the table.

"Isn't it? I love this place," I reply and wave at a complete stranger sitting at a distant table, muttering, "Oh look, it's Joanna Dubois," under my breath. I wait until the waiter has returned with our drinks and a complimentary bowl of green olives, then turn to her earnestly.

"So tell me, Diane. It's Diane, isn't it? Okay, good. So tell me, who fired you?"

"I work for the Carters. Mrs. Carter fired me."

Bingo! I feel like I'd scratched off a lottery ticket and won fifty bucks. "That's just … terrible. And what did you do for this Mrs. Carter?"

She knocks back her glass, and when she puts it down again, it's empty. I do the same and quickly signal the waiter for another round, already wincing at the damage this evening is going to do to my Visa card.

"I am—was—the housekeeper in the Carter household."

I nod. The waiter puts down our drinks in front of us. My heart is racing as I hand him my credit card. "Keep it, for the tab," I say, then wait until he's gone and whisper, "You were the housekeeper?"

Diane nods and this time only takes a sip, thank God, leaving the rim with a pale, sticky imprint of her lips.

"I was. All the way back to the first Mrs. Carter."

"There was a first Mrs. Carter?"

"Yes, but they got divorced. Mr. Carter kept me on, which was nice."

"What's the second Mrs. Carter like? Other than a complete and utter bitch, obviously," I laugh. But she flinches and I quickly add, "For firing you, that's what I meant."

She nods. "She's different. Very different from the first. I mean, the first Mrs. Carter, she had style. She was a real lady. And she was really busy, all the time, because she worked so hard. The second Mrs. Carter? She doesn't work, at all, so I don't know why she's tired all the time."

"Right, right, good question. Why is she tired all the time?"

She makes a face, like she's reluctantly admitting to something. "She's got the baby."

"Right."

"I've never looked after children, let alone babies. I don't know what to do! I said to her once, you should hire a full-time nanny, since you're so tired all the time. She looked at me like I'd suggested she send Mia to the moon."

I nod. "Like Laika the dog."

"Like who?"

"Never mind. Keep going."

She shrugs. "That's it."

"Really? Okay, well, what about Mr. Carter? What's he like?"

"Very nice. He's an old-fashioned gentleman. Mr. Carter is always calm, always kind, very patient with little Mia, too. Although he works hard, so he's not at home much. He's a partner in a law firm. His first wife was a lawyer too."

I think back to the photos of their wedding. A nice, rich guy like that? He would have been the ideal mark for Hannah. He never stood a chance.

"What's the house like? Must be something, huh?"

"Beautiful." She dabs at her eyes again. "You should see Mr. Carter's art collection. It's like a museum, only more beautiful. I took very good care of his art pieces. I was very particular with them. I know he appreciated it."

"Art collection?"

"Big colorful paintings, sculptures, and the antiques. Furniture like you've never seen. It's a beautiful place, the Carters'. But she's not from this world. You can see that a mile off. And I'm not used to babies, but I did my best, and I enjoyed it. I like little Mia. She's sweet as pie. But I have work to do, you know?"

"Of course you do. If I may, why did she fire you?"

She twirls her glass, which is empty again, and I take the hint. I'm biting my bottom lip as I signal the waiter for yet another round. At this point I don't even know if my card will cover the bill.

Small red circles grow on her cheeks. She wipes her nose with her sleeve. I put my hand on her arm. "I was only trying to help her," she says. "To explain how to behave in such company, how to run a house like that, that sort of thing. Like I said, she's not the first Mrs. Carter, and that's the truth. She just doesn't have that kind of class, you know?"

I do know, I assure her. Still, I shudder at the idea of being lectured by the staff.

"But why did she fire you?"

"I may have overdone it, I suppose." By now she's talking like someone who is not used to drinking, not so much because she's slurring her words, although there's that, but because she's talking in circles. Like what a nice man Mr. Carter is, and how tired Mrs. Carter is. How the second Mrs. Carter is not like the first Mrs. Carter. At one stage she goes to the bathroom, and I slip her phone discreetly onto my lap. It's a Nokia, one of those old-style ones that only makes phone calls and sends texts and not a lot more. There's no passcode required, so I scroll through her minimal contact list to the Carters, then take a photo of the number with my own cell.

She returns from the bathroom and drops her face in her hands. "What am I going to do?" she wails.

I'm not buying the story about why she was fired. It's too vague, for one thing. But I don't think I'm going to get any more out of her.

"I'm so sorry. Look, I don't know this Mrs. Carter from Adam, but I can see what a…" I search for the right words. "Reliable woman you are. You present extremely well, you're obviously someone who works hard and is prepared to go the extra mile. You're clearly not someone who should be fired."

I pull out a bar of chocolate from my bag, break it into pieces while it's still in the wrapper and open it with my teeth. She takes the piece I offer her.

"Maybe we should go now," I say. I don't dare ask where she'll go. I'm already constructing excuses as to why she can't come with me when she says, "I better call my sister. I'll go stay with her, in Queens. She's recovering from pneumonia, so she'll be glad for the company—and the help, I'm sure."

"Oh, good. Good."

"I think I should go and apologize to Mrs. Carter, what do you think? Maybe if I explained to her that I didn't mean anything by it. And that I can help more with little Mia, too." She nods repeatedly, her eyebrows raised like she's prompting me to agree.

"Look, Diane, I'm very sorry this has happened. I think you should go to your sister's and have a few days off. Put your feet up. Watch Netflix. Sometimes, the Lord sends these challenges to us for a reason. Maybe there's a better position right around the corner. In fact, I'm sure there is. Give it a chance. Give your future a chance, Diane."

She looks startled, and I don't know what I've said wrong. Then she reaches for her coat on the seat next to her.

"Thank you… Claire, you've been very kind."

She's getting up already, and I ask her to wait while I signal for the bill, which my card manages to cover, incredibly. It's raining, and I pull the hood of my raincoat up over my head. "Shall we walk to the subway together?"

She shakes her head. I get the feeling she wants me gone, but I follow her anyway because I can tell she's going back there. I just know it and it's making me angry. She's going to ask for her job back. She's going to say she is *so very sorry, Mrs. Carter*, and worm her way back in, but I can't let that happen. There's a vacancy in the Carters' residence now, and I want to keep it that way.

She stands outside their building on the other side of the street. Upstairs, the drapes move and Hannah's face is at the window.

I step back behind Diane and whisper in her ear. "Oh, that's her, is it? I know her. Her name is Hannah. She hates you, she told me. She can't stand you and she's been looking for a way to get rid of you."

I leave her there, looking like that wet rat a few feet away bobbing in the storm sewer, except that one is dead, so not the same exactly. That one looks like it's been run over by a bus before getting stuck against the stormwater drain.

SIX

It's the next day, not a cloud in the sky, and the air feels fresh after all the rain last night. I've only just taken my seat at the bar when Hannah's door opens and she appears with her baby in her arms. With her is an older woman with short white hair and masses of jewelry that I recognize from the wedding photos as Harvey's mother, Patsy. She's wearing a light beige raincoat, Burberry probably, and dark brown pants. She kisses Hannah on the cheek before adjusting her sunglasses, then walks away briskly.

Hannah stands there, bouncing Mia on the spot for a moment, then takes a backward step before reappearing with something in her right hand.

And then I see the baby's hands in the air. She's leaning forward in Hannah's arms, toward the mailbox that hangs to the side of the door. Her little chubby fingers open and close, trying to grasp the edge of a white envelope. I am frozen, my coffee cup halfway to my mouth, waiting for what is coming next. My heart starts to beat really fast as I watch Hannah put the key in and slide her hand under the flap. Part of me doesn't want to look; the other part would give anything to see the expression on her face, but she's a little bit too far away for that.

There's a split second where she doesn't move, and then she does this kind of dance, and it's the funniest thing I've seen in a long time. It's like she's tap-dancing, bouncing around the dead, still-wet, still-sticky-with-blood, flat-as-a-pancake rat that I squeezed into the box last night. She's shaking her hand like crazy, making little jumps on the spot. Jesus. Give her a cane and a top hat and put her on the stage, that woman is comedy gold. I lean forward to see what Harvey's mother is doing, but she's almost at the end of the street by now. She doesn't turn around, not even when Mia starts to wail.

"That must be a really funny scene you're writing," the waiter says from the next table, and I realize I've been laughing out loud the entire time.

Not wanting to brag, but the rat was a stroke of genius, hands down. Of course Hannah will think Diane, irate ex-employee, put it there. I can't wait to think up more evil little deeds that, quote, Diane, end quote, might do to her. By the time I'm done, Diane will have a better chance at being selected for the International Space Station than getting her old job back.

It's almost seven p.m. and the lights have come on in the Carters' household. All I see are shadows behind drapes passing from room to room. I know she's not going out again, but I don't want to go home yet because how often do you get a win like that? I can't tell April about any of this (How was your day? Awesome. You'll never guess what I did today!). But I want to be around people, I want noise. I'm excited and I'm happy and I want to get drunk.

So I go directly to Paddy's on Sullivan, which is a dingy, grungy old Irish pub where the lighting is dim and the drinks are cheap, and it's also my local.

I don't remember much after that, just snatches: me laughing, falling over, a tattooed arm helping me up. And now I don't know where I am. The sun is bright, streaming into the room between the brown drapes. My heart is beating too fast. My head hurts. I'm so thirsty it makes my tongue stick to the roof of my mouth.

I spot a glass of water next to the bed—at least I hope it's water—with a barely-there layer of dust on top. I grab it and gulp it down. Then I hear noises, water running, things moving on surfaces. There's someone here. I wipe a hand down my face. It reeks of sex and cigarettes. I close my eyes and try to remember what he looks like. A flash of black hair, a tattoo like ivy growing up and around his arm and along his shoulder blade. The same arm as last night in the bar. An image comes into focus. I can see myself tracing it with one finger while he takes a deep drag from a cigarette, dropping ash on his chest.

"You smoke inside?" I remember asking, rubbing the ash into his chest.

"You're awake." The sound of his voice makes me gasp.

He's leaning against the wall, his arms crossed on his chest. His hair is wet and he's clean-shaven. No trace of the day-old beard that chafed my cheeks last night. Pity. I liked that. I pull the sheet up to cover my breasts and scratch my scalp with my other hand.

"Hello," I say. I wish he'd go now; I feel fat. Ugly. Exposed.

"You're okay?"

"Kinda."

"Hangover?"

I roll my eyes, which sends a pounding ache into my skull. There's a couple of awkward seconds of silence, then he says, "There's coffee in the kitchen. See you in there."

But I don't go in for coffee. I get dressed and slip into the bathroom to pee. I glance in the mirror and roll my eyes at my own reflection. My mascara has smudged below my eyes. My face is blotchy from alcohol. I rummage through the cabinet and find some pills; I try to read the label but I can't focus, so I just take them and shove them in my pocket.

I don't say goodbye, I just leave.

Back at the apartment, I rummage through my own bath-room cabinet for some painkillers, but I can't find any. I figure that's because I finished the last bottle and never got around to buying some more. I'm pretty sure I did that last time, too, so I guess if April has stocked up, she's keeping them somewhere out of my reach.

I lie down on my bed, but my head hurts too much to sleep. I gaze lazily around my small, pathetic room. Some days I don't mind it; I think of it as a stopgap. But other days, it depresses the hell out of me. This is one of those days, so I get up again and go to work on my project.

One thing about Hannah, she almost never goes out. On the one hand, I can see why she doesn't want to take Mia with her to her therapist. Dr. Malone would charge for the baby, I'm sure of it. *Two hundred and seventy-five dollars, with ten percent off on her tenth visit. Would you like to purchase a lifetime pack for her now?*

But what about baby yoga? The petting zoo? Mommy and Baby Gym? I wonder whether Harvey keeps her locked up. Maybe he's one of those controlling husbands who likes to keep his wife on a tight leash. Maybe that's why she never buys expensive clothes; maybe he only gives her a microscopic allowance. They're not hurting, though, that's for sure. I found him in an article about "America's Most Prestigious Law Firms". The story is a couple years old, but still. His firm has offices in London and Singapore, and close to a billion in annual revenue.

Hannah does take the baby out for a stroll occasionally, and once she went to the florist up on Park Avenue, Poppies & Blooms. I got very excited to see her chatting up some guy, or maybe it was the other way around. It looked innocent enough on the outside, and not at all like a lovers' assignation, but then again, who knows what evil lies in her dark heart?

I do.

Anyway, days go by. Days! I do not leave my post in case something happens, like Diane showing up with her broken and contrite heart. Just to be sure she wouldn't be welcome, I made a few late-night anonymous (but lispy) calls. *Fuck you, Mrs. Carter.* So much fun! But I need to remain vigilant, so I call work again and say that I am sick. *Again? What's the matter with you?* I can hear the disappointment in Dr. Lowe's voice. Sometimes I have to remind myself what a creep he is.

Then, miracle of all miracles, a woman in her early fifties carrying a large buff envelope and wearing a wool coat, of all things, rings the doorbell just as I'm thinking of leaving. You can always tell people going to a job interview because (a) they wear clothes that don't fit very well and are completely inappropriate for the weather; (b) they carry a folder, or a clipboard, or some kind of leather compendium if they really want to impress, where they file their pathetic little CV, half of which is made up anyway; and (c) they look up, for house numbers, which is what this woman has just done. I've had a job interview myself recently, and all three checked out.

When she comes out again, I am already in position—with my own large folder, which is part of my props at the bar, so that's good luck there. I bump into her, silly me, because I'm not looking where I'm going, am I? I am too busy looking up at house numbers.

"I am so sorry! Honestly, this is not my day. I have a job interview in two minutes, and I must have written down the wrong address because the people at number thirty-six over there definitely do not need a math tutor! Shit… oh, I love that coat, by the way."

She frowns and puckers her lips, but not in a good way. "A math tutor? I've just been to see about the housekeeper's position"—she points behind her to the Carters' house—"but the child is only a baby. I don't think she needs a math tutor!"

I pretend to look over my notes. "Hum, no, definitely no housekeeping involved. Which agency sent you?"

She narrows her eyes at me. "HSG. And you?"

"Nope, not HSG. That's too bad, I better go. Thanks for your help, and good luck!"

SEVEN

I just need a reference and then I'm going to contact these HSG people. I'm going to tell them that I am looking for a housekeeper position, live-in, please, preferably with babies because I love them so much. And I'm very, very good, just ask my reference.

I have a cousin—a second cousin, to be precise—up in Connecticut. Her name is Emily. She's older than I am, and I haven't seen her in years, but we used to visit them when I was a kid. Then after my parents died, she took us in, and my brother John and I lived with them from then on. I didn't really bond, mostly because I was too fucked up, too sad, too lost. It's hard to cut through that, for anyone. John fared a lot better, I suppose because he's so much younger than I am. I know he keeps in touch with them, and last I heard he was in college somewhere. I don't know where, and I don't care.

One thing about Emily is that she never came to court to support us back then, but later, when I moved into her house, she asked me once, almost in a whisper, "Did he really do those things? Your father?" I could never look at her the same after that.

We exchange cards at Christmas—and by that, I mean she sends me a card, and I vaguely tell myself I might send her one next year, or not, then put hers in the trash. I call her now and then to say hello. Usually when I'm drunk.

If she's surprised to hear from me, she doesn't let on. We chat awkwardly about her kids, she asks if I've been in touch with John, I say no, she suggests I come and visit around Thanksgiving. I note she doesn't say "for Thanksgiving." She says it must be shockingly hot in the city even though it's not even summer yet, and at least they get the sea breeze. I agree with everything she says.

When we run out of things to say, she waits a beat and then asks, "Everything all right, Claire? Do you need money?"

I've never asked her for money. Ever. I have stolen some, imitated her signature on checks, that sort of thing. In fact, I became so good at imitating her handwriting that once, when I wanted to be excused from swimming lessons because I was being teased about my weight, I wrote a long and comprehensive explanation of why chlorine was hazardous for my skin and I was not to be exposed to it under any circumstances. Weeks later she found it, crumpled at the bottom of my bag. "We should get that skin condition of yours looked at," she said. I didn't have a skin condition, but she really believed she'd written the letter and then forgot.

"I don't need money," I say. *I want your love, got any to spare?* "I have a small favor to ask."

"Oh? What is it?"

"I'm playing a prank on a friend of mine. It's a long

story, but I was wondering if I could give your name as a reference. For a housekeeper's job."

"What housekeeper? What on earth are you talking about?"

It made a lot of sense in my head before, but it sure doesn't make any sense now.

"I just need someone like you, of your … standing, to vouch for someone. You just have to say you know this person, and that she was your housekeeper for three years. And that she was fabulous. You'd recommend her to anyone. Is that okay? Can you do that?"

"You want me to vouch for a housekeeper I've never met?"

"It's just a joke, Emily. It would take too long to explain, but I'd really appreciate it. If I could put you down as a reference."

"I don't know…"

"Emily, please, do this for me."

"I don't know, Claire. I don't feel comfortable about this."

"It's no big deal, just a joke, like I said…"

"Then why don't you ask one of your friends? I'm sorry."

"Emily?"

She won't budge, and that's that. So I hang up on her without saying goodbye, mutter *Fuck you* at the phone and bite my knuckle a while. Then I call Dr. Lowe. I'm resigning, I tell him. I'm applying for a new job, and I need a reference. I would like you to say that I worked as a housekeeper, for you and Mrs. Lowe. I was extremely reliable. Everything was perfect. You were sorry to lose me. At least that part is true. And I'm great with kids, too. Oh, and I took extremely good care of your art collection.

What, you don't own any artworks? Sure you do, Dr. Lowe.

"Freak," he mutters and hangs up on me.

In the end, I call the agency. This is Mrs. Carter speaking, I say. They're so nice. Really friendly people. Mrs. Carter! How are you! One moment, I'll put you through to Carlotta, they say.

I tell Carlotta that I've muddled everything, and I can't remember what time or who is my next applicant.

"Louise Martin. At eleven a.m. tomorrow."

"Ah! Yes, of course. Could you ask Louise to come at ten a.m. tomorrow instead? Like I said, very muddled! I'd lose my head if it wasn't screwed on!"

Then I set up an email account that I'll use to contact Hannah later: hsgsolutions@gmail.com (because hsg@gmail.com is unfortunately not available). I set the name of the sender to Housekeeping Solutions Group and drop their logo in the footer.

I don't bother going to the bar. I decide to catch up on some sleep instead so that by the next day, I don't look like the type of person who stays up all night drinking. I even go to the grocery store and pick up two packets of Amy's frozen mac 'n' cheese for April and me. That night we sit together on the couch and watch *House of Cards*, and when I tell her I'm going to bed, she hugs me and says, "I worry about you, you know. That's why I get mad sometimes." And it makes my eyes swim because nobody worries about me anymore, except April.

The next day, at ten a.m., I am fishing around my bag just outside the Carters' house when Louise Martin arrives, exactly on time. She's taller than I am, and thinner, too, with short brown hair, but we're about the same age. Later I'll find out that we're exactly the same age. So that's good.

"Excuse me," she says, smiling. "I'm going in there."

I look up. "Oh! Well, I better get out of your way!" I smile, then cock my head at her. "You're not the new housekeeper, are you?"

She frowns. "Excuse me?"

"It's just that I came all the way from New Jersey for this interview and now"—I jerk my thumb behind me —"she just told me the housekeeper position is gone." I make a face.

"Gone?" Her eyes grow wide.

"Been filled this morning. Thanks so much for letting me know, right?" I shake my head. "I wish the agency had told me. I've come all this way for nothing. Anyway, that's not your problem, even if it is you. No hard feelings. I hope you enjoy the job. Now where *is* that MetroCard?"

She's not happy, Louise Martin. No, she's not the new housekeeper, and yes, she too has come from far away for this interview. She's going to call someone and ask for an explanation. I commiserate. "Wanna cup of coffee? My treat," I say. I take her to Starbucks and buy her a salted caramel mocha. While we wait for our order, I go to the bathroom and call Carlotta at the agency. *Hannah Carter here. Sooo sorry, but I've hired someone for the position. Yes, that's right. Yes, please cancel any remaining candidates. No, thank you!*

Half an hour later we leave together, kiss goodbye outside and promise to keep in touch, especially in case one of us hears of anything. I still have fifteen minutes before Hannah expects to interview Louise Martin, and I've learned everything I need to know about her. I'm ready.

EIGHT

Hannah Wilson and I have only met once in person, very briefly. But we've seen each other in court and on TV. I'd been feeling confident she wouldn't recognize me, but then at four o'clock this morning I woke up in a panic. What if she did? So I went to the all-night drugstore on the corner for some hair color, then I cut my hair short in front of the bathroom mirror, the scissors hacking at it, and with every snip I thought of her.

Time for your comeuppance, Mrs. Carter.

Snip.

I told myself that if there was the slightest flicker of recognition, I would tell a lie—that I'd already accepted another position and I had come to let her know I was no longer available. Then I would leave. But one thing I've noticed about having pimple-ridden skin is that people don't look too closely. Also, people trust me. My face is a trustworthy face. It wasn't always this way; I've had some people say terrible things about me. I was called a *weirdo* more than once. But I got better at it. I learned. I practiced till I got perfect. Poker face, kind face, concerned face, trustworthy face.

It goes without saying that by the time I arrive at the appointed time, my finger poised on the doorbell outside the Carters' brownstone, I know I'm about to make a really bad, very bad mistake. I tell myself to turn around and go, that there is still time, but my legs are shaking and they're not listening, and now the door has opened wide and Hannah Carter stands there, a big smile on her face, and her hand extended.

"Hello, you must be Louise, come on in! I'm Hannah Carter." I've been looking at Hannah for two weeks now, but it's still a shock up close like this. Her skin is beautiful, like a peach, but her gray eyes look red-rimmed and tired. I suspect my late-night phone calls may have something to do with that, so that's nice. She's wearing a simple white shirt and jeans, and a pair of ballet flats. The only jewelry other than her rings is two small diamond earrings. I shake her hand limply and step inside, and I can't believe I'm here.

The foyer is gorgeous, with pale walls adorned by colorful paintings and art deco lamps, and a tiled floor with a dark mosaic design. There are two antique console tables on either side, carrying cheerful bouquets of yellow flowers. A green velvet couch runs along one wall, and at the back of the room is the circular staircase, curling up along the wall.

"I know, it's grand, isn't it? I hope it's not putting you off!"

I turn to her and force myself to focus. Hannah Carter is smiling at me. She thinks I'm a twenty-four-year-old housekeeper looking for a job. I study her face, waiting for her to recognize me, my eyes flicking back to the door, but she just looks normal, certainly not confused. I think I'm in.

"Not at all, you have a beautiful home, Mrs. Carter."

"Thank you! It has nothing to do with me, you know. I didn't decorate it. If I had, there would be a lot more color, for one thing." She winks at me. "This way. Let's walk up, it's just the one floor."

"I love color," I say brightly. But I feel a dampness creeping up my hairline, and a rivulet starts to run down the side of my neck.

We arrive in the kitchen, which is smaller than I'd expected. She indicates a stool at the kitchen island. I pull it out, and it scrapes loudly on the tile floor. There's a large notepad in the center, and she reaches for it.

"Now... Louise Martin."

"That's me." But she's wearing the same perfume my mother wore, Clive Christian No1, and it takes me back with a shock so unexpected that for a moment I can't breathe. She opens a cupboard and brandishes two mugs and asks, "Would you like a cup of coffee? Or tea?"

"Tea would be very nice, thank you." I stand up from my seat. "Here, let me. You sit down, Mrs. Carter." It's better for me to do something. It helps me hide my discomfort, and before she has time to protest, I've put the kettle on to boil, opened cupboards at random until I found a teapot, and now I have two packets of tea—one in each hand. I cock my head at her and ask, "Which one? Mint? Or Earl Grey?"

"Let's go with mint," she says. "I don't know how long the Earl Grey's been here for. Definitely before my time." She laughs.

"I was hoping you'd say mint." Then on impulse I open the trash can and throw the other packet into it. She lets out a snort of laughter, and by the time I put the steaming mug in front of her, I can tell she's relaxed. She likes me. I decide to be like a breath of fresh air. Friendly, not too obsequious, happy. Diane I am not.

She asks about my previous employers, Mr. and Mrs. Van Kemp, where I have worked for the past five years as per Louise's history.

"Your references are excellent, by the way," she says. "Glowing." She smiles.

"Thank you. I enjoyed working for Mr. and Mrs. Van Kemp very much. I was sorry to leave them."

"Why did you leave them?" she asks.

I put both hands around my mug. "My mother. She wasn't well, breast cancer. It's just her and me; my dad died a few years back. I just couldn't bear the thought of her fighting this on her own, you know?"

"Is she…?"

I shake my head and smile broadly. "Oh no, she's fine. Better than fine, even. She's in remission, thank God. But the treatment was rough. All these sessions of chemo, they take it out of you. But she's okay now."

"I'm glad," she says. Then she goes back to her clip-board, and I'm thinking, *Don't punch her. Not yet.*

"My husband is an art collector, as you may have seen on the way in here. We own a number of precious works, many of which are on display around this house."

"Yes, I see that. They're beautiful."

"Do you have any experience caring for antiques and artworks?"

I am ready for that one. "Mrs. Van Kemp, in my last posi-tion, she loved her art and she showed me what to do. It was my favorite part of the job. I loved spending time with all these beautiful pictures." I tell her some brain-numbingly boring details about protective cotton gloves and sweaty palms, acrylics versus oils, when to use a little moisture on the cloth. I rub my fingertips together. "It's the sweat that's the problem. It can leave a mark—on furniture, too. I prefer to use soft rags only. Dry ones, except if I'm cleaning oil paintings, because they attract dust, have you noticed? So much pollution in this city, it leaves grime over the years. Anyway, a bit of water on the cloth is best for those, but only very occasionally."

By now I'm starting to sound like I'm going for the wrong job. *It's a housekeeper she wants, not a conservator.* But she smiles and says, "My husband is going to love you." And I'm thinking, *Babe, wait till he sees my tits.*

She writes things down, and all the time I stare at her face and it makes my heart beat so hard I can feel it in my throat. She really has no idea who I am, which is incredible to me because I, on the other hand, am so aware of her, it's making every fiber of my being tingle, and not in a good way.

"We have a baby girl. She's asleep right now, thank God." Her eyes flick to the baby monitor on the kitchen bench. Baby Mia is fast asleep on the pixelated gray screen. "She's almost four months old. We need—or I need, more to the point—a bit of help with her." She makes an apologetic face, like she should be better at it, like she's afraid I'll think she's not a good mother.

I give her a reassuring smile. "I love children. I helped care for the Van Kemps' children. Three of them. The youngest, Bethany, was one year old when I started with the family. Mrs. Van Kemp was going back to work and I was able to help a lot, which was lovely. I enjoyed it very much." *Blah-blah-blah.* She's holding a red-and-gold Montblanc pen, flicking it back and forth between two fingers, tapping it against the marble tabletop.

"That's wonderful," she says. "Music to my ears."

But I can't stop staring at her hand, because this pen, it must cost close to a thousand dollars, and she's playing with it like it's some cheap plastic Bic from Walmart. I consider taking it away from her if she doesn't stop soon. *Stop playing with the pen! A pen like that deserves some respect!*

"Mrs. Carter?" I point at her hand.

"Yes?"

"It's just the way you're tapping that pen on the table, maybe you don't realize you're doing it."

"Oh? No, you're right, I didn't realize."

"It looks like a Montblanc. Is it?"

She turns the pen in her hand and frowns at it like she's never seen it before. "Yes. How do you know?"

I point to the tip of the cap. "That little gold symbol here, like a snow top. Mrs. Van Kemp owns one too, but hers is black and white. She's very careful with it. They're so expensive, I just thought—sorry, I shouldn't have said anything."

"No, thank you, I'm glad you did. It was a gift from my husband, when I gave birth to our daughter." She smiles. "He showered me with gifts for a whole week when Mia was born. Sweet, isn't it? He won't be very happy with me if I break it!" And we both laugh, like we're gently poking fun at Mr. Carter and his expensive gift habits.

"Even the ink is special, take a look." She scribbles on the corner of the page and holds it up to show me. "Barbados blue. Did you know there were so many different shades of blue ink?" She shakes her head like it's all so ridiculous, but she's not fooling me. I'd bet a bottle of Grey Goose that she knows exactly how much this pen costs. It looks like a limited edition. I bet she chose it.

She puts the clipboard away. "This may be a little personal, but I'm just curious. Why would you want to work here, as a live-in housekeeper, I mean? You're only"—she glances at my CV— "twenty-four. You could study; there must be other things you'd like to do with your life?"

Luckily for me, Louise was very chatty yesterday. "I'm saving money, Mrs. Carter. This is my five-year plan, or I hope it is. I love to sew and make clothes, and I can't save money if I have to rent a place myself. I'm hoping that within five years I will have saved enough to start my own business. My own clothing store, maybe in Queens." I shrug, a little coyly. "I know how crazy that sounds, me wanting my own business someday—"

"No, not at all. I understand that more than you think. I think you'd be as good as anyone else."

"Thank you. I sure hope I didn't just shoot myself in the foot by announcing my five-year plan!" I laugh.

"Of course not. I'd love to find out more about your five-year plan. You may well inspire me about my own five-year plan."

At one point, she asks, "What will you bring to this position that other candidates might not?"

I think about it. I even stare out the window. "I'm just a really hard worker." And that has to be the first time I've used those words to describe myself. I even throw in something about *work ethic*, which, considering what she did to my family when she worked for us, makes me want to hoot with laughter.

Then she tells me about the position. Five stories, six bedrooms, seven bathrooms, a million sitting rooms, breakfast room, TV room, terraces, floorboards, rugs, laundry. She goes through all the chores I'd have to do. Bathroom cleaning, kitchen cleaning, grocery shopping, running errands, surface polishing, changing linens, refrigerator cleaning, taking out the trash, taking care of plants. My eyes glaze over and I have to pinch myself to keep from falling asleep.

"Is that all good?" she asks.

I think of all the objections I could raise. Like, there's only so many hours in the day, twenty-four at my last count. And since it's only her and her husband and the baby, would they consider downsizing? Also, did Diane really do all these things all by herself? I don't think so. Diane does not look superhuman to me. But then again, why fret? Once I'm done here, the cleanliness of the place will be the last of Hannah's worries.

"Absolutely. All good," I reply.

When we walk down the stairs, I ask her, "Have you interviewed many people for the position?"

"No. There aren't that many people who are prepared to live and work with their employer full-time. That's why I asked you about that earlier. I've seen two people so far, but they weren't a good fit. Oh, that reminds me, when can you start? Because I need someone urgently."

I know then that I've done as well as I possibly could. At least I am in the running. And the funniest thing is that before she closes the door behind me, I catch her glancing up and down the street distractedly, and I know she's looking out for crazy Diane. Crazy Diane who leaves dead rats in her mailbox and calls her at night with vile, threatening words.

NINE

I leave it for thirty minutes. Any longer and she might contact the agency, maybe even gush about "Louise Martin". I pray silently that she hasn't done so as I make the call, my stomach clenched. She answers on the first ring and when I announce myself, her tone is a little puzzled, but warm, and my whole body relaxes as I breathe out.

Mrs. Carter, I hope you don't mind, the agency gave me your number, they said it was all right.... It's just that, I've been offered another position you see?... Yes, just now, but I wanted to check in case—well, I'll be honest with you, I thought you were so nice, and I love the idea of helping you look after a little one, so I wondered if you'd made up your mind about me, one way or another.... Oh really? That's awesome! I'm so happy, Mrs. Carter, you won't regret it, I promise.... No, that's all right, I'll call the agency now and tell them.... That's no problem at all, it's better for me to let them know. Thank you so much, Mrs. Carter.

Then I send the email I've already drafted from my fake *Housekeeping Solutions Group* account.

Dear Mrs. Carter,

We're delighted to let you know that Ms. Louise Martin has accepted your offer of employment as Live-in Housekeeper. Louise will start her position on Monday, blah-blah-blah, we will forward our invoice after the agreed trial period, blah-blah-blah.

She replies almost immediately, saying she really looks forward to Louise becoming part of the family, which I think is a very strange thing to say to a new employee, and under different circumstances, I think I would find it creepy.

It may be risky, all this, but not that risky. The key is to anticipate what the other party is going to do next and stay one step ahead. I'm not going to be there long, just long enough to reach my goal and then I'm out of there. I want redress. I want her to admit what she did to me and my family. To admit it was all a lie. And I want her to do that publicly. Some people might say that's impossible, but those people are not consumed like I am. This is my life's work now. And if I could make her feel miserable in the process, so miserable that she would want to die, well … that would be nice.

That night, I tell April I'm going to Pittsfield for a while. Just a week or two, I say. To stay with my cousin Mary who is convalescing. Pneumonia. Terrible illness, that.

"Oh! Will she be all right?" she asks, digging into her bowl of vanilla ice cream. I already finished mine and I'm wiping it with my finger and licking it.

"Oh yes. Eventually."

She turns down the volume on the TV. "How long will you be gone?"

I've thought about this all day, obviously. How long will it take me to achieve my plan? Let's see. Step 1: get inside the house, check. Step 2: seduce Harvey. Now, some people might laugh at the prospect of me—sad, fat, ugly me—seducing a man like Harvey, when he's got someone like Hannah at home, but it's not love I'm offering. It's a hand job, and more. It's all the things his wife won't do, and for free. Show me a man who'll turn that down.

Except it's not for free, not really, but it's Hannah who'll have to pay. Because I'm going to make some good videos on my phone, ones where I role-play the *shy, reluctant* housekeeper. If I could get him to slap me, even better. Some men like that. But anything that shows "he made me do it" will do. And that's where step 3 comes in.

Step 3 is where I turn the tables on Hannah. Step 3 is where she finds that everything she's worked so hard for is about to go up in smoke. Because if I put those videos up on YouTube, Harvey Carter's life as he knows it will be over. He will be shunned, humiliated. He'll lose his law practice, or at least the bulk of his clients. I mean, who wants to be associated with that? The Carters will be social pariahs. I can't imagine "little Mia sweet as pie" ever being accepted into an exclusive private school. I know these establishments. They'll come up with all sorts of excuses as to why she's *not the right fit*. And anyway, the Carters will be broke by then and Hannah won't stick around if there's no money. And she won't want to be part of *another* scandal. All that work snagging Harvey for nothing, and those life-long dreams of money and glamour? Irretrievably gone.

Hannah will have to consider all this when I show her the videos. But I will offer her a way out. I will delete all of it if she admits that she lied about what my father did to her. A confession. I'll film that too, of course. I'll say it's for my own security, in case they try to discredit me after I delete the videos of her husband's misdemeanors.

Step 4? Distribute her confession far and wide, obviously. I'm thinking *New York Post*, *Vanity Fair*, the *New Yorker*... maybe I'll make a deal with one of them for an exclusive. It may have been ten years ago, but it was a big case at the time. Wilson vs. Petersen. People will remember.

April is staring at me, her spoon against her bottom lip. "Earth to Claire Petersen?" she says, and for a moment I wonder if I spoke out loud.

"Two weeks," I say. "Three at the most."

TEN

That summer I had to come home to New York in the middle of camp for an orthodontist appointment that had taken months to secure. My mother picked me up that morning and drove me to my appointment, then I went home briefly to pick up some more clothes. I barely noticed the slim, shy girl in our house. We exchanged no more than a few words of greeting before my mother drove me back. Then maybe a week later, over one of our phone calls, my mother mentioned she needed to find a new nanny.

"Why? What about that girl, what's her name?"

"She's gone. She went home."

"Already? I thought she was there for the whole summer? What happened?"

"I think she was just overwhelmed. She was so young, barely twenty. She'd lived her whole life on a farm, you know, so I guess it was too much for her."

"I thought that was the point. Didn't you say she wanted to visit museums or whatever?"

"Yes, well, I don't think she did that. She was terribly

unhappy, then she asked to go home, so we called her parents and sent her back."

Then she told me other news, and I didn't give a single thought to Hannah Wilson for months. Until I found out my parents were being sued in civil court for sexual assault.

There were two things that defined my father: he was a businessman, and he worshiped my mother. I think he could never believe his luck that she'd agreed to marry him. He was middle class before he met her, whereas she was the quintessential New York high-society woman. I used to think she was the most beautiful woman in the world, head-turningly so. She was also very smart, and in many ways, as wonderful and privileged as her life was, I think she wanted something else for me. Not a career so much as a calling. Didn't quite work out that way.

But he was talented, or so we thought, and his invest-ment firm grew steadily over the years. We were rich. By any standard. Which is why she picked us.

She went home, back to her pathetic life in Canada, and told her parents that my father had visited her room every night and did things to her. She also said she couldn't tell my mother because he had threatened her.

I have no doubt that Hannah Wilson came to us with that plan already in place. She looked for a wealthy family, and she found one. She counted on the fact that my parents would not want the publicity and would quickly settle out of court for an undisclosed sum. Just a generic blackmail scam, although impressive in its simplicity.

Needless to say, my mother didn't believe a word of it. The idea that my quiet, kind, bespectacled father was capable of whatever she claimed he did was never even considered, and after the initial shock of the betrayal, she returned to her defiant self. She had done so much to accommodate that girl, and this is how she repaid us? She was adamant that the Petersens would not settle. "We will clear our good name!" she thundered.

So my parents fought back. Hard. They accused her of going after money, which, considering she wanted ten million dollars in compensation, was the truth. Hannah returned to New York accompanied by her parents for depositions and filings. They looked so out of place, the three of them, in their Sunday best and with their baffled expressions, as if it hadn't been their idea to be here, as if they hadn't made all this happen. By then the press was having a field day. My father was a monster, Hannah was a naïve young girl who had been taken advantage of. My parents countered that she was a gold digger, that she'd even conned her own parents, who looked like good people, they said.

The problem was that she presented well in court. She was young, not beautiful but pretty enough, which was probably better. She looked scared all the time. Even at my young age, I could see that she had that quality that made people want to protect her.

So I stepped in. I told my mother that when I'd met Hannah that day, I'd said something like, I'm sure I'll see you again before you go back, and she'd said, I don't think so, I don't intend to stick around here for long. I asked why that was, and she winked at me and whispered, I got what I wanted. I'm going to go home, and very soon I'll be very rich.

I said I didn't even understand what she meant but I hadn't asked because, why would I? She meant nothing to me; I just wanted to return to my summer camp.

It says a lot about the stress my parents were under that they believed me. They immediately called their lawyer, and public opinion began to shift against her. It also helped that they were generous donors, culturally as well as politically. The press remarked that my mother had even volunteered at a soup kitchen one Christmas.

My father gave a press conference with all of us by his side, outside the court where he had filed a counterclaim. He spoke words I didn't understand like "malicious prosecution," "frivolous claims" and "abuse of process," but I nodded in agreement the whole way through. We had done nothing but be kind and generous to her, and this had been a premeditated con, an attempt to blackmail us against a potential scandal not of our own doing, skillfully carried out by a young woman of dubious character. The "dubious character" was a reference to the fact that she'd been caught shoplifting two tubes of lipstick with a school friend long ago, and some clever journalist had dug up the story and made it sound like she was part of some criminal gang.

And then my father paused for longer than made sense, and when I turned around to look at him, he looked suspended in time and I'll never forget the look of terror on his face when he turned to my mother. He groaned and clutched at his chest, and before we could do anything, he'd fallen hard on the concrete steps. After that, all I remember are the screams and my mother cradling his head on her lap. By the time the ambulance arrived, he had died.

And that was the end of Wilson vs. Petersen. The press carried unflattering photos of Hannah above headlines that screamed *murderer* and *con artist*. She had killed an upstanding citizen, a man who had given so much to his family, to his church, and to the poor of this city. For a while, people rightly brayed for her head—on talk shows, in line at the checkout. There should be consequences, they said, for what she'd done. But they'd left by then, the three of them, back to their shitty little lives on their farm.

The end? No. Evil has many tentacles and it was not finished with us yet.

It turned out that the money that had funded our lavish lifestyle wasn't strictly ours. It belonged to my father's clients. It was amazing that he hadn't been found out at that stage, considering he essentially borrowed from Peter to pay Paul, without telling either Paul or Peter. I've thought a lot about the years when my life was a kaleidoscope of birthday parties, ponies and tennis lessons, and I can't recall a single occasion where my father was stressed, or him admonishing my mother for spending too much. It was the opposite, really. He was always buying us gifts. But now his clients wanted their money back, but there was no money. And that would have been the bigger scandal. Never go after rich people's money, I found out the hard way. They'll forgive you anything, except stealing from them. But my mother sold everything and settled with everyone, and under the circumstances and out of respect for my mother, no one made a big fuss.

Not long after we buried my father, my mother moved us to a cramped two-bedroom apartment in Charleston, West Virginia, where she would just lock herself in her room. I would walk in to find her lying in bed with the blinds drawn and an eye-mask over her face, like some faded film star. When she emerged there was a smell about her, acrid and unwashed. Her hair became limp and greasy, and over time matted on the back of her head. She wouldn't eat, she wouldn't speak, except to say, "I have to lie down, I have a migraine." Just like she said the day before and the day before that. We had no housekeeper then. No staff, no friends to speak of, no one to help us. I would order us a pizza and pay for it with her credit card. I would think about my dad, about how much I missed him. My little brother would cry himself to sleep.

When my mother died, alone in that room, the doctors said it was an accidental overdose, but I knew it wasn't. I think she literally felt she had nothing to live for. It goes without saying that I have often thought of doing the same, until Hannah Wilson came back into my life, and life got exciting again.

ELEVEN

I move in with the Carters the following week. Hannah takes me to my quarters, as she calls it. It's at the back of the first floor and down half a dozen steps. It's small and cramped and makes my room at April's seem like the Taj Mahal. I vaguely wonder whether housekeepers have a union.

My uniforms hang in the closet. I had been concerned I might have to dress up in some black pseudo-French frilly type, but I am pleased to find a double-breasted light blue dress with two rows of white buttons all the way down the front, and white trim on the collar and sleeves. She must have ordered some new ones specially, because there is no way Diane and I are the same size. I also find a number of pinafore aprons, all of them white. Next door to my room is the bathroom and a small gym, equipped with a treadmill, a spin bike and weights.

"That's where I live," she quips. "Harvey had it put in especially for me. Do you think I should be offended?" She chuckles, then pats her hips and adds, "Still trying to lose that post-baby fat. Some days I think it will never happen."

I'm at least twenty pounds heavier than she is, but never mind.

"You look great, you've got nothing to worry about," I say. Except me, obviously.

She smiles. "Thank you."

The last two rooms are the laundry and what she calls the utility room. In there is a cleaning trolley with cloths and spray and feather dusters, which I'm supposed to push around the place as I do my work.

"Everything all right?" she asks as we go back upstairs.

"Everything is terrific," I reply. And she laughs. We both do.

Then she takes me on a tour of the house. I make all the right noises (ooh, aah) even though part of me is a little shocked at how ostentatious everything is. The living room alone—I mean, the *main* living room, because there are a number of living rooms—is larger than April's little apartment downtown. Then there's the view. The tall windows from floor to ceiling that open onto the private terrace facing directly over Central Park. The white wood-paneled walls, covered with artwork. Even the ceiling is spectacular. It's a painted sky, all blue and white and pale gold, and it's breathtaking. Like a dream. Apart from the bedrooms, there is very little wall space in this place that isn't covered with valuable artwork.

"This is my favorite room in the house," she says when we reach the kitchen. I doubt that very much, but it's a good line. "I love this view, overlooking the trees." She stands back from the tall windows. "If you stand about here, you might even think you're in the country."

"You might have to put your hands over your ears, too," I say, and she laughs, a big genuine laugh.

Next is the nursery. It's a perfect room for a baby, with

its light-pink-and-light-gray color scheme. She tells me that the artist who did the ceiling in the main living room came and painted the mural. It's a little girl walking among wildflowers, carrying a parasol made of butterflies. Mia makes gurgling noises in her crib and Hannah picks her up. She's wearing a white cotton onesie and wriggles her feet. Hannah brings her belly to her nose and smells her, which strikes me as hilarious and makes me laugh out loud.

"I know, isn't she the most beautiful girl ever?" she coos, as if I'd been laughing out of pure joy at the sight of her. "She used to cry *all* night. Thank God we're past that now. Speaking of which…" She shows me a white object that looks like a cheap plastic radio. Like something you'd have in the shower. "Baby monitor. We have two of them, but yours is different because I couldn't find a video monitor that worked all the way down to your room."

"I have one in my room?" I blurt, panic rising. An image of me running up the stairs to Mia in the middle of night flashes in my mind. Then doing it again. And again. And then daylight.

She smiles apologetically. "It's only if I'm out. When I'm here, you can turn it off, or turn it down low. Anyway, this is yours. Audio only."

I'm still fuming over it when she says, "Here, you want to try to feed her?" And to my horror, she hands me Mia. "Sit down. I'll go and fetch her bottle."

She walks out, leaving me and Mia together in the armchair. I've never held a baby before. She doesn't cry, which is good. I lift her up, jiggle her little body, get used to her weight, figure out how to sit her down and how to cradle her, sort of, just enough so I don't look like the complete fraud that I am. Then Hannah returns with the bottle and hands it to me. I mumble something about it being the right temperature, then stick one end in Mia's mouth.

"I can see you've done this before," she says, and I'm not sure if she's being sarcastic or not, but I wish she'd stop looking at me.

"Lovely room," I say.

"Thank you. I insisted we redecorate it."

"What did it look like before?"

"Oh, let me see. Some dark-blue-and-gold damask wallpaper over on that wall, an enormous photograph of a naked woman lying down, from the back, across from a four-poster bed with a plum-colored velvet canopy and a huge glass chandelier."

"So why did you change it?" I ask, and she cracks up.

"Can I leave you for a minute? I have a call to make," she says.

"Sure."

It's just Mia and me now. We stare into each other's eyes, hers way more trusting than mine. I'm struck by how long her eyelashes are, how thin the skin on her eyelids is, almost translucent, and how utterly perfect she is. Her skin is like porcelain, but warmer. It occurs to me that babies are like a blank slate—they haven't been disappointed yet; they think the world is a happy place, that promises are meant to be kept and recycling really is a thing. What will be her first letdown, I wonder? Her mother, obviously.

She smiles at me, a wide grin, genuine and radiant with happiness, as if she were saying, *Oh, it's you, that's really great,* and it's like a current passes through—from her to me—and it makes my eyes swim. When Hannah returns and takes her from me, I find myself hanging on just that little bit harder and Hannah has to give an extra tug.

Finally, Hannah introduces me to Mr. Carter. We are in

his office, a large room with a big mahogany desk in the center, a bookshelf that takes up all of one wall and framed pages from medieval illuminated manuscripts hanging opposite. The effect is so impressive I almost curtsy.

Harvey Carter is shorter than I expected. He shakes my hand and welcomes me to their home. He tells me that he works in a law firm and he's very busy. "You'll hardly ever see me," he says. His offices are somewhere downtown and he often works late. Occasionally he'll be needed in the London office for a few days. Hannah adds proudly that he's one of the founding partners, and he coyly brushes her off.

He seems like a nice person with a big, open, friendly face, and when he looks at Hannah, that whole face lights up. I imagine that face when he realizes that he's been had —when she announces over caviar hors d'oeuvres that it's not working and she's leaving him; when he receives the demand for millions of dollars from her very expensive, very adversarial divorce lawyer; when he happens upon the cover of a tabloid and sees his ex-wife sunning herself on a yacht, her toes being sucked by some tanned, ripped stud, and he realizes he's paying for it all, stud included.

I feel a wave of outrage on his behalf, and I mentally telegraph to him that it's going to be okay, that it won't come to that. That I've got this. That I'll get to her before she has time to do any damage to him. Because while we'll make home videos, Harvey and I, I'll never use them. I only need them for leverage, that's all. I'm not an evil person, and I'd never hurt an innocent party. I mentally telegraph that too as I stand there, demure and sweet and blushing with shyness. I suspect that's his type.

TWELVE

It's my first morning and my alarm goes off at six thirty. I turn it off and go back to sleep because she said they'll get their own breakfast this morning, and what difference does it make if I get up at seven or eight or nine? But then she knocks on my door. "Everything all right, Louise?" and I have to say my alarm hadn't worked.

"Won't happen again," I say, still groggy from sleep.

They have phones in almost every room in this house. The system doubles as an intercom, which is how she can call me if she needs me. That first morning, the phone rings and I pick it up, thinking that's what I'm supposed to do, and I'm about to blurt *Carter Residence!* when I hear her voice on the line. "Hi, Dad."

My heart does a somersault. Her father. That abominable man whose ugly red face has haunted my nightmares ever since I first laid eyes on him. It should have been him who died, instead of my father. I think about that often, and then sometimes I think about killing him too.

74

"He said no," Hannah says. "Sorry."

He doesn't say anything for a moment, but I can hear him breathing through his nose, long, loud breaths, like he's gearing up for a fight.

"I'm sorry," she says again.

"Don't you want to help your old dad, then?"

"It's not like that, it's not my money. I can't make him."

He snorts. "You rich people are all the same, aren't you? The more you have, the less you want to part with it. I didn't think you'd end up like that, not the way we raised you, your mother and me."

"Dad, come on. Enough. I would if I could, you know that. It's not *my* money."

"How come it's not *your* money, when you're his wife? I don't know how they do it over there, but where I'm from, married couples share everything. They look after each other. Any money I have is your mother's. She'd know, she spends enough of it." He coughs; it goes on for a while.

"Sharing, Hannah," he continues finally. "Sharing your good fortune, and being honest with each other. That's how marriage works."

"What do you really want fifty thousand for, Dad? You're not gambling again, are you? You haven't been at the track again? Because I'm not sure you're being honest about what you want the money for."

He pauses, and it goes on for so long that I think maybe he's hung up, but then he speaks again. "Speaking of being honest…"

"What?"

"Harvey said something interesting at the wedding. I can't get it out of my mind; maybe you can help me out. He said, 'I can't wait to take Hannah around New York. I

75

can't believe she's never been there before.' And I thought to myself, well, what a funny thing to say."

"You didn't tell him, did you?" she blurts.

"That this isn't your first rodeo? Nah. I figured you must have your reasons to *lie* to your husband," he sneers.

"I have to go, Dad. Mia's crying."

"You do that, sweetheart. And don't call us back again, unless you've got some good news for us, all right? Not that you'll want to anyway. Now that you've got all that money, you should find plenty to keep you occupied. Just don't call here again, all right, sweetheart? You ungrateful witch, I can't believe you'd break your mother's heart. Again. You fucking—"

She hangs up on him, and I do the same, but way more gently. I can't believe Hannah has never told her husband about her past. Or maybe I can. Because one thing's for sure, nothing has changed in that family. They're still the same pack of hustlers.

Usually, Harvey leaves for work about eight in the morning, and before he goes, he'll spend maybe twenty minutes in his home office. On my second day, I get in there early and pretend to clean with the feather duster. I don't get the point of those things since they essentially move dust around from one location to another, inches away, but it's a nice prop. On one shelf are a number of boxes of various shapes and sizes. Some are made of wood, some are covered in cloth, some are made of porcelain. I open one at random, and it looks like an old set of painting brushes and some strange tarnished metal cigarette holders.

"Ah, I see you've found my calligraphy collection."

"Oh, Mr. Carter. My apologies, I thought you'd

already left." I'm blushing furiously as he comes to stand next to me. He takes out one of the smaller silver tubes, opens one end of it, pulling out the stopper, and drops the contents into his hand. "These are antique nibs. Arabic. See how sharp the edge is? That's how they get the type of stroke." He turns around and points with his chin at one of the artworks on the wall covered with strange lettering, then carefully puts the nibs away. "Calligraphy is a bit of a hobby of mine," he says, "although I don't use these, of course." He opens a long wooden box in which are various inks and nibs and fountain pens, all snugly set inside a dark red cushiony lining.

"They're beautiful," I say. He nods. "Did you do any of these?" I point to the various framed calligraphy works.

He chuckles. "No, I'm still working up to that. Maybe one day."

He puts the boxes back and picks up a stack of papers from the desk. I'm still feeling embarrassed at having been caught out but relieved he doesn't seem to mind. Then I figure I may as well make the most of the situation.

"I'll get out of the way, Mr. Carter. I can finish later." He returns to his papers, and I turn around and quickly undo the second button of my blouse so it gapes in the right place. Then I blow off a little speck of dust from the top of a bronze angel's head, to show I take pride in my work. I walk past him and quote, accidentally, end quote, brush my tits against his arm. He looks at me and frowns. I apologize but my eyes don't leave his.

Now, I don't expect Harvey Carter to fall in love with me, obviously. But I am hinting at a free offering. A little gift from me to the master of the house. And it's not usually that hard. I remember back when I was in high school, *public* high school, and living with cousin Emily.

Her awful kids always got great grades in everything in their *private, independent* school, where they studied things like flower arrangement and pottery. I still remember going to see my cousin Sasha perform some idiotic contemporary dance thing with flowers in her hair while her brother Todd played the violin very badly in the crappy student orchestra, and afterward all the adults agreed that they were *geniuses*. The night before the next concert I broke Todd's violin strings using a pair of nail clippers. He didn't realize until he pulled the instrument out before walking out on stage. They never figured out it was me; they accused some other kid who apparently was jealous of Todd's talent. As if those kids really had any talent to begin with.

Anyway, the point is, my own grades were not that good—orphan, public school, surprise surprise—and one day cousin Emily imposed a curfew on me until things improved.

I was fifteen years old, and the only subject I liked and was good at was creative writing. It was run by our English teacher, Mr. Clegg, who found me after class one afternoon crying in the hallway and took me back to the empty classroom, closed the door and asked me what on earth was the matter. I told him through sobs how much I hated cousin Emily. I'd fallen in love with the books of Charlotte Brontë and told him that my life was like Jane Eyre's, only much worse. He nodded a lot and kept licking his lips. He had very fat lips, thick and plum-colored. Then he asked me to unbutton my blouse so he could see my breasts. I was shocked, I said no. But then he said how beautiful I was and how he thought about me all the time, so I did as he asked. I was also a little in love with Mr. Clegg and by the time I went home I was determined to lose weight for the wedding and was picking names for our children. Mr. Clegg was already married and had children of his own, but I decided he was terribly unhappy, and that was Mrs. Clegg's fault, and that I would never ever make Mr. Clegg unhappy. When I think of this now, I cringe. Surely these were the fantasies of a much younger girl. Anyway, I didn't stay naive for long. I discovered that if you love someone, they might not love you back, but if you do what they say, they will like you for a while. And take care of your grades! Hooray!

Anyway, back to Harvey Carter. He smiles at me quickly, in the way people do when they just want to get away but they don't want to be rude, and he's gathered his papers and he's gone now. I don't usually get this wrong, and I wonder if I've lost my touch. This is very annoying because I need Harvey Carter to play his part, and I bite my knuckle hard enough to leave the imprint of my teeth around it.

THIRTEEN

It's been three days, and it goes without saying that I hate this job already. Harvey is working long hours and I haven't been able to get any time alone with him. Not even ten minutes.

I never do any actual *cleaning*, obviously. I just shake my feather duster here and there and call it work. Same with the vacuuming. Just push it around a bit. Maybe dab some fake sweat on my brow whenever she walks past. But it's still a strange feeling to catch sight of myself in the mirror, a lint-free cotton cloth in one hand and a jar of Danish wax furniture polish in the other. It makes me want to do something crazy, like eat the contents of the jar and then puke all over the Louis XV commode, see if that makes it shine. But then I remind myself why I am here, and then I feel better.

I got to check out her bathroom today, all under the cover of cleaning it. I love her bathroom; it's large and light with a Moroccan feel because of the blue-and-white tiles and the light fixtures. Visible through an arched doorway is the gorgeous freestanding bathtub sitting under the window. I imagined myself lying in that bathtub, bubbles up to my chin, turning the tap off with my pedicured toe. I found some Ambien and some Xanax in the bathroom cabinet and normally, I'd swipe them both, but not this time. I did help myself to a Xanax, though. God knows I need it.

I have to come up with all sorts of ways to hide my duplicity. I know that Hannah doesn't cook, and neither do I, obviously, but Louise Martin does. She wouldn't have been hired otherwise. Fortunately, they do their own breakfast, and Harvey isn't at home for lunch, so Hannah will usually fix herself a sandwich. For dinner I'll buy things like fettuccine in a packet and a jar of gourmet pasta sauce from Fairway, or some frozen veal cordon bleu that comes in a box and goes in the microwave. In the kitchen I'll line up ingredients more or less randomly on the countertop as if making something from scratch, just in case. I'll even drop an olive on the floor and sprinkle herbs over the stove.

Yesterday I opened a jar of tomato paste and noticed it had a small grey round of mold on the top. Now, I'm the type of person who, at this point, would throw the whole jar away. This time I carefully scooped the mold with a wooden spoon and added it to the ready-made sauce that was gently warming on the stove. Sometimes she'll come into the kitchen just to have a chat, so yesterday I said to her that I don't like people hovering when I'm cooking. I said it in the nicest way. "It's just a quirk I have. Fortunately for me, Mrs. Van Kemp didn't mind one bit."

"Oh, no problem, I'll keep out of your way, then."

If only. One thing about Hannah is that she has no friends, except for a woman called Eryn who knows Harvey from way back and is only a few years younger than Hannah, so "Harvey thought we'd make great friends, the way people do with children of the same height," is how she described it to me. "And I'm not sure, but I think she wants my husband," she added, whispering.

"Really?"

She shrugged. "Just a feeling. And the way she is around him. Like a butterfly. Although she is quite beautiful." She sighed.

"Does it bother you?" I asked. Please say yes.

"That she likes Harvey? No. Why should it? Harvey could have had her. He chose me, so…" She smiled coyly from one side of her mouth.

I don't know why Hannah tells me these things. Maybe it's because she's so friendless and lonely. She follows me around the house like a puppy. I vacuumed the stairs this morning because I'm worried she'll notice I'm not doing any work, and also to shut her up because when she's not sleeping, which she seems to do an awful lot of, she talks, like, all the time. I don't usually have people to talk to, except maybe April, and even then, it's not like we chew each other's ear off for hours on end, so being around Hannah is taking some getting used to.

It's the middle of the afternoon, and I'm fake-sweeping the terrace. It's pretty spectacular up here. The terrace runs the entire length of the building. It's large with a stone floor, and in lieu of a railing is a low wall of brick pavers with green potted plants along it. If I lived in this house, I'd spent all my days here.

Hannah appears in the French doors. "Ha, there you are. I'm making myself a coffee, would you like one? Mia is asleep, thank God!"

I follow her to the kitchen, thinking she wants me to

make the coffee, but no. She tells me to sit down, puts a plate of chocolate chip cookies in front of me and pops a capsule in the coffee machine. When we both have our steaming cups in front of us, she sits down at the stool opposite me, puts her bare feet on the bar and starts nibbling on the edge of a cookie.

"How did you meet Mr. Carter?" I ask, resisting the urge to shove the entire cookie in my mouth at once.

She smiles. "I used to have a flower store in Toronto. That's where I used to live. He was visiting on business, and he came by to buy some flowers."

"Is that it?" I ask after a moment. She laughs.

"It was the end of the day and I was locking up, and suddenly he was there, knocking on the door, breathless. He gave me the same spiel I'd heard so many times over the years: 'Please don't lock up! I need to buy some flowers! It's an emergency!' Invariably, the emergency is that they've only just realized it's their wedding anniversary and they need flowers. Right now."

"Makes sense," I say, reaching for another cookie.

"I said no, the flowers are already in the cooler. I told him to go to the supermarket, they have flowers there. He was very insistent. He wanted something special. He said that a colleague of his had just had a terrible day and needed cheering up. At least that was different, so I asked what had happened, and he said her cat had been run over. I had a cat. I loved my cat, so I gave in. I brought out an arrangement of birds of paradise and calla lilies. He said it was perfect, and he couldn't thank me enough. Then he came in again the next day and bought a small plant for the apartment he was staying in. He explained he was only here for a short time, on business, and the apartment he rented needed cheering up."

"Like the colleague with the cat," I say.

"That's what I said! I asked if the bouquet was well received, and he said, 'Absolutely. My colleague feels much better because of them, and I expect my apartment to do the same.' Which I thought was pretty funny. Then he came a third time, and this time he asked what my favorite flowers were. I don't have a favorite flower; they're all special in their own way. But I played along. I love violets, but they don't last long. Sweet peas are one of my favorites, but I didn't have any to sell. Tulips are special. An underrated flower that comes in all sorts of varieties. People don't like them in vases because they tend to droop; they think the flowers are dying but that's not true. That's just the way they are, which makes very beautiful cascading bouquets if you cut them in different lengths."

She pauses to take a sip of coffee, and I'm trying to understand why we are talking about flowers, if we will ever get to the point, and if there is a point at all.

"I showed him the Burning Heart variety," she continues, "yellow and red, with big swirls of color. He bought two dozen of them, then after I'd finished preparing the bouquet, he offered it to me with a flourish. Will you come out with me, he asked, for a drink? I'd just been dumped by my not-very-nice boyfriend. His name was Barnaby, and by the time I found out he was cheating on me, it had been going on for months. Which made me 'not the brightest tool in the shed,' as my father would say." She rolls her eyes.

"So Harvey walked into my life, brandishing a bouquet of Burning Heart tulips. That first night, he took me to the Ritz-Carlton for cocktails and Jacob's for dinner. I can safely say I'd never set foot in such places. My dates so far had been more of the *Let's have a beer at the local sports bar, it's curling night.*"

I laugh at that.

"Would you mind if I had a cigarette?" she blurts.

"Here? Now?"

"It's the coffee, it makes me crave nicotine. If it bothers you, I won't. I shouldn't anyway. Oh, and Harvey thinks I've given up. Which I have," she hastens to say. "I didn't smoke at all once I found out I was pregnant. But I've been sneaking one here and there lately. He'll kill me if he found out."

I shrug. "It doesn't bother me, it's your house."

She gets up and pulls out one of the cookbooks on the shelf and retrieves a pack of Marlboro, a lighter, and an ashtray. Then she opens the window and sits down again.

"Promise you won't tell?" she asks, cigarette already in her mouth.

"My lips are sealed."

"Thank you." She takes a drag. "That's better," she says, exhaling a thin column of smoke. "I wasn't used to men like Harvey. Men who open the door for you, who help you put your coat on."

"I hate that," I say. "It just makes it harder."

She smiles.

"So what happened? If you were there and he was here?"

"I didn't expect our little romance to go beyond his business trip. But then he extended his stay. When he left, he promised to come back. I didn't really believe him. But he did come back. Then every time he'd leave I'd think, okay, this is it, this is the end, but he kept coming back to me. We spent many wonderful nights together in my small apartment. He was different, he made me laugh. He was charming and interesting and kind. Then he asked me to marry him. What can I say? By then I was in love. Head over heels. And pregnant with Mia." She smiles, but there's something sad at the edges of her eyes. She stubs out the cigarette.

Of course she was pregnant. I can just imagine how she made herself into everything he wanted, seductive and sweet at the same time. She'd gush that having sex in the missionary position for five minutes was the most thrilling experience of her life. Then, somehow, against all odds and statistics, she got pregnant, *accidentally*, and Harvey being a gentleman, well ... as they say, the rest is history.

"I was thirty years old when I met him. It's not old but still, I thought my life's direction had been set by then. I did begin to worry about whether I'd ever have a family. I hadn't met the right man yet, and while I wasn't holding out for Prince Charming, I thought it would be nice to meet someone reliable, someone who could hold down a job, someone who didn't feel the need to lie all the time. So while I might have expected the compass needle of my life to swing a few degrees here or there, a few minor detours, I sure didn't expect this. I didn't expect Harvey."

"I bet you had a nice wedding."

She smiles. "I can barely remember it. Even when I look at the pictures. In the church, we had to do away with the tradition of his side/her side of the aisle, as I had only a smattering of people attend. Harvey had a list of over two hundred, although I think at least half of those were acquaintances of his mother's. 'People we must invite, Harvey, darling. They'll never forgive us,' Patsy had said."

I'm surprised at the sharpness of her tone when she talks about Harvey's mother. "I take it you're not close?" I ask.

She lights up another cigarette. "She doesn't like me. I mentioned it to Harvey once, early on, and he said I was being overly sensitive. His mother doesn't like a lot of people, he said. I don't know why he thought that would make me feel better, considering she adores his first wife."

"There's a first wife?" I ask, innocent-like.

"Serena. I never met her. She moved to London after the divorce. But his mother took a long time to forgive Harvey for divorcing her—*such a lovely woman, and beautiful, too. A true sense of style*, is how she referred to Serena at my own wedding."

I raise my eyebrows. "Awkward."

"That's one of the reasons Patsy doesn't like me. Harvey left Serena for me, you see."

My eyebrows shoot up. "Harvey was still married when you met him?"

She cringes a little, then recovers quickly. "I didn't know he was still married. By the time I found out, they were already going through the divorce. But it didn't take long. It was amicable."

Yeah, right.

"Anyway, my parents came to the wedding, of course. In all the photos, they look really happy, which is a miracle in itself. My mother in her green silk dress and, oddly, white gloves. My father with red cheeks in his light gray suit, the same gray suit he brings out for every special occasion. I remember thinking it was stretching worryingly around his waist, just like me!" she chuckles. "Still, it was sweet. They kept telling me how proud they were. Like I'd achieved something really significant."

Of course they were proud. She'd finally caught the big fish. Then I think of the phone conversation she had with her father and I wonder how he feels now.

Hannah empties the ashtray into the trash and says she's going to lie down. I guess it's all the lies that take it out of her. I tell her not to worry, I'll feed Mia when she wakes up.

Still, that was a good story, and she told it well. If I didn't know any better, I'd almost believe it.

FOURTEEN

The next day, Hannah goes out, I don't know where to. To her therapist, no doubt. It's the first time I'm alone here, and I've been dying to go through her things, especially her bedroom, but of course I haven't because she's always here, so the moment she leaves I almost run upstairs.

I start with the dresser. It's clearly hers, some kind of antique thing with a big mirror on top and lots of little drawers. There's a photo in a pretty silver frame, of her with Harvey on a vacation somewhere. He looks very relaxed, very proud with his arm around his wife's waist. She's heavily pregnant and her face is more puffy than it is now. She stands with one hand on her stomach, looking at him in puppylike adoration. I pick it up to take a closer look at her. You'd never know, looking at those big eyes and that pretty smiling mouth, what an evil heart she carries within.

She's got some nice beauty creams, which I help myself to. I try on some green eyeshadow and pocket a Dior lipstick from the back of the drawer.

They have two walk-in closets, his and hers. He has

conservative tastes, it must be said. Nice suits, hanging according to season and color. Lots of shirts, white ones, some with stripes. Her clothes, on the other hand, are surprisingly ordinary and barely fill a third of her space, although I notice some new shoes, very nice, expensive, definitely, then I get it. Of course, she's trying to lose weight before she splurges on a new wardrobe!

I spot the dress I saw her buy at Bergdorf Goodman's the day I followed her. It's a black lace cocktail dress with a nice edge to the décolletage, and a brilliant idea flashes in my mind. Since she's so insecure about her weight, I'm going to sew inside the seam. I'm already laughing at the thought of her putting it on and finding it doesn't fit anymore.

I take it downstairs to the laundry. There's a sewing machine there, all set up on the bench. It takes a bit of Googling to figure out how to use the machine, and I use a dust cloth to practice on. Then I line up one edge under the bit of metal and press the pedal, and within seconds the dress is getting pounded by the needle, like a doll-sized jackhammer, but it's not right and I pull on the fabric to release it, but it's stuck. The thread has knotted itself into a tight ball. I'm starting to sweat. This is not going the way I imagined. This is turning out to be a really bad idea. What if she comes home now? How am I going to explain this? I can't exactly say it required mending; by the looks of it, she's never worn it before. I wish I'd popped another one of her Xanax before I started this, because it's really stressing me out.

But Mrs. Petersen did not raise a quitter, and an hour later it is done. I return the dress—looking a little worse for wear, it must be said—where I found it, and then I go to check on Mia. She's awake, and perfectly happy. I pick her up, and she giggles at me, puts her little chubby hands on my face and frowns in concentration, like she's exploring me. I keep her in my arms while I search the rest of the house, although without much urgency. But I do find a credit card statement belonging to Serena Carter, from a UK bank, hidden between two of Harvey's legal books on the shelf. She doesn't spend much. He's scribbled "paid" on one of them, and I note that the statement is only six months old. Which means Harvey Carter is still paying his ex-wife's bills, and he's hiding it from Hannah. Now *that's* interesting.

Mia yawns and rests her head in the crook of my neck, and it feels so nice that I stand there, swaying slowly and even forget about Hannah for a while, so when she comes home I barely have time to put the statements back.

Maybe Harvey Carter is still in love with his first wife. Maybe he's suffering from buyer's remorse. Why else would he hide the fact that he's paying her bills? In fact, why else would he pay her bills in the first place? They don't have children, she's a professional woman, surely she earns a good living. Maybe Hannah can sense it. Maybe that's why she has this thing about Serena.

I had another go at seducing him yesterday, in a less subtle manner because time is not on my side. He was in the small sitting room downstairs and Hannah was in bed —where else?—so I walked in with the top three buttons of my uniform undone but this time I wasn't wearing a bra. Any more than three buttons and my tits would be falling out. I leaned against the doorjamb and put one hand on my waist, in what I would call a very suggestive pose, one that left little to the imagination.

"Is there anything I can do for you, Mr. Carter? Anything at all?" I asked, chewing on a fingernail. He looked up from his newspaper, blinked a few times and blushed. Then he went back to reading and said, "No, thank you, Louise. Maybe Mrs. Carter would like some herbal tea." I turned around, too angry to be embarrassed, and left him there. I didn't check whether Mrs. Carter wanted some tea. It goes without saying. But it's beginning to look like I'm wasting my time here. I'm almost at the end of the first week and no closer than I was when I started. Except here I am, changing her sheets because apparently that's on my schedule, and she had to remind me because I didn't do it last Tuesday. So I guess the joke's on me.

I need a different plan. I liked the original because using Hannah's own strategy against her had a nice symmetry to it. But maybe I'm overcomplicating things. Maybe I should just point a gun to her head and get her confession that way. I wonder where I could get a gun. I bet she owns one. Harvey would have bought it for her. A nice, compact little thing. A Glock, most likely. Something pretty and feminine, just like her. Maybe with a pearl handle or something.

I peer over the balustrade but there's no sign of her. I figure she's still downstairs at her computer, where I left her earlier, so I search Harvey's closet first. I'll say I'm tidying up if she comes in. I run my fingers along the back wall behind the hanging suits, I check the shelves and inside the shoes, but there's nothing that doesn't belong there.

I do the same in her walk-in closet, and behind the bottom shelf, I see a line in the wall that shouldn't be there. I look more closely—it's some kind of panel. I run my fingers along its edges, my pulse racing. I push softly, and it clicks open. I'm grinning. I'm thinking, gun, obviously. Totally. Gun. Again I make sure she's nowhere near the bedroom, then I pull open the panel and reach into the cavity.

It's not a gun. It's a leather notebook with a thin leather strap—as thin as a shoelace—wrapped around it. I untie it, and a cream-colored card falls out. I pick it up, turn it around. It's her wedding invitation. I open the notebook and flick through the pages.

It's better than a gun.

It's her diary.

I still wake up some nights wondering where I am, but it's different now. Before, I would run my hands over the sheets with their one trillion thread count and smile to myself. I'm in our bedroom, in our enormous bed. I'm home. Then I would reach out until my fingers brushed against some part of Harvey, his back probably, or his arm. He would be asleep because he always sleeps, no matter what. I would press myself against him, maybe move one of the many down pillows and shift it under my head. Or I would raise myself on one elbow and whisper sweet nothings into his ear, kiss his neck softly.

Now, more often than not, when I wake in the dead of night, it's because my heart is hammering and I am overcome with the absolute certainty that something is very wrong. I don't reach for Harvey because as much as he tries, he can't help me. He'll tell me that I'm dreaming and that I should go back to sleep. He doesn't understand how relentless and absolute this feeling of doom is. Like we're drifting toward disaster, gathering up speed and we're all blindfolded. I don't even know what the danger looks like, only that I have to stop it before we reach it.

Harvey says I've been like this ever since Mia was born. I don't think I have. Mia is almost three months old now, but I was fine after she was born, I'm sure of it. I tell him that, but he just shakes his head. He says Dr. Malone is excellent, the best, and she can help me. He says that I'm suffering from anxiety attacks. He says everything is going to be fine. That he's there for me, no matter what. It's normal, he says. It will pass.

Dr. Malone has very small eyes, like two black buttons too close together. But it gives her a weird piercing quality. Like she has laser focus and can read my mind.

"Is this what maternal love feels like?" I asked, then with a chuckle, I added, "If so, it's going to be a very long eighteen years!" I meant to lighten the mood. Look at me, I'm fine, I can crack a joke so let's get off the crazy train, but she looked at me with her little eyes and said, "How long have you been feeling this way?" Then she asked all these questions like she was on a fishing expedition. Did I think the nurses at the hospital were going to hurt Mia? No. Did I have mood swings? Hmm, let me see, I just had a baby, what do you think? Instead I just said "probably." Are they getting worse? No. Do I experience any hallucinations? Aural or visual?

No. But I know where you're going with this, I thought. Postpartum psychosis. I looked it up, too.

I did my best to reassure her I didn't suffer from acute paranoia. I leaned forward, trying to see what she'd written down. I have enough problems without her trying to send me to the psychiatric ward, thanks all the same.

Maybe it's physical? Maybe I should get some tests done? Sometimes my pulse is so slow that merely standing up makes me feel like I'm about to faint.

She says it's probably just stress and that I should take a few days off. But all I have are days off. I'm beginning to think everyone is in on it, whatever this is. This thing that is killing me.

She asked me if I was sad. All the time, I said, and I could feel my tears well up as I said it and it made me laugh. Look at me, I'm a walking cliché.

She gave me a prescription for Xanax.

That's the last entry. It's not dated. None of them are. They're more like notes, random and mostly hastily hand-written. But if Mia was almost three months when she wrote it, then it must be a month ago, give or take.

I flick through the earlier entries. The notebook begins with her wedding. It's gushing and ordinary and I can't stop reading, because this is gold. There must be something in there that shows what she's like. What if she wrote something about her plans for Harvey? Something that proves that she's only after his money? I could use that as leverage in exchange for her confession. But then I hear her on the landing below, calling me, and reluctantly I tie the leather cord around the notebook and shove it back in its hiding place.

FIFTEEN

I am almost at the house, grocery bags filled with ready-made spinach and ricotta cannelloni from the frozen section of the supermarket (three minutes on high in the microwave!) and an ordinary Greek salad from Allegra when Diane jumps out of a doorway and lands in front of me.

"So it's you!" she screeches. She looks me up and down. "Why are you here? Are you the new housekeeper?"

I almost laugh, I can't help it. The sight of her like that, with her arms outstretched like a scarecrow, is just hysterical. I have to put my groceries down to wipe the tears of laughter. "Diane, you're the best. You really are. What are you trying to do? Hug me?"

She recoils, one hand on her chest, her features going through a multitude of expressions like she's demonstrating how face gymnastics can smooth out those pesky wrinkles. But then I grow serious because this is not good.

"Of course I'm not the new housekeeper. What a funny thing to say! You okay, Diane? How's your sister? Is she better? What about you? How you doing?"

She squints at me. "You're wearing my uniform."

"No! I—look, I'm just helping out, that's all. I'm sure I told you last time that I know these people. You remember?"

She stands back and grows taller, like a puppet slowly hauled up by the puppet master who suddenly remembers he has a job to do, and from her full height she says, "Your name isn't Claire."

Of all things, this is the most unexpected, since my name is, in fact, Claire.

"I called Mrs. Carter—"

I feel my heart drop and my stomach clench. "You did what?"

"Mrs. Patsy Carter. I have a good relationship with her, I'll have you know. And she said your name is Louise."

She looks triumphant with her little scrap of misinformation. But the horror of what she just said is making me clench my fists. I'm too close to the finish line to have crazy Diane ruin it for me. Then I remember that she's not crazy, that it's me who made out like she is, with the rat and the phone calls, and yet that's how I think of her now. Crazy Diane. Go figure. But my temper has gotten the better of me, and suddenly I'm poking a hard finger into her sternum.

"You know nothing, now get away from me and never come back here, or I'll call the cops, you understand? I'll sue you for harassment. I'll tell everyone that you're a vindictive, bitter old woman who got fired because she's about as competent as a one-armed violinist and batshit crazy to boot. Get out of my way now, while you still can, Diane."

She nods, startled, and moves out of my path. I leave

her there, my heart thumping, fully aware I'll have to deal with her later. Diane is a threat now.

Once inside, I find Hannah in the smaller seating room that comes off the foyer. She's sitting at the desk, doing something on her laptop, with Mia on her lap. Mia is holding a stuffed yellow-and-black tiger and sucking on its ear.

"Did I tell you I was a florist before I came here?" Hannah says.

"I believe you did," I reply, trying to stop my eyes from rolling.

"Well, I was thinking about your plans to open a fashion store. And you've been inspiring me." She smiles. "There's a shopfront for rent on Sixty-Ninth that would be perfect for a flower store. I'm thinking of specializing in— and please don't laugh, okay? Promise?"

I make a serious expression and point to my face. "No laughing matter. Understood."

"Okay, well, here goes: flowers for children. I could run workshops; they can learn to grow things in pots. I'm a bit vague about it all but I'm very excited. I'm researching flower markets right now. All thanks to you." Then she studies my face for a moment and grows serious. "Everything okay, Louise?"

"I've been accosted by a strange woman," I say. I watch that happy, excited face fall and turn anxious. I sit down on the chair by the wall, next to the desk. Mia smiles at me.

Hannah bites a fingernail, even though it's a nice French manicure and she only had them done yesterday. "I think I know who that is. What did she say?"

"I was just about to walk in the door with the groceries when she came right behind me. She put her hand on my shoulder, she really scared me. Then she said, 'Don't trust her, mark my words, she's a real…'" I stop.

"Bitch?" Hannah asks.

"Yes! How did you know? You know her? She has black hair, very thin, a bit taller than me—"

"Oh God. Yes, I know her. I'm so sorry, Louise. It's my old housekeeper, Diane."

"Really?" I open my eyes wide. "What's wrong with her?"

"I had to fire her. She didn't take it well. She's been behaving erratically."

"How awful!"

"I know. But I hadn't heard from her over the last few days, and I honestly thought she had started to move on. I was just beginning to relax." She shakes her head. "But this is not fair to you. I'm very sorry she accosted you like that."

I wave a hand in front of my face. "Oh, that's all right. No harm done. I gave her a piece of my mind. Told her not to come around here again." I say this in the tone of someone who has endured a few battle scars and isn't intimidated by some whacko on the street. I want her to think of me as being on her side. Her protector. "Should I call the police?" I ask, thinking, *please say no*.

"No, don't. I'll tell Harvey when he comes home. That won't be for a few hours." She checks her watch. "My husband has been reluctant to do anything about Diane out of some deluded sense of loyalty. But if she's beginning to harass you, then I think it's time he took charge." Then she sits back in her chair and bounces Mia on her lap. "She's called here twice, very threateningly. But Harvey doesn't believe it's her. He says they're kids, prank calls."

"But how do you know that they're from Diane?"

"Oh, please, Louise, don't you start."

"No, I mean it. How do you know?"

"I know it's Diane because she has a slight lisp. And like I said to Harvey, kids who make prank calls don't call me Mrs. Carter."

And then the doorbell rings, and we're not thinking straight, either of us, because she points her chin toward the door and says, "You go," and I open it, vaguely expecting a deliveryman and Diane is standing there, her mouth distorted like she's in pain, and I'm shouting "Get out!" and trying to close the door on her but she's gone crazy. She's kicking my shins and banging her fists against the door, screaming like some wild caged animal in a zoo. Hannah stands there frozen, clutching the baby in her arms, and she looks terrified.

"What are you doing?" she cries.

Diane looks right at her, her eyes wild and red-rimmed, pointing her finger at her. "She's evil!" she's shouting, her voice raspy as though she's finding it difficult to get the words out.

Hannah's whole body is shaking. "Diane! Stop! Please!" Mia's wail slices the air and it's chaos, everyone is screaming and it's like trying to hold back a bear or a wild dog. She's too strong for me. The strength of fury—like a patient in an asylum lifting the therapist above his head and throwing him across the room. I give up trying to shut the door and stand right in front of Diane with both hands on her chest, pushing her out. Hannah is pleading with Diane to stop but it's as if she doesn't hear her. And yet she's looking right at her over my shoulder, her whole arm pointed at her like she's trying to grab her, her face burning with rage and fury, desperate to explain and to be understood. "She's evil! She's a liar! Liar! She's not who she says! She's a liar! I know who she really is! Liar! Liar!"

"Stop it!" Hannah is shouting and sobbing at the same time. She's shaking so much I'm afraid she'll drop Mia, who by now is hysterical. Then I give one more shove and Diane stumbles backward, enough for me to slam the door shut on her.

I turn around and lean against it, my heart beating so hard it makes my uniform quiver. "Go upstairs. Lock yourself in the bathroom." Hannah nods maniacally, and meanwhile, Diane is banging on the door behind me so hard I worry it's going to jump off its hinges. It's like a scene from a horror movie, except I'm living it.

"Go, now!" I shout. This time, she bolts and runs up the stairs, half falling, catching herself with one hand and holding Mia tight with the other.

When Hannah has disappeared, I open the door and push Diane so hard she stumbles back in surprise. I hiss at her with venom. I raise a fist and tell her that I'm going to kill her. I frighten her so much she takes off running down the street, but she's not very fast. She runs the way people do when they never run, throwing their legs sideways like a duck.

SIXTEEN

Hannah is still locked up in the bathroom upstairs, so I sprint into the office, my heart still pounding. I need Diane's cell number right now. I know I'm making too much noise, but I can't help it. I bang drawers open and shut and rummage through the antique filing cabinet. I'm about to give up and try somewhere else when I find it. Diane's employment file. I grab a pen from the desk and jot her number on my thigh. I call her from my own cell phone while listening out for Hannah. I can hear Mia crying upstairs, which means I'll be able to tell if Hannah opens the door.

When Diane picks up, at first I think she must be on the subway, just from the noise, like wind rushing through a tunnel, but then I realize it's her breath, loud and pained from running.

"It's me," I whisper. And she hangs up. I call her again immediately, and she picks up but doesn't speak.

Then she says, "I'm calling the police."

"Diane, listen to me!" I hiss. "Hannah just tried to call the cops on you! Just now! I had to stop her. Honestly, what you did back there? That was assault! That's a criminal offense, Diane! You'll go to jail if the police get involved! I told Hannah—"

"Hannah?"

"That's right, like I said, she's a friend of mine. I told her, don't call the police, it's not her fault. You were upset, but you're okay now, right? Because you understand that was forced entry just now, and you screaming like that—"

"But I just wanted to warn her!"

"About what?"

She hesitates; I can hear her crying. Finally she blurts, "About you."

"About me? You've got the wrong end of the stick there. I'm a friend of hers. I'm just helping out until they find someone else. And I'm sorry about before, the things I said. That was uncalled for, and I apologize. I just overreacted, you understand? You seemed to accuse me of something, and I tend to overreact when people falsely accuse me. It's a thing I have. I'm working on it. But you need to move on, Diane. You can't come back here, okay? I might not be around to smooth things over next time, and you definitely do not want the cops involved. Remember what I said—that was assault. And forced entry, too. With witnesses. Think of your sister. By the way, how is she?"

"My sister?"

"Yes, the pneumonia?"

"Be—better," she stutters.

"Great, that's great news. I'm really happy for you. And for her, obviously. Now I think you need to take a breath, okay? I'll make sure that Hannah doesn't report this to the police, okay?"

She breathes in a long, scattered breath. "I'm sorry, I—"

"It's okay, don't worry about it. Just take it easy. And don't come back here, all right?"

"All right."

"Okay, take care. Bye now."

Upstairs, I knock on the bathroom door. "It's me, it's Louise." I have to speak loudly to be heard over Mia's screams.

"Oh, thank God." I hear her fumbling with the lock on the other side. "Thank God," she says again. She puts one arm around my neck, and I quickly take Mia from her because she's shaking so much I worry she might drop her.

"Are you all right?" we both ask at the same time.

"Where is she?" she asks.

"She's gone. I went down the street after her, but I lost her."

Hannah sits on the edge of the bathtub and starts to cry. "I can't do this anymore. What's wrong with her? What does she want?" And I'm kind of surprised, because I really expected her to ask me questions, like *What did she mean, you're not who you say you are?*

"I thought she was going to come up and kill us, I really did," she says. "I was so worried about you, but every time I went to open the door, I had an image of her standing there, brandishing a fire poker over her head."

"It's okay now," I say gently. "She's gone." Then I hum to Mia, softly, the way my mother used to with me, and Mia stops crying, just like that. She looks at me with big round eyes, and there's only the sound of her hiccups and Hannah's raspy breath. "I'm going to put her to bed," I say. Hannah nods and puts both hands over her face.

After Mia falls asleep, I join Hannah in the kitchen. In

two strides she's put her arms around me. "Louise, you were amazing, the way you held her back like that, I—I don't know what to say. I'm very grateful to you, really. God, I need a drink." She releases me and points to a bottle of Pinot Grigio she's just retrieved from the wine cooler. "Join me?"

"Sure, that would be good," I say. But this is too weird. Surely she should be asking me questions about what Diane said. She pours me a glass and gives it to me. If anyone had told me that I would be chatting away with Hannah, sharing a bottle of Pinot Grigio, I would have laughed till my nose bled.

"Will you call the police now, Mrs. Carter? Or would you like me to?" I ask.

"Please don't call me Mrs. Carter. It's Hannah. And, no, don't call them. I'll wait until Harvey comes home," she says, and I think, okay, that makes no sense whatsoever, but whatever.

As if reading my mind, she continues. "I wasn't well after Mia was born. Only because Mia didn't sleep those first few weeks, like, at all. Honestly, I remember being so tired I could barely lift my arm to brush my hair. But Harvey kept saying I was being overly anxious, like I was having a nervous breakdown and that it was very normal after having a baby."

"I'm sorry, I didn't know. What did you do?"

"I said to him, is that what happened to you when you had a baby?"

I laugh. "Good for you."

"The thing is, I've never been an anxious person. I don't scare easily. That's not to say I'm brave and fearless. I mean, I've never gone bungee jumping, or paragliding, or parachuting, because all these things are scary and dangerous, and I'm not crazy. But even when I was pregnant I was very relaxed compared to some people. I loved being pregnant. I took to it like a lotus to water. I was like a happy Buddha, constantly rubbing my belly. I mean, sure, I wasn't crazy about the part where I looked like an elephant, but I didn't let it worry me. But after she was born, honestly, at one stage, whenever I saw Harvey asleep I wanted to shake him awake and laugh hysterically in his face. We'd have huge fights about this. But then Harvey insisted that I see someone, a psychiatrist, because of it."

"I see," I say.

"The night after I let Diane go, Harvey was away in Chicago and I was by myself with Mia. I thought it would be nice to have her next to my bed, so I put her in the smaller crib, the portable one."

I nod. "I know the one."

"I was sure she'd sleep like an angel, aware in some primal, subliminal way that her mother was nearby."

"Makes sense."

"Except it had the opposite effect. For hours I'd been watching her little red face wrinkle with fury, feeling more and more powerless to help her. I'd pick her up, I'd sing to her, I'd put her down again, I nuzzled her, I didn't nuzzle her. I left her to it while I paced the room, then I picked her up again. It just went on, and on, and on, and any minute I was going to join her in this screaming fest. I honestly started to think that she preferred being alone. That she hated me."

She looks up at me quickly to gauge my reaction. "It's not uncommon," I say. "Mrs. Van Kemp had terrible problems with the youngest one. I don't think she slept for a year, so you're miles ahead." I top off her glass while I'm at it, and she takes a gulp of it.

"Suddenly, just like that, she stopped crying," she resumes. "It was like the power had been cut. I was sitting on the side of the bed with my head in my hands when it happened. I thought she was taking in air, getting ready for the next onslaught, but when I looked at her, she was completely still, her little fists suspended in midair. Then I realized what she was doing."

"What?"

"She was listening."

"To what?"

"There was someone in the house."

I gasp. Then I look around and stare at the window, because for a moment I think maybe Diane's in the house right now.

"I thought I was going crazy, because of course no one was in the house. It was maybe midnight, and Harvey wasn't due back until noon the following day. But then we heard it again and Mia made the tiniest sound, a little gasp. We looked at each other, and I put one finger to my lips, a part of me thinking how wonderful it would be if it were so easy, the other part thinking we're all about to die, and I went to check."

"And was someone there?" I whisper.

She shakes her head. "But something was different. There was a light on downstairs. I leaned over the balustrade and looked down the spiral staircase. I always turn out the lights, all of them. Not because I'm worried about the bills, but because I don't believe we should waste our planet's resources, no matter how much money we have."

As if Hannah cared about anything but herself, but I manage not to roll my eyes, so that's good.

"There was a light on. Two floors down. So I went to have a look, of course—"

"I don't know why you say, 'of course.' I wouldn't have."

"Yes, well, you're smarter than me, then. I was halfway down the steps when I thought, what am I doing leaving Mia upstairs? At the very least I should have taken my cell phone with me, but I didn't even know where it was. Then I remembered some news item about a celebrity who locked themselves in the bathroom to call the police because there was someone in the house. I remembered thinking at the time how lucky it was that they had a cell phone in the bathroom." She laughs. "Except it wasn't luck, was it? It was forward thinking. Unlike me, prize idiot going down the stairs in bare feet, in my tracksuit pants and one of Harvey's old T-shirts."

She twirls the stem of her empty glass and I go to refill it, but the bottle is empty.

"Would you…?" she begins.

"Hold it right there," I say. I rush to the wine cooler and hold out another bottle. "This okay?"

"Perfect."

I pour her another glass. "Okay, keep going. The suspense is killing me."

"I'd reached the landing by that point, and I called out, 'Who's there?' But no one replied. I told myself I was over-reacting. That I must have left the lamp on myself without realizing. But it was the one with the stained glass shade and the small brass pull chain hanging from the socket, you know the one? Next to the phone?"

I nod. I know the one.

"I don't usually have it on. But I was standing in front of it and I could see my reflection in the window. Then the phone rang, and I thought I was having a heart attack. It was a blocked number, but I picked it up, and it was her."

She leans forward, and I do the same. It's dusk now. Neither of us has turned on a light and everything in the room is losing its color.

"What did she say?" I ask.

"Fuck you, Mrs. Carter. I hope you hate your life."

I sit back, speechless. Maybe she is crazy, maybe Harvey is right to send her to a psychiatrist, because I did call her that night, and I did say those things to her, but I didn't go into her house and I sure didn't turn a lamp on.

She sighs. "Predictably, Harvey said I was overreacting. He said it was my anxiety getting the better of me. That I needed to relax. That obviously, I left the light on." She stands up and tears off a sheet from the roll of paper towels, then blows her nose into it.

"Maybe Diane still had keys," I say.

"Exactly. I said that to him. 'How do you know Diane didn't keep one of the keys before returning them?' But he said he checked."

"Maybe she made copies," I suggest.

"I said that too, but he says you can't just go and make copies of these keys. They're security keys. In the end we had a fight, right here, in this room." She chuckles. "Anyway, I got him to change the locks."

"Well, that's a relief," I say.

"Harvey and I made up, of course. We made up that night—we were both apologizing, although I still don't know what I did wrong exactly. It was such a stupid argument. We haven't spoken of Diane since. We pretend that I never said the things I said about her, that I no longer think she's a danger to society, so we don't need to mention her ever again. But I always worry that she's biding her time, that the next time she does something it will be even worse. Every time I step outside, I search for her, but so far, she has stayed in the shadows, where she skulks about, no doubt, ready for her next strike. Have I told you about the rat?"

I tilt my head at her. "The rat? No."

She tells me about the rat in the mailbox, how it happened after she fired her. How she was holding Mia at the time and it was a miracle she didn't drop her. Also that rats have terrible diseases—I hadn't thought of that—and she had to wash her hands with bleach!

"What did Mr. Carter say?"

"He wasn't there. His mother was there, but she'd left before I found it. And you know why she was there? Because Diane had called her and she had come to ask me to change my mind. She would take Diane's side against mine."

I shake my head. "Did you tell Mr. Carter about the rat?"

She nods. "He said it was kids, playing a prank."

"Kids have a lot of time on their hands around here," I say. "Maybe you should consider moving downtown."

She smiles sadly. Then she gets up and turns on the overhead lights, and the room suddenly becomes normal again. I move to the window and pull the blinds down.

"So what happened after that?" I ask when we're both back at the table.

She shrugs. "Nothing. He assured me it couldn't possibly be Diane, that it wasn't her style. He said he's known her a long time. Nothing I say will convince him, so I've given up."

"Well, once he hears about this, he'll feel terrible for not believing you sooner."

She hesitates. "If you don't mind, let me tell him in my own time."

I'm waiting for her to say something else, but she reaches for my hand and squeezes it, and it's so unexpected it makes me blush. "I'm so glad you're here, Louise. I can't thank you enough." She lets go of my hand. "After tonight, I feel like I owe you my life!" she laughs. "And since you seem to double as a bodyguard, I'd like to give you a raise. I know it's awkward, please don't say anything. I'm really very grateful. For everything. I want you to know that."

"Thank you. That's kind of you." But something is wrong here, because why would you wait for the right time to tell your husband that some lunatic tried to break into your house, clearly wanting to harm you and your child, and thank God Louise was there to stop her? She should be calling him right now. She should be screaming into the phone. *See? And I have a witness! So you believe me now?*

"You're welcome," I say.

"Thank you. It's complicated," Hannah says. "So if you don't mind, I'd appreciate it if—"

"Hannah, honestly, it's none of my business. I won't mention anything to Mr. Carter."

"Just not until I get a chance to do it, that's all."

"You have my word," I say, thinking I can't wait to call her again later tonight. I might even wait until she's asleep if Harvey isn't back by then.

Bitch. You're a horrible person. I know what you did.

"Thank you," she says. "I appreciate that."

SEVENTEEN

Ever since Diane burst through the door like the Big Bad Wolf in the "Three Little Pigs" story, I've been on edge. I can tell Hannah is too. We don't speak about it, but we both scan the streets whenever we step outside. We both jump at the sound of a phone ringing. Any phone. We have our own reasons, but we're both scared of her and I have more reason to be than Hannah. All it would take is for Diane to change her mind and get in touch with Hannah, or even Patsy, and tell them my real name. They'd call the agency and be told that, no, whoever your housekeeper is, it's not Louise Martin. I still have the image of Diane screaming that I'm a liar imprinted on my retinas. And I still don't understand why Hannah hasn't confronted me about it.

It's Saturday, my first day off, and I am lying on my bed watching TV with a bottle of vodka I swiped from the bar upstairs. I can barely keep my eyes open. This job, if I were to do it the way it's intended, would be like being trapped on a hamster wheel. By the time you finish cleaning the house you have to start again from the beginning.

Hannah complained this morning that she's not well. She's worried something is wrong with her. She says she can't think straight and that she feels like a radio constantly trying to tune itself but looping through endless static instead. I thought, as an analogy, this one has probably passed its used-by date. Does anybody even own a radio anymore? Is static still a thing?

I said, "Really? But you've been doing very little, hardly anything. Maybe you should go to the doctor! What does Mr. Carter say?"

Because all the while I'm thinking, I'm the one who has to wake up at six a.m. every morning, and you're telling me this? I'm so tired all I can do is shuffle slowly through the house, cataloging the things I'll steal when I leave. Unless she's around, in which case I might scrub some imaginary speck of dust.

Anyway, I open the bottle of vodka, thinking I should have opted for some red wine because I don't have a refrigerator in my room, not even a bar fridge, and warm vodka is not the same. I pour some into the glass that normally holds my toothbrush and surf through the various channels. They don't have Netflix or Hulu or anything like that. I wonder if I should ask for it, as part of my employment package. In the end, I settle on a shopping channel, and I am plowing through my second bag of corn chips when she knocks on my door.

"Hello! Louise! You in there?"

I freeze for a second, then put my glass slowly on my bedside table, straighten my T-shirt and open the door a fraction, just enough to squeeze my face through. Like that poster of Jack Nicholson in *The Shining*.

"Hi?"

She's wearing her denim jacket and black jeans, her hands in her back pockets. "I know it's your day off. I thought maybe we could go out together? Shopping, maybe? If you felt like doing that?"

I grip the edge of the door harder. "That sounds like fun, but I'm going out soon."

"Oh? Of course! Sorry."

"Maybe next time?" I say.

"Sure, okay. Next time. Oh, and there's another thing."

"Yes?"

"There was an issue with your W-4 form—your Social Security number doesn't match. Can you give it to me? I'll resubmit it for you."

I stare at her for a moment, and no words come out. The silence goes on for just a little too long until finally I shake my head. "Sorry. I can't think today," I say, laughing a little too loudly. "Okay, Social Security number. I'll find it and give it to you."

"Great, no rush, whenever you can."

"But it's going to take a while, isn't it? If you have to resubmit it?"

"I don't know, why?"

"I was wondering, could you pay me cash instead? Maybe just for this month? I don't know if I can wait, that's all."

"No, you won't have to wait. Even if the W-4 is late, it won't affect your salary. I'll make sure you get paid into your account, regardless."

"Right, but I forgot to say, I've got an issue with the bank account on my application."

"Oh?"

"It's stupid, but I closed it down recently. I just haven't had the time to do anything about it. So just for this month, if you could pay cash, I'd really appreciate it."

She blinks a few times like she's confused, and I'm about to say, okay, fine don't worry about it, Hannah, but she nods.

"Sure, I'll organize it. Enjoy yourself today."

I smile, thank her, and manage not to kick the door shut in her face. Then I drag myself to get changed and put the bottle of vodka in my bag. I consider going to see April—we could order pizza, maybe? But then I imagine all the questions she'd be asking: *OMG! Where have you been? Why didn't you return my calls or my texts! How's your cousin? What's Pittsfield like? What do you do all day? Hey, I don't mean to nag, but do you have my rent yet?*

So, I end up back at Dominic's place, on the off chance he's home. I haven't remembered his name is Dominic at that point, but I remember where he lives. He opens the door, sizes me up, and says, "You left without saying goodbye."

"I know," I say. "I'm sorry. That's why I'm here. I've come to say it now. Goodbye."

He chuckles, and we stand awkwardly at the door, and I'm just starting to think this is a really dumb idea when he puts his hands all over me, hugging me, groping me, which feels nice after Harvey not even being tempted. So I kiss him.

After we have sex, he gets up to get glasses for the vodka, and I use the time to snoop around his apartment. It's brighter than I remember, and surprisingly tidy. I open his laptop, which asks for a password, so I close it again. I vaguely consider stealing it, then change my mind. I turn my attention to the black soft bags of various sizes and folded tripods in the corner.

"What's all this?" I ask when he returns.

"It's my job." He hands me a glass, then opens one of the bags and pulls out a camera, very professional-looking. He points it at me but doesn't take the cap off.

"You make porno?" I ask, and he laughs.

"I'm a photographer."

"What, like weddings?"

"Sometimes, but mostly I do things like still life, for the larger stock image libraries. Then I'll do events. Art openings. Some catalog work, the occasional gig with the *Post*." He tries not to smile, the way people do when they're really pleased with themselves but they pretend it's no big deal.

"How did you get into that? Photography, I mean."

"I don't know. I fell into it."

"Really?"

"Yeah."

"What did you do before that?"

"You really want to know?"

"Sure I do."

"I took drugs."

I chuckle. "We all take drugs, Dominic."

"I sold them, too. It landed me in jail for two years. Feel free to show yourself out."

I cock my head at him. "Is that true?"

"Yes, and I'm not ashamed of it, in case you're wondering. Shit happens."

I laugh. "I know shit happens, buddy. So what now? You're cured?"

"I'm in recovery."

I snort. "And they let you into posh events? Art openings? The occasional gig with the *Post*? No way! Oh wait, is that how you buy drugs? Is this your gig, you get in and steal stuff? That is wicked, my friend. Congratulations. I'm impressed." I take the last swig off my tumbler.

He crosses his arms over his chest and frowns at me, like he's confused. He doesn't know if I'm joking or not. Neither do I.

"I don't steal stuff. I don't buy drugs either. It's my job. I also teach—in prison. I help kids who are incarcerated, so they can get their high school diplomas. So they can get past their mistakes and go to college when they get out. I teach them to give up drugs and get a job. Get a life. You got a problem with that, too?"

I put one hand on my waist. "Wanna fuck?"

When I return the following day, Hannah has gone to lunch with her friend Eryn. I'm sitting on her bed, shaking and confused, and it has nothing to do with my hangover. It's because I have her diary in my hand, and I have to read the entry twice because the words are jumping and they're making me ill.

I woke up last night, and that horrible fear had me in its grip again. I had to rush out of bed to Mia, but when I got to the nursery, complete silence. By the time I bent over the crib, I had twisted myself into such a panic that I was almost surprised to find Mia in it, lying peacefully on her back. I placed my palm over her round belly and felt her breathe. Only then did I let my own breath out. I'm going crazy. I couldn't decide whether to laugh with relief or howl with despair at my own neurosis.

I stood there, pulling myself back together, the heel of one hand between my eyes and the other gently resting on top of my baby, and maybe that was why I didn't hear her.

"*Everything all right?*"

And for a second I thought it was Diane, and I opened my mouth to scream, then quickly clasped my hand over it.

"*Louise, shit, you scared me to death.*"

"*Sorry,*" *she whispered.* "*I didn't mean to. I just heard something.*"

"*Yes, me,*" *I replied. She came to stand next to me, so close I could smell her soap. She bent over the crib and rubbed my daughter's cheek with her thumb. A little sound escaped Mia's lips, like a bubble.*

"*She's all right now. Sorry I woke you. Go back to bed, Louise.*"

She straightened finally and pulled her hand away, but I could tell she didn't want to go. Mia let out a short, displeased cry. We both froze, but then she sighed and we both chuckled softly. "*I'll bring you some tea, it will relax you,*" *she whispered. I was about to say no, her teas always make me sleepy and I don't need any more of that, but then I changed my mind just to get her out of the room.* "*That would be great, thanks.*"

I dragged the armchair next to the crib, tucked my feet under me and pulled the throw over my shoulders. But a part of me wondered, did Louise really come in because she heard me? Because it felt like she was already there, in a dark corner of the room. Waiting. Silent. Until finally she announced herself. She seems to do that a lot, appear suddenly out of nowhere when I least expect it. Sometimes I wonder if she's spying on me. I should probably say something to her. Ask her not to do that anymore. It's creepy.

At least those awful phone calls have stopped, although I fear it's a case of the calm before the storm. I try to distract myself, go for walks in the park. It makes me feel better to be outside. Louise and I took Mia out together the other day. We went to the conservatory garden, which I love. On the way back I pointed out the foxglove and explained how toxic it is. She was fascinated by that. She couldn't believe that a plant that lethal could be found in the middle of the park. I suppose she has a point.

I wish I could talk to Harvey or Dr. Malone about Louise. Explain that it's a feeling I have about her, and it's not a good one. She's making me nervous. But I can't, of course. It would just confirm what they already think about me. That I'm paranoid, overly anxious, sick.

I feel so alone, I want to cry.

None of this is true. I've never been to the conservatory garden with her and Mia. I've never laid eyes on foxglove. I wouldn't know what it looks like if it slapped me in the face.

That scene she describes in the nursery, her coming in to check on Mia, me in a dark corner of the room, staying silent, being creepy? Never happened.

It's her who's always following me around, not the other way around. I'm constantly trying to get away from her. I try to remember a single time when she might have been surprised to see me, and I can't.

She's lying. She's writing down lies about me and I don't know why.

EIGHTEEN

She walks into the kitchen as I'm unloading the dishwasher. I can't bear to look at her, and when she says, "I'll give you a hand," I tell her I'm almost finished. I'm afraid I'll hit her if she gets too close.

She's going to a fundraiser this evening, a gala for research in something or other.

"Do you know it's my first proper outing with my husband since moving to New York? Harvey says he can't wait to show off his new bride to his acquaintances, although part of me thinks he's just making that up."

I can't even tell if she's telling the truth anymore. I think from now on, I should just assume she's lying. Nothing she can say to me now will make me change my mind. Clearly, the only way to deal with this new reality is to go along with it.

"Don't be silly," I say, still not looking at her. "He's so proud of you. Anyone can see that."

"No pressure, then," she says. "I'll have my hair done all the same."

"You sure you're excited? You don't seem excited," I say.

"I'm just, you know—"

I do know. I know before she says it. *I'm tired.*

Is she lying about that too? I mean, she doesn't work—she does nothing, pretty much, except spend time with Mia. She wakes up late, and when she's up she drags herself from room to room like a post-op patient. Harvey even asked me about it the other day. How did I find her? She's a little pale, I'm worried about her, he said. He asked me to make an appointment for her with their family doctor. "She won't do it otherwise. I keep asking her."

"Leave it to me," I said. Then I made soft eyes at him, but he was already gone. I didn't make the appointment. I don't give a shit.

Then Harvey calls to say he can't go to the gala. Some drama at the office. I'm putting the last of the glasses away, pretending that I'm not eavesdropping.

"But the tickets are a thousand dollars each. Can we even give them away this late?" she whines, although I suspect that mentally, she's dancing a little jig. Then she says something about Eryn.

"Everything okay?" I ask when she hangs up.

"He can't make it. Some emergency meeting, contracts that have to be redrawn, and unfortunately there's nothing he can do about it. But he's asked Eryn to go with me instead."

"Eryn?"

"Harvey knows how much I wanted to go, and he didn't want me to be disappointed," she says. Clearly, he doesn't read his wife very well. "I wish he'd asked me first. I know he means well, but the whole point of me looking forward to it was to go out with him. Anyway…"

"Can you cancel?" I ask.

"Not really. She's coming to pick me up at six p.m. Oh well, I'm sure it will be fun," she says in the tone of someone who is sure of the exact opposite. She checks her watch. "I should go. I have a hair appointment and a manicure. I'll be back around four."

I have hours to myself. Mia is asleep, and I actually consider kicking my shoes off, grabbing a chilled bottle of Cristal champagne from the wine refrigerator and drinking straight from the bottle. I could even take a bath in her beautiful bathroom. She has a jar of Laura Mercier Crème Brûlée Honey Bath that comes with a special wooden honey spoon, and some eye-wateringly expensive face mask made out of caviar or something. She probably wouldn't even notice if I used her things. And even if she did, I could always blame Diane.

But I don't do any of that. I check her notebook, but there's nothing new, so I go downstairs and take a nap.

I'd forgotten about the dress until Hannah called me into her room. She'd just returned from her shower and was wearing her silk robe. She held up the dress, still on its hanger, and the sight of it made my stomach lurch. I expected her to say something like, what on earth did you do, Louise? And I was all set to blame Diane, but instead she handed it to me and asked me to give her a hand with it. It gave me a little thrill all the way up my spine, because that dress, it's not going to fit, and how nice is it that I'll be here to witness that?

She pulls her robe down so that it sits halfway down

her back, and I'm a little taken aback but she's wearing some very nice underwear, so all is good. She admires herself in the full-length mirror, says that she's lost some weight, she's been working out. I wonder if she expects me to agree. To tell her how fabulous she looks. I wonder if she expects me to care.

"Will you help me put it on, please?"

I take the dress off the hanger, my heart beating faster because I sure hope I get away with this, and when I look up again my eyes are drawn to a spot just above her bra. There's an odd mark there, like a scab. She catches my eye in the mirror and quickly shrugs her robe back on.

"Close your eyes," she says. I do as I'm told, but not before I see her cheeks go pink.

What was that? I wonder. What else has she been up to? Then I hear her swearing under her breath.

"What's wrong?" I ask, my eyes still closed, even though I know exactly what's wrong.

"This is stuck," she says. "Would you give me a hand?"

I open my eyes and I know I've overdone it. I'm looking at her from the back. The dress is bunched up over her thighs, and even unzipped it looks like it's about to bust open. Still. It's hard not to laugh.

"I guess it's too small."

She swears under her breath and starts to pull at the sleeves. I tell her to relax while I pull the dress up and over her head. It gets caught in her newly styled hair, so that was a complete waste of time.

I tell her to calm down while I untangle her hair. Finally I manage to get it off. She quickly reaches for the silk robe and puts it over her shoulders.

"Maybe I should tell Eryn that I'm sick. I've got fat person flu."

I don't reply. I try to imagine what this scene will read like in her journal. *Louise told me I was really fat and then she pulled my hair!*

But then something occurs to me. I could save her, again. Just like I did with Diane. I could make myself *indispensable*. Every time something went wrong, I could be there, ready to make things right, like Mary Poppins. I'll get her to confide in me eventually. I'll get her to trust me. I'll find out what the fuck she's up to.

"I'll tell you what, let me have a quick look and see what I can do, all right? I'll be back in a sec." I leave her there, shaking her head, on the verge of tears.

It's a heck of a lot easier to undo the stitches than it was to put them in. Even the little tears in the lace are not obvious because, well, lace.

"Let's try again," I say now, brandishing the dress.

"That was fast! What did you do?"

"You'll see." I want to slip it over her head, but she does that whole "close your eyes" thing like we're not both female, and I'm not twenty pounds heavier than she is. Whatever. I just humor her. Although I would have liked to take another peek at that mysterious mark.

"Oh my God!?"

I open my eyes. It's perfect. I zip her up and admire my handiwork. As in, my undoing of my handiwork.

She gushes for the next ten minutes. What did you do? You're a genius! But how?

I ask if she had it altered when she bought it.

"Well, yes! Just a tuck here and there, nothing major."

I raise my arms. "There you go! Every time! From now on, always use Marco's downtown. Less glamorous maybe, but impeccable work."

There's no Marcos downtown, obviously.

She hugs me, which is awkward, and kind of revolting. I stand with my arms dangling by my sides until it's over, and she says, "Wait, I forgot, here." She opens a drawer and pulls out an envelope. "Your pay. In cash, like you asked. I put a bit extra."

She presses it into my palm, and I weigh up whether to count it right here and now, but then the doorbell rings.

I guess my mind is elsewhere with all that business with the dress so when Eryn comes in, I don't look at her closely. I look at her, because how could you not? She with the long, tanned legs of a supermodel and the face to match. Just not closely.

I serve them champagne on the terrace, and even then I don't pick up on the way she's looking at me. I figure she's just curious because Diane is gone and I am her replacement. I listen inside the French doors as Hannah describes some of the things Diane had done, like the rat and the calls, and how Harvey hasn't been very supportive. Then Eryn asks about me, and Hannah gushes about how wonderful I am, and how I can sew, and I'm the best cook, and Mia loves me, and so on and so on. Eryn cracks a joke about stealing me, and Hannah says no way, you can have my husband if you like, but hands off my housekeeper, and I don't know why but it makes me angry. I want to tell them that they're a couple of hypocrites, that I bet they think they're so progressive and I bet they vote liberal and they sign all the petitions about health care and work conditions, but back inside their ivory towers they make jokes about whether they can steal their friend's maid and shriek in mock outrage. Not my maid! Have my husband instead! But then I remember that I'm not the maid, I'm not the housekeeper either, I'm just pretending. I don't know what's the matter with me.

Hannah goes to fix her makeup, and Eryn waits for her downstairs. When I walk past with the tray of glasses and the empty champagne bottle, I say something like, have a good evening. She squints at me, like she's near-sighted and has forgotten her glasses. It makes my hairline tingle.

She narrows her eyes at me and tilts her head. "Do I know you?"

"I don't think so, ma'am," I say, but something about her eyes. It tugs at something on the edge of my brain. *Eryn…* And then it comes to me. I can't believe I didn't recognize her sooner. Eryn. The Johnson girls. Eryn and her sister Bella. Eryn and I were in the same year at school before we moved away.

"Where did you work before? Maybe that's where I know you from."

I almost blurt it out. *I worked for the Van Kemps. For years.* But I catch myself just in time because what if she knows the Van Kemps? Spent the last ten Christmases at their house? Had met the real Louise Martin? All she'd have to do is make a call on the way out, *Darling, remind me, that housekeeper of yours, you had her for years. Yes, Louise, that's it. Did she have big boobs?*

"Dr. and Mrs. Lowe," I reply, my chin lifted in defiance. "A very nice family."

She nods slowly, her eyes still narrowed, and I can smell a whiff of stale alcohol emanating from her. But it's in her eyes. She's going to figure it out. I can see her little brain working. *Tick, tick, tick…* I'm getting nervous. She's just staring at me, and my mouth is set so tight it's making my lips tremble. She's going to say it.

Oh, I know! Claire Petersen! That's it! Groton. Freshman. Remember me? Eryn Johnson?

If I weren't carrying the tray, I'd grab her right now. I would put my hand behind her long neck and shove her into the open elevator. I would press the button for the basement before she'd have the time to fight me off. I can see myself doing it. I'm considering it. There's a boiler room downstairs, next to the laundry. It has a lock and I know where the key is. I could keep her in there. I could tie her up, leave her down there until I have what I came for and all this is over.

She's still thinking about it, tilting her head this way and that, when Hannah arrives and pulls her by the sleeve. "Come on! We'll be late!" And that's enough to make Eryn's mind move on to the next thing, like a goldfish. Before they walk out, Hannah whispers in my ear. "I probably don't need to say this, but please don't let anyone in."

"Of course."

I can hear them all the way down the street as I stand at the door—which I do not close until they're out of earshot, in case Eryn says something about me.

NINETEEN

Philippa Davenport and I had been best friends since third grade. We'd sit on her pink satin bedspread and do each other's nails and listen to Mariah Carey on repeat. She had a cook called Anna who would bring us crepes with Nutella and ice cream and slices of strawberry cheesecake. We were in love with Justin Timberlake and Harry Potter, and we spent countless hours planning our weddings in minute details, from tiaras to profiterole cakes (we were obsessed with profiterole cakes).

Philippa's fourteenth birthday party was to be held at the Pierre Hotel, in a sumptuous, grand circular ballroom. The theme for the party was the Debutante Ball, which to us was the most exciting thing in the world. The real Debutante Ball is an invitation-only formal affair, where young ladies of distinction from upper-class families are presented to high society. We were all such young ladies of distinction, and the real ball was still at least three years away for us, but this was the next best thing.

Philippa and I prepared for it for months. We talked nonstop about what we would wear, even though it was a given that every girl would wear more or less the same thing: a white satin gown and matching gloves that went all the way past our elbows.

Hannah had been and gone from our lives by then. There had been some confusion as to why, having made such a fuss of coming to New York, she'd only stayed for a week before begging to be sent home, but I wasn't interested. She was a blip on our landscape, a kink in our road. As far as I was concerned, she may as well not have existed at all.

The adults were also invited, but at the last minute, my father didn't come. Something about him not feeling well, and I was vaguely aware of something going on at home—hushed voices behind closed doors, my mother looking teary, my father shaking his head a lot. My mother and I walked in the gorgeous room lit by enormous chandeliers, like a rain of crystal drops cascading from ornate glass frames and adorned by a series of painted angelic scenes in gilded frames, as exquisite as if Raphael had descended from the heavens to paint them all himself. The room was enchanting and the most glamorous room I'd ever stepped in.

My mother joined the adults for cocktails while I went searching for Philippa. There was a photo to be taken of all of us girls, and I was instructed to join the others. I saw them giggling and jostling each other as the photographer and Philippa's mother organized everyone. I had never felt so beautiful in my life, in my white dress like a soft cloud and my blond hair in soft curls held up with diamanté combs.

When I think about that day, I try to stop there, before the titters of laughter that had begun farther down the line reached me. Before I leaned forward into the closed group of girls and asked, smiling, already laughing in anticipation, what the joke was all about. Before I caught sight of Philippa hurriedly scrunching a piece of paper and shoving it into her tiny white purse.

Something about the way they were laughing, with their gloved fingers almost touching their lips, the glances they were throwing at each other but not at me, made me pause. "What is it?" I asked again, this time directly to her. She didn't answer. Something wasn't right. My heart beat too hard in my throat as I snatched Philippa's bag from her and grabbed the crumpled paper from it.

"Hey!" she shouted. I dropped her bag to the floor, and a Tampax rolled out onto the carpet and came to a stop against my toe. Just like that, everyone was quiet. They all watched me as I smoothed out the creases from the page. It was an article, torn out of some shitty tabloid.

Wilson vs. Petersen. Did He? Or Didn't He?

It took me a moment to understand why I was looking at a photo of my father. It was a headshot, one I'd seen before in his firm, framed on the wall of the lobby.

Did he, or didn't he what? I turned around, away from their prying eyes and stifled giggles, and I read on about Hannah Wilson's claim that my father had tried to rape her in our home, repeatedly, that he had touched her, and it got so bad that the family had to send her back. The Wilsons were suing for millions.

The room was spinning. It was no longer glamorous and sumptuous, it was grotesque. Some cheap set in a suburban fair where the music was too loud and the people waltzing looked like demented clowns. They were laughing again, now that someone had picked up Philippa's fucking Tampax and no one needed to be embarrassed by that anymore.

There was a tug at my elbow, but I couldn't move. I couldn't read either because the article was shaking too violently in my hand.

"Claire, honey." I turned around slowly to look at my mother. She was white as a sheet, her mouth set into a tight line. "Come on, honey, let's go home."

But I was trapped on the merry-go-round, with the room still spinning and the orchestra still playing and the clowns still dancing, and the noise of laughing growing louder and louder around me.

I dropped the newspaper cutout and let myself be dragged away, hot tears stinging my eyes and shame burning my face.

Funny, I'd forgotten Eryn Johnson was there that day, laughing at my humiliation right in my face.

I'm pacing around the kitchen, biting the skin around my nail, with Mia looking at me from her chair. I've screwed up. I've been complacent, enjoying seeing Hannah miserable. I've wasted so much time, and now I'm about to be caught. What if Eryn asks Hannah about me? What if Hannah tells her that I worked for the Van Kemps and Eryn knows them? What if it comes back to her, just like it did with me? Surely not. She couldn't possibly associate me now—the Carters' overweight, plain-looking, boring housekeeper—with someone she briefly went to school with ten years ago. I don't even *look* like myself. And even if I did, it's not enough to jump to conclusions, surely. But none of that makes me feel better. It's clear to me that the only solution is to get Eryn away from Hannah.

I grab my cell and call Dominic. He's in a bar, he can't hear me properly and he has to go outside. I wait, trying to come up with the right words. When he comes back on the line, I can hear traffic in the background.

"Hey, stranger," he says. Dominic has sent me two texts since we last saw each other. I didn't respond to the first because I didn't know what to say. Then I made vague promises to catch up soon in response to the second.

I tell him I was thinking about him, especially about the other night. He laughs. That's nice, he says. I think about that a lot, too.

"Where are you?" he asks. "We could catch up if you like."

"Baby, I want to, but I can't. I have to be somewhere. I'm sorry. I miss you." I cringe. Was that too much? Too soon? But then he says he misses me, and there's a smile in his voice.

"I have a favor to ask," I blurt.

"Okay, what is it?"

"It's a silly thing, but bear with me, okay?"

"Sure, hit me with it."

"Do you have a press pass? Like if you wanted to get into a charity function, invite-only, lots of money, could you do it?"

"It doesn't work like that, you get your credentials on a case-by-case basis, but yeah, I have a couple of passes. I can usually get in wherever I need to."

"Do you think you could get a pass for the Children's Garden Ball?" I ask quickly.

"The Children's Garden Ball? That's on tonight."

"I know."

"Jeez, babe, I don't know, it might be too late. Why? You want to go?"

"No, not me, but could you try? Please?" I sound all wrong, so I give a little chuckle, then I say, "My friend and I have this running bet. We try to get the worst possible photo of each other, and at the end of the month, our friends vote on who really is the worst. It's a social media thing, celebrities are doing it, too. Anyway, she won last month. And you should see the photo she took of me!" I laugh. "On second thought, you shouldn't. Too embarrassing. And now I just found out she's going to the Garden Ball tonight, and getting a picture of her there doing something silly, like picking her nose or whatever, would be perfect. It would be a hoot."

This has to be the longest shot since man decided to fly to the moon. I sound like a teenager telling her boyfriend about games I play with my girlfriends. Or it's worse than that. I sound like this is the most important thing in my life: getting an embarrassing photo of my friend so I can win the monthly bet.

"Those tickets are super expensive," he says. "Who's your friend?"

"Hannah Carter, you know her?"

"No, should I?"

"No, not at all. But you could get in, right? As a photographer with your pass, could you follow her around? Try and get the worst possible photo? You'd have to do it undercover, like James Bond."

He laughs. "I don't know, Claire. I've got a night off, I'm here with the guys… I don't even know what she looks like."

"I'll text you a photo—" But Mia begins to cry. She has dropped her stuffed tiger onto the floor. I pick it up and brush it off, hand it back to her, and talk to her softly until she's happy again.

"Who's this?" Dominic asks.

I sigh. "It's my friend's baby. That's why I can't come and see you tonight."

"You're the babysitter?"

"Just doing a favor for my friend, so she can go to work. She's just lost her husband and I'm helping get her back on her feet."

I feel bad lying, which is an odd feeling. But now Dominic wants to know all about Mia. How old she is, and what she's like. Turns out that Dominic has a niece; she's almost a year old now. His sister is on her own, too. The father left.

"That's tough," I say.

"Sure is. And I'm sorry to hear about your friend's husband. That's much worse. You should get your other friend to help out, the one who can afford a ticket to the Garden Ball."

"It's funny you should say that," I say. "Because while my friend never asked her to help, they do know each other. And my other friend, the one going to the Garden Ball, she's got a lot of money but she doesn't like to part with it much, I noticed."

"Maybe you should get new friends," he says.

"Maybe I should."

In the end, he makes no promises, but he lets me text a photo of Hannah. I send him one from her Instagram profile, a selfie from her honeymoon in Paris.

TWENTY

When Hannah comes downstairs the next morning, she looks terrible, like she's aged ten years overnight. Her eyes are red-rimmed and puffy from crying. She's got a jacket on and she's putting Mia in the stroller.

"You okay?" I ask.

"No, not really. Can you help me out here?"

She's trying to shove a beanie on Mia's little head, but Mia is fighting her off. I step in and take it from her. I pretend not to notice that her hands are shaking. I gently pull the beanie down low over Mia's ears and tuck the blanket around her.

"Can you come with me?" Hannah asks quickly, putting her large sunglasses on. "I'll pay extra," she whispers. Then she blushes. "Sorry, what a thing to say. I make it sound like I'll pay extra if you'll be my friend?" She laughs wryly. "I sure could use one."

I could say no, I have things to do, I'm incredibly busy. But I need to finish what I started. I need to make sure she stays away from Eryn.

"Sure, I'll come with you. Where are we going?" I ask,

as if there's nothing wrong with her, as if she's not a complete mess. She squeezes my hand.

"You know that stupid mothers' group? No, maybe you don't. I can't remember if I mentioned it. Anyway, I'm meeting with them now, if I can ever get out of the fucking house—sorry—over in the park. I'm already late."

"Okay, can I ask—why do you want me to come with you?"

"Because I need moral support. I know, don't say it. I'm a loser. Anyone who needs moral support to go to a mothers' group up the street is a loser. I just want to check them out. If it's weird, I'll leave. We can walk around the park instead." She laughs almost maniacally.

"Hannah?"

"Yes, Louise?"

"Maybe you should stay home."

She quickly wipes her cheeks with both hands. "It's not an option, unfortunately." And the way she glances behind her makes me think it has to do with Harvey even though he's gone to work already. I suspect he wants her to go.

I nod. "Okay. I'll get my jacket."

We barely speak on the way, other than me asking again if she's all right, and her shaking her head. Her eyes are darting everywhere, and I wonder if she's looking for Diane.

We walk to the gates of the Billy Johnson Playground. "Harvey is pushing me to join this group," she says, just as I suspected. "These people, they're Eryn's friends…" She doesn't say Eryn's name as much as she spits it out. She wipes her cheek again with the back of her hand. "Fucking Eryn," she mutters.

"What happened?" I ask.

But then we see them in the distance—a group of women in full workout gear, strollers in their midst, the three-wheel type people jog with. Some women are stretching their legs, others are doing squats.

"Shit," Hannah mutters, and I don't think it's just because she's dressed in jeans and a loose top. These women look fabulous. These women, with their perfect physiques and their pretty smiles, they look happy, they look like they belong. I bet most of them have jobs, too, important jobs. Like Serena. Partners in law firms or business owners or financial managers. It occurs to me that Hannah really does feel insecure in this world, and it's not just an act.

She guides me by the elbow, dragging me along as we take a sharp left. "I need to sit down," she says.

"Okay." We sit on the first bench we spot, overlooking the lake.

"Before I begin, if you see anyone with a camera pointed at us, let me know, please, okay?"

"Of course."

"Eryn called this morning," she blurts.

Mia stirs, and I rock the stroller gently. "And?"

"There's a photo of me circulating on Instagram."

I stop moving. "Okay, how bad is it?"

She shakes her head. "I don't know. At first I thought, not that bad. But the way Harvey reacted, you'd think I'd gotten completely blind drunk, taken my clothes off, and set the place on fire."

I frown. "But you didn't?"

"God, no. It's a photo of me smoking a cigarette."

"I don't understand."

She takes a shaky breath. "Last night at the gala, after

dinner, Eryn and I went back outside. She asked me for a cigarette, and yes, before you ask, she knows I started smoking again. But Harvey doesn't know. I mean he does now, obviously." She snorts. "We found a quiet corner. Somebody took a photo and put it on social media."

"And that's it?"

"Hello? Mrs. Harvey Carter, smoking behind the bike shed at the annual ball for children's cancer?"

"Oh, shit."

"Yeah, shit." She presses her hand hard between her eyes.

"How did Eryn take it? Being in the photo?"

"That's the thing, she's not in the photo. It's just me. She got cropped out. And before you ask, we don't know who took it. But I have a very good idea." She gives a wry laugh.

With a trembling hand, she fishes around her bag and pulls out her cell. "Look." She shoves the screen under my nose.

I've already seen it, obviously, since I'm the one who put it up. I didn't even know Dominic had been to the gala until he texted the photo of Hannah and Eryn smoking. He sent it with a text: *I hope you win your bet. Go get some new friends.*

I wasn't expecting him to send anything. It was such a stupid lie, a last-minute desperate attempt to rope him in, just so I can make Hannah look bad. What are the odds that he'd get a photo? And I didn't think he'd really believe it. *My friend and I have this bet...*

When he texted it to me at eleven p.m. last night, my first thought was, I must introduce Dominic to April because honestly, those two are the most gullible people I know and they are made for each other. Then I thought, wait, I like this guy. Sorry, April. Still, I'm going to have to teach them both about trust and common sense.

He sent another one, too, of Hannah laughing at an odd angle that made her face look like a demented rabbit. Cute, funny. Not what I was after, though. Not ugly enough or embarrassing enough. But the smoking one? Honestly, I was astonished that those women would even do such a thing at that event.

I cropped Eryn out of the shot, not because I wanted to protect her from the fallout, but because I wanted Hannah to suspect her of being in on it. I created a brand-new fake Instagram account, then put a bunch of hashtags and tagged all the right people, including Eryn. Within minutes the post had twenty-five likes, and half an hour later it had over thirty comments. Looking at it now, it has over four hundred likes and is the top post on the hashtag feed #childrensgardenball.

I turn to stare at Hannah. She's biting her fingernails and shaking like a drug addict. "You can barely see your face," I say. "No one would know it's you." I point to the photo where she's bent down, the cigarette in her mouth, leaning into the lighter that Eryn is holding. The only part of Eryn you can see is her hand. Hannah is squinting, and the flame is throwing shadows on her face. She looks... I don't know, nasty. Vicious.

"Are you fucking kidding me?" she hisses. "They've got my name all over it!"

I go back to the screen and read through the hashtags, which obviously I know by heart.

#mrshannahcarter #justsayno #theregoestheneighborhood #hypocrite-much #hellomrscarter #wheredidhefindher #mrsharveycarter #han-

*nahwilsonrememberher #toomuchmoney #whocaresaboutthekids
#gobackwhereyoucamefrom #nqocd*

"That one I had to look up," she says, tapping on the screen. "Turns out 'nqocd' stands for *Not Quite Our Class, Darling*. Nice, isn't it? Then there's the caption." She taps the screen with her finger, and it makes the image zoom right in. Then she tries to zoom it out with two fingers, but she's making it worse, so that now the screen is filled with her big puckered lips around a giant cigarette.

I take the phone away from her and zoom it back out. Then I pretend to squint at the caption.

You can't put a bitch in a dress and call it a decent person

"Ouch," I say. Then I read the various comments below. *Who is this?*

WTF???

Can someone tell this moron smoking gives you cancer?

Did she even give any money to the cause?

What an idiot

Stupid bitch

"I think it's Diane," Hannah says.

I nod, tapping around the screen. "Okay, so the poster is some stupid username and it's their one and only post. She must have created it last night." I keep staring at it like I'm deep in concentration. "But how the hell did she do it? Surely she wasn't at the fundraiser. Didn't you say the tickets were a thousand dollars each? Can Diane afford that sort of money?"

She shakes her head. "I doubt it. And, no, of course I didn't see her. I would have come straight home if I had."

"Did you see anyone who could have taken the shot?"

"We were only a hundred feet from the marquee. We weren't even hiding exactly, just trying to be discreet. We

140

walked away toward a darker corner and sat down on the first bench we came across, along the path and under a tree. I don't remember anyone else nearby. There were photographers, as there would be at that sort of glittery event. But they were nowhere near us. I just don't know.

"I just had a massive fight with Harvey about exactly that. I said to him, I'm not punching anyone or raving like a lunatic. I'm smoking a cigarette, for Christ's sake. I told him he was more upset about the fucking post than about the fact that his wife has a stalker. Then he started yelling, 'A stalker? Oh, that's right! I forgot! It's Diane who took the photo! Did she put the fucking cigarette in your mouth, too?'"

She winces, rubs a spot along her arm.

I nod sagely, an expression of concern on my face, but really, inside, I'm having a party. This fight with Harvey is just an added bonus.

"So how did Eryn know about this?" I ask.

"She's tagged in it."

"Diane tagged her?"

"Yes!" She waits a beat, then says, "You don't think it's Diane?"

"Put it this way. If it really was Diane, would she have cropped Eryn out of the shot? And would Diane even know how to do that? Did she know you were going?" I shake my head. "I don't know. Maybe someone saw you two smoking and took a photo, uploaded it. The end."

"Are you even concentrating here? Because as you yourself pointed out, this is a brand-new account, created for this one post. This isn't some lucky potshot at me. This is a deliberate attempt to humiliate me, all this shit about Mrs. Harvey Carter. *Not quite our class, darling.* What the fuck? And if it isn't Diane, then who? I can't think of anyone."

She closes her eyes but doesn't speak. I keep going. "It does seem like some kind of setup, don't you think? Let's look at this for a moment. Eryn knows you're going. She knows Harvey isn't, since she took his ticket. She's the first person to tell you about it. And of course, she's not in the photo. Very convenient." We sit in silence for a moment, then I try again. "Why are you so certain this is Diane?"

She closes her eyes briefly. "I want to tell you something. I haven't told anyone since I've moved here. But I have to know I can trust you."

I'm impressed that Hannah can say things like that with a straight face.

"Of course," I say.

"There's a tag on that post. Hannah Wilson, remember her. That's what it says. That's my maiden name."

"Okay."

"Oh God, this is so complicated. You see, I never told Harvey about this, I don't know why, I just didn't! And then it was too late. And his mother hates me, so that sure doesn't help. I told you I was pregnant before we were married; well, she thinks I did that on purpose to ensnare her son."

"Hannah, I have no idea what you're talking about here. Start at the beginning. Hannah Wilson. Your maiden name."

I've been gently rocking Mia, and I get up to make sure she's still in the shade. Behind me Hannah slides across the bench to where I was sitting.

"I'll do it," she says. She takes hold of the handle and starts to rock the stroller. I want to tell her she's doing it too fast, I want to ask her to be more gentle, but I don't.

There's no way I'm going to interrupt her now. I just walk to the other side of the bench, sit down and adjust my sunglasses.

Let's hear your version of events, Hannah Wilson. I'm all ears.

TWENTY-ONE

"When I'm asked how I came to be a florist," she begins, "I usually say that it was a simple, accidental and fortunate path."

I have to stop my eyes from rolling around inside my head. I don't think I could handle another lecture on tulips right now.

"High school diploma at eighteen," she continues, "then straight to an apprenticeship, after which I found a job in a shop in Toronto. But you see—and no one knows this about me, not even Harvey—I desperately wanted to be an artist. I used to draw all the time. I thought I could study at art school. My parents own a small farm and they assumed I'd work with them after I graduated. I managed to convince them to let me have the summer off first. I wanted to travel, see a bit of the world, and most of all, I wanted to see the famous works of art. But to do that I needed a job, and the only job I'd ever had, other than on the farm, was babysitting after school. My mother had a nephew who had married a New Yorker. She mentioned to her I was looking for a job, babysitting, somewhere abroad. I don't know how they did it exactly, but next thing I knew I was offered a job as a nanny for the month of August with a family in Manhattan. They needed help looking after their nine-year-old son and would provide a place to live as well as a small wage."

She stops talking for a moment, and it's unbearable. But I don't prompt her. I wait patiently, my heart thumping in my chest, until finally, after an eternity or two, she resumes.

"The family was lovely, at first. They lived around the corner from here, on Park Avenue, in an enormous apartment on two levels. I'd never seen anything like it. The mother was very kind—" And for a second there I want to punch her. *Don't talk about my mother.* She continues. "The father was a short, round-faced, balding man who was always reaching for his wife's hand."

Just like Harvey.

"The boy, John, was sweet, and very good looking for a child his age—with dark curly hair, a thin pale face and blue eyes. He was a lovely boy, easy to get along with, eager to please. But I was too young, too immature, too shy. Everything overwhelmed me: the noise, the crowds, the air so thick and sticky I could barely breathe. I was afraid of leaving the apartment, terrified that I would get lost, that I wouldn't know how to catch the subway or which bus to take. It just seemed easier to put it off, this great adventure, until I found my feet, maybe even the next day, or at most the next week."

She rubs her hand on her forehead, like she's got a headache. "I woke up one night, not long after I'd arrived. It was dark—pitch black, even. The covers had slipped off me, or that's what I'd thought, and my nightdress was pulled up to the top of my thighs, high enough to reveal the beginnings of my pubic hair. Then I heard it, the sound he made, a quick intake of breath, over and over. It was him, the dad, sitting on a chair by the bed, so close I could have touched him. I was so shy and inexperienced, I didn't know what he was doing. I thought maybe I was needed, my mother's instructions echoing in my head. *Be polite, always say please and thank you. I won't have a daughter of mine be ungrateful or rude to her bosses.*" She laughs bitterly.

"I quickly pulled my nightdress down and swung my legs out of the bed. I was about to ask what was going on when he reached across and lifted my nightdress again, kept it up with one hand so that I remained exposed while he finished masturbating. It only took a few seconds, but instead of fighting him off, I sat there frozen, my face burning. I couldn't move. I didn't know what to do, I couldn't even comprehend the situation I was in. Then he patted my knee and left. I lay down again, crying with shame. The next day at breakfast, she asked if I was all right. He was there, too. He glared at me, then in a loud voice, he said, 'Are you not very happy today, Hannah?'"

She stops speaking, then turns to me and says, "You okay?"

I snap my head up. "Sure, why?"

"You just made a funny noise, that's all."

"I'm okay. Keep going."

"To this day I don't know why I didn't say anything, only that I was paralyzed by shyness, and by the parental instructions I'd always heard, that the adults were in charge. That you should always answer when spoken to. My room didn't have a lock on the door, and it happened again two days later, and then the night after that. That time I cried, I told him to leave, I said I'd tell his wife. He said that no one would believe me. I was here without a proper visa, I was working illegally. Did I know what that meant? It meant that if the authorities found out, I would go to jail. The wife would ask me, her forehead all scrunched up in worry, 'Are you sure you're all right, Hannah? Is there anything we can do?' I'd just shake my head. No, nothing. Thank you. But I just wanted to vomit all the time. In the end she couldn't bear it anymore, this sad and surly girl that even her little boy, who liked everybody, seem to recoil from. Eventually I told her I wanted to go home. She called my mother, and two days later, he drove me to the airport. He patted me on the knee, said that they would miss me, and wished me luck."

She stops there, like she's lost in her thought. My leg is shaking and I have to press my hand down on it to make it stop.

"I cried when I saw my mother," she says. "I told her about the father's nightly visits." She sighs, picks at the skin around her thumbnail. "She told my father. I was summoned to the living room. It was like someone had died. They were both sitting on the sofa, my mother clutching a handkerchief. My father wanted to know everything. I told him my sordid tale once more, looking at the floor. He was furious. I'd never seen him like this. I begged him not to say anything, not to do anything. To let it be. It was over. What was the point in getting upset?

"But he was so angry, understandably. He said he didn't care how fucking rich and uppity these people were. That we may be the Wilsons from Ontario, simple farming folk, but we were honest, hardworking folks and we would not be used and discarded, just because they had so much money. Because that's what it came down to, in the end. If his daughter had been perved upon by a poor old creep with no fortune to his name, he wouldn't have made a fuss. He might even have told me not to get so worked up over nothing. But these were very rich people, and to this day, I swear I don't know if he saw an opportunity, or if he genuinely thought that my honor was priceless. My dad has a gambling problem. He's always looking for an angle. He calls me asking for money all the time. He wants me to ask Harvey for thousands of dollars, but I won't do it. I just tell my dad that Harvey says no, and that's that."

I'm surprised that she would even admit to that. Then it occurs to me she might have known I was listening in on the conversation, and she's weaving it in as part of her narrative.

"A lawyer showed up," she continues. "I repeated my story again for a third time. I was terrified of the consequences. But I couldn't resist the power of my father's determination. He'd put forms in front of me. Sign here, he'd bark. And here. And here. We'd go over my story again and again, and each time he'd ask, 'Did he touch you? You know, on your private parts?' and I would die, right there, of humiliation. Eventually they filed a complaint in civil court in New York. It was my word against theirs, essentially. By then the press was covering the story, and for a time they were on my side. We went back to New York a few times, the three of us holed up in one room in a cheap hotel, my father pacing back and forth on the brown carpet. There were depositions and filings, and the more they fought back, the harder my father went. We were asking for ten million dollars in compensation. But there was an older sister who had been away that summer. I only met her once, very briefly. By now she'd told everyone that I'd told her I'd planned the whole thing, that I was after their money, and the father had never done anything to me. As if. But then the father died of a heart attack. And that was that. Case closed."

Case closed? In your dreams, Hannah Carter née Wilson. Case not closed. Not by a long shot.

"My father didn't say a single word all the way home, but his knuckles were white on the steering wheel. My mother looked out the window. I cried in the back seat. When we arrived back home, my father wouldn't even look at me. He went to get changed into his overalls while my mother took off her gloves in our small living room and turned to me, glaring, and said, 'Tell me now, Hannah, did you make it all up?' And just like that, my parents distanced themselves from the debacle they had helped create at my expense. My mother pursed her lips for at least a year whenever she saw me, like it had all been my fault. If I tried to defend myself—*But I never wanted this!*—she would just shake her head. 'Let's not speak about this anymore.' My father barely said a word to me, and when he did, it was usually to tell me that I'd broken my mother's heart. So when the florist in town advertised for an intern, I applied because I couldn't wait to get out of there. If none of that had happened, I would have done what my parents expected of me. I would have worked with them on the farm, married a local guy and taken over when they retired. So that's how I became a florist. And you know my biggest regret?" She laughs wryly. "I never went to a single museum. I didn't even try to become an artist. I just gave up."

She wipes her cheeks with both hands.

"I have to go to the bathroom, I'll be right back." I

don't wait for an answer. I run over to the restrooms by the zoo and lock myself inside. I only just make it before I throw up.

"You okay?" she asks, frowning, when I return. It's all I can do not to punch her in the face. Because she is the greatest liar I've ever met. She knows very well that's not what happened. And I don't just mean her justifications for her actions, her claims that my father really did those things to her. I expect nothing less from her. But there's something about the way she told the story. There are too many lies. Too many things that don't add up.

I nod. "I have a sensitive stomach. Nothing to worry about, keep going."

"Do you remember that day Diane came to the house, the day she went crazy?" she asks.

"How could I forget?"

"She said I wasn't who I said I was. Clearly, she found out about Hannah Wilson. She came over to threaten me. That's why I didn't want to tell Harvey about her coming over, you understand?"

It takes a moment for it to sink in. Hannah thought Diane's big crazy outburst was about *her*. She believes Diane was threatening to expose *her*, her past. *I know who she really is. She's a liar. She's evil.* She had no idea Diane was talking about me. I think back over what she said right afterwards. *I'd like to give you a raise, since you double as a body-guard.* That was a bribe, pure and simple. *Don't tell my husband.*

"Have you told him now?" I ask.

She shoots me a small smile, then opens her lips as if to say something. She blinks, shakes her head imperceptibly. "Not yet," she says and quickly adds, "but I will. I have to. I just want to get over this latest drama first." She puts her hand on her forehead and stays like that a while.

The award for best actress in a real-life drama goes to…

"The part that really worries me, Louise, is that I feel like I'm losing my grip on reality. I wonder if that's why Mia is always upset when I'm around."

"She's not always upset," I say.

"With me she is. Babies, children, they're attuned to their mothers. I worry sometimes I'm doing something wrong with Mia. Something that will matter later."

I nod. "When I lost my mother—" But then I immediately stop talking.

"Oh, Louise, I thought your mom was okay? I thought she'd recovered after the treatment? Did something happen?"

"Oh yeah, I meant when I *almost* lost my mother. I thought she was going to die, I told you that, didn't I? That's why I had to take time off work and look after her."

"Of course. I remember. But she's okay now, isn't she?"

"Yeah, she's good."

"Okay, good to know. You had me worried for a moment."

She rummages through her bag for something and pulls out her phone.

"We should go," she says, still not looking at me, and I think I detect a blush on her neck.

"Sure. You okay?"

"Yes. I am now." She turns to face me. I study her face, but she seems normal again. "Thank you for listening."

"You're welcome, but I'm still not sold on the Diane angle. Just saying. If I were you, I'd keep Eryn at arm's length for a while. Something's not right about that woman."

She stands up, hoists her bag over her shoulder and adjusts her sunglasses. "That's funny, she said the same about you."

TWENTY-TWO

Back home, Hannah announces she'll put a cheese platter together for us, which is fine with me. I'm always nervous around mealtimes, especially if Hannah is hovering nearby, so if she wants to do it, I'm not going to stop her. I still have leftovers from a Greek salad I bought the day before, so I pull that out of the refrigerator. It's in a bowl because I'm very careful not to keep the original packages. They get immediately thrown in the trash, even the recyclable plastic ones. I put them in a paper bag and take them out to the trash in the street.

I serve the Greek salad and put out some saltines to go with it as she pulls out a bottle of Shiraz. "I never drink at lunchtime, but today I'm making an exception. You want to join me?"

"I think it's an excellent idea." I pull out two glasses for us.

"Don't tell Harvey I didn't go to the mothers' group, please."

Don't tell Harvey… Don't tell Harvey… "I won't."

We eat silently for a moment. "Can I ask, why did you

fire Diane?" I ask without looking at her, like I'm just making idle conversation.

"Because she threw out my mug from Canada," she says.

I look up then. "She threw out your mug from Canada?" I repeat, to make sure I heard her right.

She sighs. "It was more than that, of course. Diane never liked me. She was always comparing me with Serena—"

"Ah."

"And maybe that's why I let her go. Because I'm insecure. There. I've said it. I let Diane go because she made me feel bad about myself."

"Bad how?"

"Oh God, so many things… One time, Patsy was here and Diane told her, in front of me, that I'd been asking people how much things cost, and she didn't think it was appropriate."

She pops a piece of cheese into her mouth.

"Seriously?"

"Uh-huh. Patsy wanted to know what I'd asked, and to whom. I had to explain it wasn't like that. It was because Eryn was here, I don't remember the occasion. I was looking at her ring. Beautiful. Diamonds and rubies. I chided her because I thought she must have a new man in her life. She said no, it's a present to myself, that's what she said. I was ogling the ring, and blurted out something like, 'That must have set you back a few bucks!' Behind me, Diane made some tut-tut sound. Then she leaned over and whispered, 'Mrs. Carter, people in your position don't comment about what things cost.' In front of Eryn. I was so embarrassed…"

I burst out laughing, which threatens to turn into

hysterics. Maybe it's the shock of the day, having to listen to her endless lies, that's made me tied up in knots. But I am laughing so much I'm crying, and now Hannah is looking at me like there's something wrong with me.

"I'm so sorry," I say finally, getting my breath back. "It's just so outrageous, it's funny!"

She makes a face, but then she smiles.

"Don't stop now," I say, filling up her glass. "Tell me more."

"Well, I would move something—for instance, you see how the spices are lined up over there on the shelf? One time, I put them all near the stove and moved the coffee machine over here, and all those white cups and saucers from over there, I put them where the spices used to be. The next day, she'd put everything back the way it was before I changed it."

"Really?"

"Really. This was the kind of game Diane liked to play, except I didn't know what the rules were. As far as I could tell, it went like this: I put something somewhere, she moves it back. I know the kitchen was her domain, but I live here, too. I just like to stand here in the morning and have my coffee, and I just put the cups and the coffee machine within reach. That was all. She walked in that morning, greeted me, and I asked her, Did you move the spices back? And the coffee machine? And you know what she said?"

I shake my head. "What did she say?"

"She put on her stupid apron, and she said, 'Mrs. Carter always liked it this way, with the cups over there and the spices here.' She meant Serena, of course."

I snort, but I'm eating, and an olive pops out of my

mouth and bounces on the table. I grab it and throw it in the sink.

"I *am* Mrs. Carter! I told her."

"What did she say?"

"She apologized." Hannah imitates Diane's voice. "'Sorry, Mrs. Carter. I mean the first Mrs. Carter.' I told her yes, I know what you meant. But I thought, she meant the *real* Mrs. Carter. The one who truly belongs here, in this beautiful home, the one who drinks her morning coffee out of fine white china, just like Harvey. The one who looks like she's stepped off a *Vogue* cover instead of, well, me. Do I look like I belong here? Don't answer that. I'm working on it. And the funny thing is that I tried so hard to get along with her. I even asked her, in the beginning, to call me by my first name. Call me Hannah, I said, back when I thought we could get along. One time I helped load up the dishwasher and she complained to Harvey that it wasn't appropriate and it made her uncomfortable."

"You can do my job, if it makes you feel better," I say.

She smiles. "So as you can imagine, Diane never did call me by my first name. Instead she seized every opportunity to make me feel inadequate. She told me once she'd read an article about how breastfed children are better at math, would I like to see it? Even though she knew very well I hadn't been able to breastfeed. I'd love to breastfeed, but I can't. I have to rely on formula instead. As you know."

"That's not nice," I say, but all the while I'm liking this Diane more and more. I clearly misjudged her.

"No, it's not. And this is from someone who, as far as I know, has not had children. Another time I put sunflowers in the hallway, and she came to me, and she said, 'The first

Mrs. Carter always puts white roses on the console table, I thought you'd want to know.' Well, you thought wrong."

"Are you serious? Again with the first Mrs. Carter?"

"Yes! I told her I was a florist before I came here, and she said, 'Oh really? How terribly interesting,' like it really wasn't."

I really can't blame Diane on that one, but still, I make the right noises, like I'm outraged on her behalf.

"But the way she looked at me after that," Hannah resumes, "I knew I'd screwed up. I'd just slid a few rungs beneath her on the ladder of respectability. I was a *merchant* now, not a proper upper-class wife. I may have scored a big fish and married above my station, but I was only one divorce decree away from yelling out prices at the whole-sale market."

"Did you do that? Yell out prices at the wholesale market?"

"Well, no. It's a figure of speech. But that day, when she moved all those things around again, I went to get my favorite mug—"

"Ah, the famous mug from Canada."

"Exactly. It had a picture of a maple leaf, very tacky, and the words *I heart Canada, and your ass too* plastered all over it. It was a silly thing, but it was a going-away present from my friend Lucy. And I was standing there, looking for it, and I said to her, do you know where it is? And she said no. No idea. I looked for it everywhere. In every cupboard, everywhere. I was getting more and more frantic, and she was watching me like I was unstable. Which I probably was. I found it, in the end. You know where?"

"Where?"

"In the trash. Broken in pieces."

"Seriously?"

"She said she didn't know. I didn't believe her, I said, we're done here. I think you should go. I don't think we're a good fit, you and me. I even said, 'Maybe you should talk to Serena and see if she has a position for you. I think you'll be a lot happier.'"

"I thought Serena lived in London now," I say, like it's no big deal.

She colors a little, unexpectedly. "She does, I was just making a point. I was just sick of hearing about fucking Serena. Even Harvey—" She stops abruptly.

"Even Harvey what?" I ask. Even Harvey still *adores* Serena? Just like his mother? And his housekeeper?

She shrugs. "When I moved in, there were still lots of her things around the place that she hadn't bothered to pack."

"Like what?"

"Photos of the two of them dotted around the place. Some clothes of hers in the laundry. Some of her jewelry, even. I asked Harvey about it. Is she ever going to get her things shipped? Or am I supposed to live with them? I was a little offended, you know? In the end he had to do it himself and he wasn't very happy about it. But at least I don't have to see *beautiful Serena*'s face anymore."

I think back to what she said about the divorce being amicable, and now I wonder. Leaving these traces behind for the new wife seems kind of insensitive. Could Serena have done that on purpose?

"Anyway," she sighs. "I guess I'm just trying to justify why I got so angry with Diane. I told her to go, that we'd give her a month's pay in lieu of notice. And that was that! Next thing I know, I heard the door slam, and she was gone."

"What did Mr. Carter say?"

"At first I thought he'd be angry that I'd let Diane go, but he was good about it." Her face relaxes. "He was about to pour me a glass of red wine when I told him. He froze, the bottle in the air. He couldn't believe it. I told him she was creeping me out. That there was something not right about that woman. I mean, who does that? Throws your employer's things away? Constantly comparing me to your first wife? He winced at that, which I didn't mind one bit. I swear, she made me feel like what's-her-name in *Rebecca*. With Diane in the role of Mrs. Danvers, waiting for the right moment to push me out the window."

"Last night I dreamed I went to Manderley again…" I muse before I can stop myself.

"That's the one," she says. As if there's nothing strange about a twenty-four-year-old housekeeper knowing her classics.

"Then he said, 'I have a secret to tell you,' and I was like, what now? I'm not the second Mrs. Carter, I'm the third? The first one is buried in the cellar? Or holed up in the attic? You know what he said?"

"What did he say?"

"He said, 'I broke the mug from Canada.'"

My hand flies to my mouth.

"And then," she resumes, "he said he never liked Diane, and that she used to creep him out, too, so he was glad she was gone. I couldn't believe it. I thought she was some kind of family heirloom. That she came welded to this house, no matter who moved in. So there you go."

She takes a swig of wine, then she leans in, and I do the same, so that we're very close to each other. Her eyes are glassy, and it dawns on me how drunk she is.

"Then Harvey went upstairs to his office, and I was gazing out the window without looking at anything in particular. It was raining, really hard. And there was a shape across the street, completely still and exposed without an umbrella, and it was Diane. She saw me looking at her, and she looked right into my eyes, and it was like she hated me. Pure hatred."

She sits back and finishes her drink. "It made me drop my wine. There was glass everywhere on the floor. And you know what? Harvey didn't believe me, that she was outside, standing across the street. He said I was dreaming, that I was confused because I'd drank too much."

"Well, good riddance."

"Cheers to that," she says, and we clink.

"But I still don't think she had anything to do with the Instagram post. Sorry. Call it a gut feeling. Just watch your back with Eryn. Like I said before. Arm's length. Cool the friendship for a while and see what happens."

If she thinks this is rather forward advice for a house-keeper, she doesn't say. She just gazes out the window and sighs.

TWENTY-THREE

That night, Harvey takes her out for dinner. A kind of peace offering, I suspect. While they're out, I take another look at her journal. I go over some of the older entries. There's one immediately after Diane has gone, before I started working here.

It doesn't help that I'm on my own, and to say I'm not coping would be merely pointing out the bleeding obvious. My husband comes home late, he's tired, he expects a meal and I can hardly blame him.

I found a recipe online for clam chowder, which I know Harvey loves. I managed to shop for all the ingredients, familiarizing myself with the local food stores, enjoying everyone cooing over my baby in the stroller. I had the potatoes boiling on the stove when Mia started wailing. I rushed upstairs and by the time she was changed and soothed, the kitchen had been engulfed in smoke. I was so frazzled I couldn't even figure out where to order takeout from, or even what Harvey might like. I racked my brain, trying to remember those early weeks in our relationship. There was no cook or housekeeper, although we did go out a lot. What did we eat? What was his favorite food? I remember laughing over a seafood paella at the Spanish restaurant around the corner we frequented so often. The Mexican bar where we'd get chicken wings and knock back margaritas. The Italian restaurant where he showed me how to eat pasta with a spoon and fork, which I never mastered, not without streaking tomato sauce over the walls in a pattern that would have made a forensic investigator rub her hands together with glee.

In the end I ordered pizza online.

Then the last two nights Harvey has come home with Chinese in white cartons, just like the movies, but without the cheerful banter. "Diane called again," I said. He mumbled something about having the number changed, but he won't do it because he doesn't think it's Diane. I don't know if he even believes me anymore. We're more like the couple who has been married going on fifty-seven years and has well and truly run out of things to say. I tried to imagine this scene if Serena were here instead of me. I bet they'd be eating out of elegant hand-made gold-leafed pottery or something. Which is when I remembered the gorgeous Asian dining set in the pantry on the top shelf, and I had to resist the urge to face-palm. I saw it the other day, still in its box—white with blue swirls of feathers, and delightful little squares of porcelain for the chopsticks so they don't stain the linen. The whole set is exquisite, and I kicked myself for not remembering it before. I bet Serena would have remembered. I bet she would have laid it out beautifully on a white linen damask tablecloth. They would have eaten in the dining room, of course, with a multitude of dipping sauces in pretty lacquered dishes and fragrant jasmine tea in small round cups.

I peered at him over my chop suey and tried to read his face. How long before he realizes this is hopeless? Before he turns around and tells me that he was on the rebound when he met me and selected the person who looks and acts least like Serena? Someone *plump instead of slim, dark-haired instead of golden blond, dim-witted instead of intelligent and educated? All so that he wouldn't be reminded of her every minute of the day, except that it's not working at all, and he's terribly sorry but we're going to have to call it quits.*

It doesn't help that I barely sleep, especially after the other night. I'm so tired that I'm afraid of going to sleep in case Mia needs me and I don't wake up. The house is a mess because I just don't have the energy to do anything about it. When I woke up this morning, I told myself that no matter what, I would burst this bubble of resentment wide open. I got so mad at myself I started to shake. And then, we were having breakfast, sitting at the same table, both of us poking at our fried eggs with the tips of our fork. Then without warning my inner voice said, Is it because of Serena? which would be all right, normally, since I have wondered that. Except that this time, my inner voice said it out loud. Harvey looked up with a look that I'm becoming depressingly familiar with. A look somewhere between puzzlement and irritation.

"Why are you so obsessed with Serena?"

Because she is everything I am not. Because you loved her more than you love me.

I don't say that out loud. But I'm glad she's gone. I'm glad I did what I did.

"I want you to be happy," I said softly. "I'm frightened, I guess. That I'm going—"

"Honey, you need to go and see Dr. Malone again, please. Do it for me, okay?"

I didn't get to finish the sentence. I was going to say 'crazy.'

TWENTY-FOUR

Hannah is up early for once. I'm pretend-cleaning her bathroom so I can grab a Xanax when I hear her out there calling me.

"Ah. There you are." She puts one hand against the doorjamb. "I'm feeling better today. And I was talking to Harvey this morning—he thinks we should start Mia on solid foods."

I'm on my knees, elbow deep in the bathtub. I sit back on my heels and push a strand of hair out of my eyes.

"What?"

"I know, I don't know what's gotten into him. He says I'm babying her too much."

"Are you serious? Harvey said that? She's four months old, Hannah. She *is* a baby."

She flinches. "I know. But what can I say? Come on. It will be fun! We can experiment with flavors, textures … do you think we should make pureed vegetables from scratch? Although the prepared ones might be better, the ones in little glass jars—do they still exist? They have added vitamins, that's good, right? We could always try both, see what Mia thinks. We could do a tasting, put little portions in little spoons, we could line them up on the table, and give it to her one by one, then come up with a rating system. Like minus one point for a nose twitch, plus five for a smile, plus ten for a giggle, minus one hundred if she cries, although it has to be real tears."

"You okay, Hannah?" I ask when she finally stops talking.

"Sure, I feel great, why?"

"You're talking really fast."

"Am I?" She cocks her head at me. "I just want to start Mia on solids today, okay? Harvey said so." I wonder if she's on drugs. She's smiling, but it's a frozen smile. A pretend smile.

"Come on, let's go to the grocery store. I'll meet you downstairs." And just like that she's out of the room.

I get up and immediately reach for the Xanax, but it's not there.

I thought we'd settled on mass-market baby food, but when I tell Hannah I'll quickly pop by Morton Williams and pick something up, she says, "Come on! This is the very first time she'll eat something other than formula. Surely her first experience should be wholesome, rather than processed?" So now we're going to the organic grocery store on Third Avenue. I told her once that's where I like to shop, because it's organic. I never shop there. It goes without saying.

The store is packed, mostly with young women in Lululemon and young men with full beards and no socks. We're standing in front of a box of yellow zucchini, next to two women who look like they've just returned from playing tennis. They both wear matching short white pleated skirts with a thin blue band on the side, and white polo shirts.

"I'm so pleased this is where you shop. We're really supporting the local economy," Hannah says, as if we were United Nations delegates in an emerging country on a visit to a local market. I have to look at her to see if she's joking or not, and I still can't tell. "I guess they know you here, huh? You're so lucky to have a connection to this neighborhood."

I smile with tight lips and leave her to check the ripeness of the avocados. I slide past the checkout line of people staring at their phones and right up to the woman at the register. "Hi, I shop here all the time," I whisper. "What's your name again?"

"Oh hi," she says, then narrows her eyes at me, like she's trying to place me. I half expect her to say, "Mmm, no, you don't," but maybe because she's very busy, she whispers back, "I'm Mel. Sorry, I forgot your name!"

"Louise. Like I said, I shop here all the time." Then I add, "But I've been busy, so I haven't been here in ages." Thereby contradicting myself. "You know how it is."

She gives me a quick confused nod, clearly wanting me to get to the point. I just smile at her warmly. "You're busy, I'll leave you to it." Then I join Hannah by the potatoes. On the way I pop some carrots and kale into a basket, to show I've been doing something.

"Ready?"

When we come to pay, I greet Mel brightly. "Hi, Mel! Nice earrings!"

"Thanks, Louise!" she chirps, and Hannah gives me a bright toothy smile that makes her eyes squint, like she's proud of me.

We're outside now, and because I'm on a winning streak, I tell her what a nice place this is to shop, and that Mel is lovely and always tells me what the freshest vegetables are.

Hannah frowns. "Aren't they all fresh?"

"Yes, of course. I mean some are fresher than others, at any given time—" And then I stop speaking, midsentence, because I just heard my name. My real name.

"Claire?"

It's behind us—not too close, maybe thirty feet away. It's April. I smile at Hannah tightly and hurry my pace. But Hannah is pushing the stroller, and it's a nice sunny early autumn day, and we're having such a nice time, and she's in no hurry, so I have to slow down again to stay level with her.

"Claire!"

Go away, April. But she won't go away, will she? Because this is April, and she's not the type to give up. I'm sweating. I am rambling about nothing, about the trees, about the squeak from the wheel on the stroller and how I'll put some oil on it when we get back. Then I hear her again, "Claire!" More insistent this time, and it's all I can do not to turn around and yell at her. *Go. Away.*

Of course Hannah has turned around and now she's frowning at me and I don't know if it's because I'm being weird or because she can tell it's me April is after—although she doesn't know it's April, obviously—and I can see she's puzzled that I pretend there's nothing to see here. We're about to cross East Sixty-Third when the red hand signal comes up, but there's no way I can stop now. I take hold of Hannah's elbow and keep walking, and the traffic light turns green when we're only halfway through and a taxi honks angrily. It's not a good look, considering we're pushing a stroller with a four-month-old baby in it. By the time we step on the sidewalk, cars are zipping past behind us and a woman makes a tsk sound at us.

"Jeez, Louise, what's the rush?" Hannah says.

I try to smile. "Sorry, force of habit. I'm always in a rush." But we're at the house now, and Hannah fiddles with something on the back of the stroller, so I quickly unclip the straps and pick up Mia.

"I'll take her," she says, extending her arms. I can't believe it's taking so long to get inside. But I fold the stroller in one quick gesture and risk a sideways glance. I can't see April, and when I close the door after me, I lean against it in relief.

In the end, we don't puree kale and carrots and put them in teaspoons and rank Mia's favorite according to some weird rating system. Hannah decides she's tired after all and goes to lie down. I put the food in the fridge and then change my mind and boil some carrots.

When Harvey comes home that night, I mention to him that I've prepared some pureed vegetables for Mia and that I'll give it a go tomorrow. That's nice, he says distractedly.

"That's what you wanted, isn't it, Mr. Carter? That I should put Mia on solid foods?" and the way he looks at me, I may as well have been speaking Swahili. He has no idea what I'm talking about.

TWENTY-FIVE

I'm like a drug addict. All I can think about is getting back to that notebook. I wait until they're having dinner downstairs and slip into her closet for my fix. As soon as I open the notebook I see there's a new entry, and this one is dated. It's from yesterday. It begins with the usual, *I'm tired, I can't bear it anymore, I don't know what's wrong with me... blah-blah-blah*, but then she writes:

> *Every day I scour Instagram for something else. I log in with my fingernails in my mouth, my pulse racing, but there's been nothing. I told Eryn that Louise suspects her to be behind the post, and she got really angry. She swore on her mother's grave that she had nothing to do with it. Same with the phone calls. She wanted to come over and give Louise a piece of her mind, accusing her like that, and I had to beg her to leave it alone. I don't want this drama in my house. I said I'd talk to Louise about it myself. But the truth is, I don't know how I feel about Louise, and not just because the house is getting more and more untidy. The other day Harvey pointed out*

the baseboards in the main sitting room. "When's the last time Louise vacuumed up here? And have you seen the carpet on the stairwell? She needs to up her game or we'll have to get someone else, I mean that. This place is starting to look filthy."

I wouldn't have said filthy myself, but I know what he means. I am here, all the time, and I don't remember the last time I even heard the vacuum cleaner. In fact, the only time I see Louise these days is in the kitchen. I never see her in any room in this house except for the nursery. If she ventures anywhere else, it's not when I'm around. And God knows I'm around.

Then this morning she said Mia should be on solids from now on. Mia is barely four months old. I'm pretty sure that's a little early, she's only just started to sit up on her own, but for some reason Louise was adamant that we should try. I went along with it, even going as far as shopping with her at the grocery store, but when we returned I said I wanted to check with the pediatrician first and asked her to wait until I'd done so. She tried to hide it, but I could see that it made her angry. I don't know why.

I think I should talk to Harvey about this. Louise is getting increasingly obsessed with my child and I think I should tell someone. I'm beginning to think I shouldn't leave her alone with Mia so much. I hate to think what she might do.

She knows. I can feel it, twisting my gut. It's the only thing that makes sense. She's writing all these lies about me, inventing moments that never happened, twisting the truth. Later, when it's all over, Hannah will want me to see how much smarter than me she is. How she toyed with me. That's why she told me that bullshit story about wanting to be an artist and working as a nanny. She won't tell her husband what supposedly happened to her, but she'll tell me? Her housekeeper? No. It doesn't add up.

Hannah Carter is a liar. And all this time I thought I was the cat, turns out I was the mouse.

TWENTY-SIX

I ring the buzzer at April's apartment. I could have used my key, but it just didn't feel appropriate. It crackles to life and her voice comes on. "Who is it?"

"It's me. Claire."

Upstairs she's waiting at the door, already in her track-suit pants, her arms crossed over her chest.

"I'm not at my cousin's in Pittsfield. I don't have a cousin in Pittsfield."

The kitchen is pristine in its cleanliness. It makes me feel like I don't live there anymore. I sit at the table and put my head in my hands.

"What have you done to your hair?"

"I cut it," I reply without looking up.

"I liked it better before. I don't like the color either."

"Thanks, April."

"You have my rent?" she asks. I retrieve the cash from my back pocket and put it on the table. She softens visibly and takes the chair opposite.

"Why did you run away from me? I know you heard me. You pretended you didn't, and you ran off with your friend. What the hell, Claire?"

"Do you have something to drink?"

She shoots me a disappointed look but gets up anyway. She opens the freezer and pulls out an unopened bottle of vodka.

"I didn't know you liked vodka?"

She drops ice cubes into two tumblers, fills them up and sets them on the table in front of us. "I don't. I'm making an exception. I got it for you. For when you came back."

I say nothing for a moment, waiting for the punchline. She doesn't say anything else, just takes a sip, watching me over the rim of her glass while I knock back a swig of my own.

"I'm not an influencer," I say, biting my bottom lip. I expect her to laugh, slap the table with the palm of her hand and yell out, *No shit!* Instead a faint blush grows in her cheeks. She shrugs one shoulder. "I thought some things didn't add up."

Some things? I want to take her by the shoulders and shake her. I want to bore into her eyes and tell her, April, honey, you need to be more discerning about who you trust. If it sounds completely implausible, it probably is.

"I'm in trouble, April."

I tell her everything. I tell her about my parents, about where I grew up, about Hannah Wilson coming and ruining our lives. I've never spoken about this to anyone, ever, and it's hard. It gives me a touch of vertigo, although that could be the alcohol. It makes it hard to breathe, but it's strangely cathartic, not unlike throwing up.

I tell her about the day of the job interview and how I

found Hannah again. I don't tell her about all the stalking I did. But I do tell her I've managed to get hired as her housekeeper, and Hannah thinks my name is Louise Martin.

"A housekeeper?" she asks, eyes opened wide, as if that's the most shocking detail of my story. She shakes her head, cups her hand around her tumbler. "I don't under-stand. What are you trying to achieve by working there? Do you want to hurt her?"

"No! Of course not!" *Don't I?* "I mean, she is a sick woman, April. She's on the evil side of the spectrum, trust me." I laugh dryly. "And if I happen to cause her unhappi-ness, then sure, all the better. But I'm not going to hurt her deliberately! Physically? No!"

"Okay."

I twirl my glass between my fingers, feel the corners of my mouth turn down. "I want her to tell the truth. Is that too much to ask?"

"But how?"

"What she did to us, to me, I wanted her to experience it. To live with it, like I did." I lean forward. "I wanted to seduce her husband, have sex with him. I was going to video it on my phone, make it sound like he made me do it. I wanted to see her face when she learns that her husband is a sexual deviant who has been forcing himself on her housekeeper."

I sit back. It's strange to have said it out loud. To feel the shape of the words on my tongue.

"Is it true? He did that to you?" she asks.

"No, obviously. Jesus, April, pay attention."

She tops off my glass. "Fine. So it's a lie. You don't think that's going to hurt her? Or him?"

"That's not the point! I wasn't going to do anything

with that video, I just wanted her to believe it. It was my leverage, you see? If it came out that her husband has been assaulting their young housekeeper every night, he'll be done. He'll lose his partnership for sure. They won't be able to show their faces anywhere. All that money, it will be for nothing. Do you think Hannah Wilson would put up with that? Of course not. She'd want me to name my price. You watch."

She pauses, absorbing it all. "And your price is?"

"I told you. Tell the truth. She admits that everything she said about my father was a lie, and she did it to blackmail him."

"I see."

"And I want it on video."

"Do you think she'd agree? It seems unlikely to me."

I think about this for a moment. "I could go easy on her. I could give her an opportunity to justify her actions and let herself off the hook. In her version of the story, she implied her parents pushed her to do it, her father especially. He's a gambler—and not a good one, apparently. She could make a statement and say it was her father's idea, and that he pushed her to do this. Trust me, anyone who knows the guy will believe it. He's one greedy prick. Even now, he wants money from Harvey because the guy had the misfortune to marry his daughter. You should hear him, berating her on the phone because she's not paying up fast enough. So that would be my compromise. She can blame her past deeds on her naivety and a misguided obedience toward her father. As long as she admits it was all a setup."

"And in exchange?"

I shrug. "Her husband remains the upstanding citizen that we know and love."

"I don't know, Claire. Sounds pretty crazy to me. I think maybe you're in over your head there. I think you should give it up, just quit. Come back here and forget about the whole thing."

"Even if I wanted to, I can't. Not now."

"Sure you can. It's not too late. Just tell her you got a better job, whatever. Get your things and—"

"I can't. She knows exactly who I am. And she's framing me, April."

I tell her about the diary and the lies she's been writing about me. "It's more than lies, it's like she's fucking with my head! Because the things she writes about in her journal happened, but she twists it around. Like this business about Mia's food, and going to the grocery store together, that's the day you saw me. It did happen, but it wasn't my idea! Why would she say it was? It makes no sense whatsoever! And the story that I was in the nursery spying on her or whatever. It's a complete lie! When she says I make her cups of tea that make her tired? I have no idea what she's talking about! And then she writes that I'm obsessed with Mia, and she's afraid of leaving her alone with me? She's afraid of what I might do? It's a lie! She's always shoving Mia into my arms. She's constantly saying she can't cope, but I'm so good with Mia. Nothing has changed."

"So why would she write those things about you? Have you given her any reason to worry?" From the look on her face, April is considering that I might be the one who's lying. I can hardly blame her.

"No. Of course not. You have to believe me, please. I have no one else to turn to."

She's silent for a moment. "I want to, I really do. But you said it yourself, Claire, you lie all the time. You've lied to me the entire time I've known you. Why should I believe you now?"

"I know, and you're right, but everything I've told you just now, it's the truth. I give you my word." She gives me a look as if to say, what's that worth exactly?

"You said she's trying to frame you. For what?"

A wave of despair comes over me. I open my mouth, but I'm scared of saying the words—in case they're true, in case I make it real.

"I don't know, but I think she's going to hurt her baby," I whisper.

She gasps. Sits back. This is too much now—she's going to tell me to go, she can't help me, she won't want to get involved in this fucked-up scenario, with her fucked-up roommate and her fucked-up history. But her face grows serious and she tops off our glasses.

"Did she say that? In her diary?"

"No, but that's the point, you see? She keeps saying *I* might hurt Mia. That she's worried about *me* being around her baby. But when Hannah and I are together, she's the opposite. She *wants* me to take care of Mia. She keeps telling me what a great job I'm doing and how helpful it is to her. She finds it hard. She's tired all the time. Maybe she's incredibly depressed. Maybe she only got knocked up to get Harvey. Either way, I don't think she wants her child anymore. And she's figured out who I really am, but she's not telling anyone about that. Instead she's writing down these lies about Louise"—I make air quotes around Louise —"and her behavior towards Mia. Maybe she's telling Harvey that she thinks 'Louise' is obsessed with Mia. Then one day, Mia will disappear, or something terrible will happen to her, and Hannah will point the finger at me, and everyone will find out that I'm not Louise Martin after all,

I'm psycho Claire who hates Hannah's guts! And Hannah will get away with it!"

I drop my face in my hands.

"You really believe that?" April asks after a long silence.

"I don't know," I say between my fingers. "I don't know what to think, but whatever she's trying to do, she's got me in her sights. She's setting me up for something, I'm sure of it."

After a while, she says. "Someone called me asking questions about you."

I snap my head up. "Who?"

"I don't know, but it was a woman. She said she was from the Department of Health and this was their annual survey. She asked me a bunch of innocuous questions, like my full name and address—"

I close my eyes briefly. I can just imagine April answering questions truthfully, as thoroughly as she possibly can. I brace myself for the rest.

"—and how many adults live here. I said two, since technically you still live here. She asked for your full name, then she asked for your occupation—"

"You didn't say I was an influencer, did you?" I blurt out.

"No! I said you worked in a doctor's office. She asked how much time you spend here; I said you live here, but right now you're staying with your cousin in Pittsfield." She shoots me a look.

I look at my hands, pick at the skin around my nails. "Sorry."

"Whatever. She wanted to know how long you'd been gone, what your phone number was, your Social Security number—as if I'd know that! But at that point I said, is

Claire sick? Because her cousin has pneumonia, and they're from the Department of Health, so maybe it's more than just pneumonia—maybe it's a terrible infectious disease, like Ebola or something, and they're trying to isolate it. Maybe you're in quarantine."

I cock my head at her. "Really? You thought that?"

She waves a hand in front of her face. "Anyway, she didn't reply. I mean, she didn't say whether you were sick or not. But then she asked what you look like."

"How long ago was this?"

"I don't know, a week I think, maybe more like ten days. It just didn't sound right. I said to her, what do you care what my roommate looks like? Are you sure you're from the Department of Health? But she hung up on me. So weird. I Googled it, and it turns out that the Department of Health really does do an annual survey. But they're automated. I mean, they don't use real people; it's more like 'press one for this and press two for that.' And they don't ask personal questions."

"Why didn't you tell me?"

"Hello? Are you kidding me right now? I've sent you so many texts, Claire! I left you messages! Either you don't reply, you don't text, or when you do it's like, I'll talk to you later. And when I call your name on the street, you pretend you don't hear me and run away from me!"

"Sorry. I'm sorry. You're right."

I think back to ten days ago. This would be after Diane showed up screaming. After she mentioned the issue with my work form, and after I asked to be paid cash.

"She's known for a while."

"I think you should go to the police. Tell them everything you know."

"I can't do that. She'll deny it. She'll say as far as she's concerned, my name is Louise Martin." I scoff. "It's me who'll get arrested."

"Why won't you just leave? Go back tonight, and tomorrow get your things, leave a note that you're not coming back?"

"Then what's to stop her from hurting her baby tomorrow and say I did it?"

We decide that there's nothing to be done right now, and it's late. Almost four in the morning. But at least, no matter what happens next, April knows and that means the world to me. "You need to find proof," she says. "Take photos of the diary. Document everything you can. Let me know of anything I can do, okay?"

I don't know what I've done to deserve April.

I stay the night there, in my old room. When I leave the next morning, April hugs me and doesn't let go. "You can always come back here. You know that."

"Thank you," I mumble into her hair. She still doesn't let go, and I can safely say this is the longest hug I've had since I was thirteen years old.

TWENTY-SEVEN

I pull my cleaning trolley out of the elevator on the top floor. But whereas normally I'd leave it on the landing like a prop and put it away an hour later, now I look like I've remembered what my job is. Cleaning is what is going to get me into every corner of the house, and not just the bedrooms. Like April said, I need proof. If I could find something that shows she knows who I really am, that would be a start.

It's good timing, too. I'm in the main living room or whatever they call it when Hannah appears in the doorway.

"Louise, when you have a moment, could you take a look along the baseboards here? Harvey noticed it needed vacuuming, and you know how he is around his art. I know you haven't been here long, and I understand it takes a while to get settled in. There's an awful lot to do in this place. Let me know if there's anything I can do to help."

"Sure thing," I say.

She blinks. "Did you have fun last night? I noticed you went out."

"Is that a problem?"

"No, of course not."

"Well, then, I'll get on with the baseboards."

"Thanks. Is everything okay?"

"Everything is fine, thank you."

She nods. "Also, Harvey asked about his shirts. He says they haven't been laundered in a while."

"I am not superhuman, Hannah."

She chuckles as if I'm joking, then she grows serious and cocks her head at me, one hand on her hip, the way she does. "Excuse me?"

"Maybe you could send out for the shirts, and everything else that needs to be laundered. That's what my previous employer did. No one expected me to be the cook, the cleaner, the nanny, and the laundromat all rolled into one."

"Your previous employer did that? Sent the laundry out?"

"Yes."

"Oh, I see. All right, we can do that. That's no problem."

Then I remember something April said. *Just behave as normal. Don't let her think that you know. Just concentrate on finding out what she wants from you. What she's setting you up for.*

I run my hand over my face. "I'm so sorry, I just had a bad night. My mother…"

"Oh, Louise, no! What happened?"

"She's really upset. I was with her." I sigh. "It's back."

Her hand flies to her mouth. "The cancer?" she blurts out.

"Yes."

"I'm so sorry, do you want to take the rest of the day off? Take a couple days if you need to."

I put one hand up. "No, it's fine. Really. I need to get back to work. It's the only thing that will distract me right now."

She looks at me with something like pity, hands laced together. "All right, let me know if there's anything I can do, okay? And of course don't worry about the shirts. I'll get it organized."

She has one foot out the door when she turns around and says, "And when you have a moment, your Social Security number?" And I swear I see the trace of a smile.

I'm woken by Mia crying; it's coming through the receiver next to my head. It's so strident, it jolts me out of bed and I run upstairs in my bare feet.

She's in her crib, her little face purple from screaming. She's kicked her blankets off, and when I put my hand on her head, I find she's burning. I pick her up and walk her, gently bouncing her, but she doesn't calm down. I don't understand why Hannah isn't here. I put her back in the crib, whispering promises—*I'll be right back, I'm not going far, I'll just go and get Mommy*—and tiptoe into Hannah's room and stand next to her bed. I remember then that Harvey is away overnight and it's just Hannah. She has a pillow over her head. For a moment I wonder if she's dead.

I raise a corner. "Hannah?"

"What?" she mumbles.

"It's Mia."

She pulls the pillow off her head but doesn't open her eyes.

"What's wrong?" Her voice is thick, and I wonder if she's been drinking.

"She's got a fever."

I expect her to get up now, but instead she mumbles, "There's some baby Tylenol in the bathroom." She still hasn't opened her eyes, and now she drags the pillow back over her head. I consider pressing down on it with both hands for a few seconds, maybe even a minute, see if that'll get her attention. Then I shake the thought out of my head, because the leap between me thinking of doing something and actually doing it isn't so much a leap as a stumble.

Mia's one-piece sleeper is damp from her sweat. I take it off, change her into a clean diaper and a lighter T-shirt, then I find the thermometer. Her temperature is 100°F exactly. I bring her downstairs to my room so I can look up on my phone whether I should call a doctor or not. I give her some Tylenol, and after some Googling, I decide to wait. I close my door to keep her out of the draft, and we sit on my bed—me leaning against the wall, rocking her slowly in my arms. I try to remember what my mother sang to me when I was little, but nothing comes up. All I can think of is the theme song to *Orange Is the New Black*, so I sing that. Mia watches me with eyes wide open—not even blinking—and just as I decide that is not a good sign, her eyelids close like one of those old-fashioned dolls. Only her little chest is heaving with the aftermath of her sobs.

"You're better now?" I ask. I take her temperature again, but I can tell she's cooled down. 98.5°F. "Okay, that's great."

Every time I stop talking or singing, her eyes open again and her little face crumples, so I keep talking. I ask her what she wants to do when she grows up. I throw out a few options. "Race car driver? Astronaut?" But these are all very dangerous occupations, so I instruct her not to even think about it. Instead I suggest president because they have lots of bodyguards.

Her eyes snap open, and I sense it, too. Like a shift in the air, the flutter of a wing. I turn to the door. The light underneath is interrupted by a dark patch. A shadow. I squint, trying to figure out what it is, and then it moves, making my heart explode.

"Is someone there?" I say. Mia is still warm and fluttery, so I leave her on the bed, one pillow on either side of her. The shape is gone. I open the door slowly and peer outside.

"Is someone there?" I whisper again, my heart pounding behind my ears.

Mia has gone back to sleep, a little bubble of sound popping from her lips. I go out into the corridor and close the door behind me.

I move silently, quickly, and when I get to the bottom of the stairs, I see something, a fleeting shadow. I think I'm going to be sick. I remember Hannah telling me about a night not unlike this one, when she found a lamp left on, even though she could swear it was off. She insisted Diane had been there that night. What if she was right?

I ball my hands into fists as I slowly go up the stairs. I reach Hannah's room without running into any burglars and go inside. She's asleep, or pretending to be, because the covers are different than they were before, like she's thrown them off and put them back on hastily. I'm tempted to pull them off violently, like a magician revealing his assistant who was there all the time, and in one piece.

I bend down and peer at her face. Her mouth is slightly opened, and I feel her breath on my chin.

"What the fuck do you want, Hannah?" I whisper.

. . .

When I get back downstairs I have to rest against the door and let my heart slow down, get my breath back. I check Mia's temperature again; it's down to 98°.

I have some vodka in the drawer, and I'm about to take a swig straight from the bottle, just to calm my nerves, but my eyes fall on Mia and I put the bottle back untouched. I'm pondering whether to take her back upstairs and put her in her own bed or keep her here with me when something catches my eye by the foot of my bed. I crouch down on all fours to pick it up. I turn it around in the palm of my hand. It's a pill, dark red, with the letter *A* followed by a tilde etched onto it. I have no idea where this pill came from, but I'm fairly sure it's not from me, so I guess it might be left over from when Diane was here. I pop it inside an empty candy wrapper and slip it in the top drawer.

TWENTY-EIGHT

I've thought about it all night, and I think I know why she didn't come into my room. She must have come to see about Mia, then realized everything was fine—I was on top of it, so to speak—and she may as well go back to bed before I realized she was there. By the time I came up, it would have been ridiculous and embarrassing to admit any of it.

But this morning I am waiting for her to say something, because Mia slept with me all night, and I barely closed my eyes. She's awake now, back in her crib, and has no temperature anymore. She flashes a happy smile at me and does that thing she does with her hands, lifting them in the air and wriggling her fingers. I grab one hand and kiss it. She laughs. She tastes of milk.

Hannah walks in, still in her silk pajamas, smiling. "Good morning, Louise. Did you sleep well?"

I have to say, I'm impressed. It takes a certain discipline to look so sincere, so totally sure of yourself, even though you know you've been caught. Sometimes I think Hannah is made of steel.

"Not really. Mia was not well, as you know. I stayed up all night with her."

"Oh God, you should have woken me!"

I tilt my head and look at her. "I did, I tried."

"Really? I don't remember. You couldn't have tried very hard. What was wrong with her?"

I squint at her. "She had a fever. You told me to give her some baby Tylenol. I did."

"Oh, thank you. I don't know why I don't remember any of it." She laughs, and I'm thinking, *because you're batshit crazy, I'd say.*

Then later she says, "I'm going out this evening. With Eryn." She puts a hand up. "I know… don't say anything. You don't think I should trust her. But I still don't believe she had anything to do with it. We're having dinner, then we're going to a show. I haven't told anyone else, so if there's a shocking Instagram post of me snorting cocaine tomorrow, I'll know you were right!" she laughs. I just pull my lips away from my teeth in what I hope is an approximation of a smile.

"Anyway, if you're going out this morning, would you get more baby Tylenol from the pharmacy? There wasn't a lot left to begin with."

I manage not to tell her to fuck off, so that's good.

At the pharmacy, I pull out the tablet I found under my bed. I show it to the woman behind the counter, can you tell what this is? I ask. She says she has to get the pharmacist. I drum my fingers on the counter and wait. She then returns with a thin woman in a white lab coat and glasses. I show her the tablet, which she sets down on the counter.

"Where did you get it?" she asks.

"I found it, in my bedroom. I can't remember what it is. Can you tell?"

"Zolpidem Tartrate. Brand name Ambien. Controlled release. You have a prescription for this?"

Ambien. "That's a sleeping tablet, right?" I put my hand out for it, but she doesn't give it back.

"It's a sedative, yes. Was there anything else?"

"No, thank you."

Hannah is having her bath, so I get my phone ready to take a photo and take the notebook out of its hiding place.

I'm on the floor, on my knees, and suddenly I hear her. She's out of the bath and I was so engrossed in what I was reading I forgot to listen. I quickly take photos of the pages and shove the journal back in the cavity. I could walk out, empty-handed, pretend I was tidying something, whatever. I could hide behind the coats. Or I could kill myself, right here and now.

But then I hear the taps again and I know she's back in her bathroom, so I hurry out of the room, my heart clattering, and back in my bedroom, I sit on my bed and check the photos I took.

I'm really, really worried. Last night, I woke up in the middle of the night and went to check on Mia, but as soon as I entered the nursery, I knew something was wrong. I leaned over her crib and she wasn't there. I can never describe what that felt like, seeing the crib empty like that. It's the most frightening thing in the world. I cried out and ran downstairs to wake Louise, and there was Mia, asleep on Louise's bed. I almost fainted with relief. When I asked Louise what she was doing there, she mumbled something about

Mia being sick. *"Why didn't you wake me up?"* Surely I should be woken if Mia is sick. She made up excuses that made no sense, like Mia had a temperature. But when I picked her up, she was fine. Just asleep. I took her out of there immediately because that's the other thing, her room is like a pigsty. I know that technically, it's her room, and I wouldn't want to intrude on her privacy, but this was just too much. Dirty underwear on the floor, I even spotted a bottle of vodka poking out from under the bed. It wouldn't surprise me if it was one of Harvey's.

This morning I woke up woozy and sick. I had a shower cold enough to make my teeth chatter. But it's better than a hot shower, which would leave me even worse, slow and confused. I try not to look at myself in the mirror, but how can I avoid them? There are too many of them. I'm so pale, I'm grey. I have dark rings tinged with purple under my eyes even though I sleep all the time. I know that today is Monday, and that I should check with Louise when my next doctor's appointment is. She said she'd organized it, then I ask her about it and she says she already told me. But she hasn't! Has she? Is it me who's going crazy? She brought me tea again this morning, even though she knows I prefer coffee. But she says I can't have coffee, that's what the doctor said. I don't understand why. And anyway, when did the doctor say that?

I took the cup downstairs and put it in the dishwasher. The coffee machine was almost pulsating to me from the counter. Just one, it said. What harm could one little cup of coffee do? It didn't have to be strong, it would help me focus. I did it, threw caution to the wind. Even just smelling the aroma made my heart flutter, but that's okay. Just little sips. With a bit of luck, I finished it before Louise returned. I know she means well, but I wasn't in the mood to be scolded.

I'm going to tell Dr. Malone when I see her next. She'll know what to do. Because I'm frightened. Really frightened. I don't know *if it's me or her. Is it normal to wake up in terror that your baby is about to—what, be taken? Be sick? Die?*

Maybe she'll think I've got that thing, what is it again? Postpartum... I can't think anymore. My brain, it's not working as it should. If I tell her that I'm scared someone is going to hurt Mia, what will she do? Will she tell someone? Will they take her away from me?

No, surely not. And anyway, Mia is fine. It's me who's turned into a zombie version of myself. It's me who's afraid of the dark, afraid of my own shadow, afraid of the phone ringing. Afraid of a knock on the door.

Afraid of what Louise might do to all of us. Mia, Harvey, me.

Louise wants to hurt all of us. She won't give up until she hurts us all.

I throw my phone on the floor and it lands on a discarded pair of jeans. It doesn't even break.

TWENTY-NINE

That's it. I can't waste any more time. She's crazy. And dangerous. I should have seen this before. I should have done what I set out to do as soon as I got here. Now I think I didn't try hard enough with Harvey. Like an idiot I got caught up in seeing her up close. I wanted her to suffer. I ended up playing stupid games at her expense, like the Instagram post and the scary phone calls. I was being petty, and petty has landed me in deep shit. Now it's me that's being played, but I don't know how or why, and it's scaring me. If she's going to use me to hurt her family, I need something to stop her. I should have tried harder, but that doesn't mean I can't get it done now.

Hannah leaves for her date with Eryn, and I'm on my own. I slip into Harvey's study, quickly assess the room. The best view of the desk is from the shelf behind the door, and that's where I position my cell. I'll get it down as soon as he gets home. There's a photo of Hannah on the desk, in a simple silver frame. She's standing on a beach, her hair blown by the wind. I put it facedown. Upstairs, I check on Mia, then get changed into my special lacy bra

192

and panties—the ones balled up at the back of the drawer —and my black uniform. It used to be tighter on me, but now there's at least an inch of loose fabric around my waist. I unbutton the top, down to below my breasts so there's no misunderstanding this time. I also undo some buttons at the bottom so that when I walk you can see most of my thigh. I wonder what Dominic would say if he saw me like this. Not much, probably—he'd be too busy tearing my clothes off.

What else? Mascara. I'm not used to putting it on, and some of it smudges on the corner of my eyelid, but it gives me a kind of slutty look, so I match it on the other side. I finish the look with a quick swipe of red lipstick.

By the time Harvey comes home, I'm ready. I'm in the kitchen, leaning against the breakfast island. He calls out hello, but I don't reply. He drops his keys on the console table and takes the elevator upstairs. I glance at the video monitor and watch him walk into the nursery. He doesn't stay long, maybe five minutes, then silence. I begin to worry. I won't have another opportunity like this, just Harvey and me alone in the house, and I don't want Hannah to come home and find me dolled up like this. God knows what she'll think. The truth, most likely.

Finally, he comes back downstairs, and I let out a breath of relief. I am already in his office and I set the video to record, then I lean against the wall opposite with both hands behind my back.

He doesn't see me at first. He sets his leather bag on the desk and walks around to his big leather chair.

"Jesus! Louise?" he blurts. He adjusts his glasses.

I smile sweetly, innocently, but not too much. "Hello, Mr. Carter." I walk up to him slowly, making sure to display as much leg as possible. I play with the top buttons of my blouse, but my eyes never leave his, and when I reach him, I place my hand flat on his chest, then take his tie and pull him up, playfully.

"I've been looking forward to this, so much," I whisper.

"What are you doing?"

"You'll see."

We're at the front of his desk now. I know from the sound of his breathing that everything is going to be fine. I get on my knees, already undoing the buckle of his belt. "I've missed you, Mr. Carter. I've been thinking about you. Every night."

"Louise…"

I slowly unzip his pants.

"Louise! Enough," he snaps. He pulls me up and fumbles with his zipper.

I cup my hand over his. "No, don't." I put the tip of my tongue on the side of his neck. I can taste his sweat. "We're going to have so much fun…" I whisper.

"That's enough," he says again. He holds me at arm's length now. "I love my wife."

I let out a laugh, like a bark, and try to get closer to him, but he won't let me. "It has nothing to do with your wife. Or love." This is not going the way I wanted, and I can't let go. I need this moment to happen. I need this on tape. It's my whole fucking plan, right there, and I'm groping for him but he is pushing me away, and there are hands everywhere flapping at each other.

"Come on, let me, I want you," I whine, as if this scene is anything other than pathetic and desperate.

Suddenly he has both hands firmly on my shoulders and he shouts, "Stop!"

So I slap him.

He puts his hand over his cheek, his glasses askew and a stunned look on his face.

I clasp my hand over my mouth. "I—I'm sorry. Oh my God." I start to cry, both hands over my eyes. Great big racking sobs that make my whole body shake.

He pats my shoulder softly. "Come on now. Enough of that." Without meaning to, I start to lean into him. I let myself go and with my face still hidden behind both hands, I rest my forehead against his chest. He smells faintly of aftershave, something spicy and old-fashioned. I have an overwhelming longing to be held.

"It's all right. There's no need to cry. I don't know why you did that, or what happened to you, but it's not like that anymore. You're safe here. You never have to do anything like this. Never. You understand?"

I nod frantically. I'm sorry, I say. I say it over and over. "I'm a terrible person," I cry.

He pats my back. "No, you're not. Don't say that. Never say that, you hear?" It's awkward and warm and reassuring and cringeworthy all at the same time.

I don't know how long we stay like this, but I can't stop crying. He says it's going to be all right. That he understands maybe some people I've worked for have expected this of me, and the world can be a really terrible place sometimes. But I don't need to do this to keep my job, not here and not anywhere else, do I understand? I am not a terrible person, he says, and I'm thinking, how would you know? But I nod into his crisp white shirt. Good, he says. Don't ever forget it. And all I can think is that I don't remember the last time someone was kind to me like this.

THIRTY

I didn't need to ask for his discretion. I knew he wouldn't mention it to Hannah, but I asked anyway. "It's forgotten," he said. Then he added, "Thank you for the great job you're doing with Mia. It hasn't been easy for Hannah. You've been a great help."

By the time I returned to my room to clean myself up, I looked like a sad clown with mascara-stained tears streaking down my face and lipstick all around my mouth. I had to wait until he left his office to retrieve my phone. The thought of him finding it before I had a chance to take it back made me want to crouch in a corner and howl. He'd think that I'd done all this to blackmail him when that couldn't be further from the truth. When he left the house an hour later and I got my phone back, I immediately deleted the video without watching it.

And just like that, my grand plans of revenge and redress are over. I've wasted almost three weeks of my life and I'm even more screwed up now than when I got here. I didn't think that was possible.

. . .

It's now been two days, and both mornings I've woken with the memory of my shame still flaming my cheeks. It overcomes me in random moments and makes my stomach flip. I feel dirty, unworthy. Maybe that's why I've been cleaning like a mad person, pushing the vacuum cleaner until my arms ache. The windows are so clean it's like they're not there. It's helped me avoid him as much as possible—which is the point, let's face it—but once, we both arrived on the landing at the same time and I froze. He gave me a small nod and an amused smile, and a single pat on my shoulder as he passed me, like this was our secret, but it wasn't a heavy one, and it made me want to weep with gratitude.

"We're off to the Hamptons this weekend," Hannah says. She looks awful. Her face is pale, and there's a random shake to her, like she's in the early stages of Parkinson's. But that means I'll have all weekend to turn this place upside down. Whatever it is she's hiding, I'll find it.

"Where to?" I ask.

"Patsy's beach house. Although *castle* would be more accurate." She chuckles.

"That will be nice," I say.

"I hope so." She sighs. "I always feel like I'm trying too hard around his mother. I turn into some demented cheerleader, bouncing around with pom-poms. I gush at everything, and I mean—everything. The whitewashed walls! The pale timber floorboards! The beachy vibe! The dog! And I haven't seen her since the Instagram post, so that's going to be interesting."

"Does she know?"

"No idea. Probably."

"Awkward," I say, because I don't know what else to say.

I help her pack, and by that I mean she tells me what she wants to take and what Harvey wants to take and I fold everything as best I can and put it in the suitcase. She does throw me a funny look at one stage and refolds one of Harvey's shirts. I tell her I have a cold, as if that explains why I don't have a clue how to pack a suitcase properly.

"Do you want to come with us?" she asks. Immediately I wonder if it's because she wants me out of the house. Is she scared of what I might find? Maybe she just wants me to look after Mia while she's there, so she can sun herself on a chaise lounge without the irritations of motherhood.

I chew my fingernail and pretend to think about it. "I don't think so, but thank you. I was thinking of seeing my mother this weekend."

"Oh, Louise, of course. How silly of me."

"That's all right, Hannah." This is the new me. I am very polite and very pliable.

"Could you make some sandwiches for the trip, please? Harvey wants to take a picnic." She rolls her eyes in a friendly-jokey fashion, then asks for ham and mustard on rye. She also wants a little vegetable puree for Mia, kale and sweet potato, in a plastic Tupperware container. I almost say to her, wait, don't you think she's a little young? Shouldn't you talk to a pediatrician first?

In the end, I just do as I'm told. I want them all out of here so I can get on with my own life. Because after this weekend all this will be over, one way or another.

I gather Mia's traveling bag, which is larger and better stocked than anything I've ever traveled with, and load everything into the back of the Bentley. I make sure Mia's car seat is securely clicked in. She puts her chubby fingers on my cheek and laughs. I realize with a start that I might not see her again, and the thought makes my eyes swim.

"I've put your picnic in here, Mr. Carter." I lift the basket to show him. "There's everything you need."

"Picnic? Right. Thank you, Louise. I don't know if we'll have the time for that, but it's very thoughtful of you."

Okay… did I get this wrong? Or is she up to her usual weird games again? I look around for her, but she's still inside. When she comes out, she squeezes my hand and gets in the car. When they drive off I almost wave at them before I catch myself.

I'm inside, I'm on my own, and I'm on a quest. I begin my search with the smaller sitting room she considers an office. Her desk is a narrow antique table with thin drawers. My goal was to break into her laptop, although I didn't hold much hope of success since I have no idea what her password might be. Not that it matters, because there is no laptop—only the power cord, still plugged in, its connector dangling loosely next to a couple of pens and an empty glass. Still, I go through the desk inch by inch, but only find a few invoices and an old auction catalog. The rest of the beige, spartan room doesn't hold anything of interest, and I begin to feel overwhelmed with the conviction I won't find anything, and I won't know what she's trying to do to me until it's too late.

I sit on the last step of the staircase and press the heels of my hands into my eyes. I keep going back to Hannah's diary entries. The lies she wrote about me. How did she find out about me? She must have been in contact with the agency. Maybe she emailed them about me, something about my Social Security number. They would have replied with something like, "We don't know who's in your house, but it's not Louise Martin, so no, you can't have her Social Security number." In which case, that evidence would be on her laptop.

I go up to her bedroom and sit at her dresser. I rummage through her drawers one by one: makeup, hair clip, some costume jewelry. I have a vague feeling of something missing and it takes a few minutes to put my finger on it.

The photograph. There should be a photograph of her and Harvey on a beach. It's always there, to the left of the mirror. I look around for it, but I can't see it. Maybe she took it with her, which seems over the top. They're there together, it's not like she's going to miss him and needs his photo on the pillow next to her.

Then I see her Montblanc pen on the floor near the leg of the dresser. I pick it up and turn it around in my hand, wondering whether I should steal it. She might think she left it behind at the Hamptons. She'd be sorry to lose it, for all her bluster that day, when she interviewed me, pretending she had no idea it was so expensive.

Oh, this old thing? it was a present from my husband, one of many, when I gave birth to our daughter. Sweet, isn't it?

I repeat the words in my mind: ...*when I gave birth to our daughter*. But that makes no sense. If she's only had this pen for four months, how did she use it to write every entry in her diary, dating back almost a year? Because her journal begins with her wedding, and she didn't own the pen then.

In the closet, I pull it out and flip through the pages, back and forth. There's no doubt about it, she wrote every page with this pen. It's the same ink, that unusual aqua shade. *Barbados blue. Pretty, isn't it? I never knew there were so many different shades of blue!*

Hannah wrote all these entries, every single one of them, in the last four months. Or more likely the last three weeks. Either way, she made it look like they spanned ten months. The wedding. Mia. Hannah's gradual descent into some vague, undiagnosed postpartum depression. Then me. All this shit about me. All lies. All of it.

I'm so tense that my jaw aches. In her bathroom I reach for a Xanax, but of course, they're not there. They haven't been there for a while. I close the door but immediately open it again so fast it bounces on its hinges. The bottle of Ambien—it's not there either.

THIRTY-ONE

I hunt through the mess that is my room, my stomach clenched. I pick up crumpled underwear from the floor and throw it on the unmade bed. I lift the mattress, then let it drop with a thud. My foot bumps against an empty bottle under the bed and sends it rolling. I crouch down and peer underneath, but there's only a pair of dusty sneakers and a bus ticket.

It's here, somewhere. I know it is. I turn to my clothes spilling out of the open closet and shove them out of the way. Then I carefully inspect each shelf, running my hands along the top, but nothing jumps out that shouldn't be there. I'm about to give up, but on the very top shelf, my fingers brush against something. I stand on tiptoes and reach farther, feeling the edge of something sharp, metallic. With the tip of my fingers, I pull it toward me. It's the missing photo inside the pretty silver frame. The one of her and Harvey that she keeps on her dresser, but her face is scratched out, like someone has taken the tip of a knife to it.

I sit on the edge of my bed, take the photo out of the

frame and study it closely. It's like her face has been lacerated. Obliterated. It was done with such force that in some places the tip went through and scratched the base of the frame, leaving angry score marks behind. Am I supposed to have done this? Of course I am. This is all part of the setup. I throw the whole thing against the wall and hear the glass crack.

I turn my attention to my own dresser, which is mostly empty. The bottom drawer holds a bottle of Shiraz, half-full, a wrinkled glittery T-shirt I never wear, a bag of chips and a half-eaten candy bar. I kick it closed out of frustration, but it doesn't go all the way in, which I hadn't noticed before, probably because I don't bother closing the drawers. I give it another push, but something is stopping it.

I get down on my knees and pull it out all the way. Then I reach in the cavity. My fingers feel something in the corner. A small square bottle. I know what it is, even before I retrieve it: the bottle of Ambien that used to be in the bathroom upstairs. It contains exactly the same pills as the one I found on the floor, although now it's almost empty.

I close my eyes, press my fingers on my forehead. It's like putting a puzzle together but missing half the pieces.

It's obvious why she's hidden her scratched up photo in my room. At some point, in front of witnesses, she will find it. She will be shocked. She will exclaim, OMG! What is that doing here? Oh boy! My housekeeper sure hates me! But if so, why hide the Ambien in my room, too? And then the words from her journal dance in front of my eyes.

I'll bring you some tea, it will relax you. I was about to say no, her tea always makes me sleep.

It made no sense to me at the time, so I just filed it away as part of the fabric of her lies, a detail she added to make it sound more authentic. But now I see it's more than that: she's always tired, it's her default state. Anyone who knows her will attest to that. Except it's a lie. She's been pretending to be exhausted and, at the same time, sprinkling evidence that I'm feeding her sedatives. All part of the narrative. The Ambien bottle in my room is for the police to find. And I'm so angry I want to punch the wall.

She's not interested in me, she's using me. For all I know, she doesn't care who I am. Maybe she really thinks I'm just some maid called Louise who happens to work in her house. She just wants to make it look like her crazy housekeeper has taken such a dislike to her that she wants to *hurt them all*. But it's her husband and her child that are the target. I'm sure of it. I can feel it. She's going to get rid of them—while miraculously surviving herself, it goes without saying—and she's setting me up to take the fall.

Well, bad luck to you, Hannah Carter, because two can play this game, and I am one step ahead of you. By the time I see you again, you will be begging me to leave you alone.

I call Dominic and he answers on the first ring. I tell him I'm housesitting for a nice couple who have gone away for the weekend. Come on over, I say. It'll be fun. They said to help ourselves to anything we like, I say. Then I take her journal and put it in my small suitcase, along with the photograph, her Montblanc, and the sleeping pills. Later, I will take them to a dumpster somewhere, or an incinerator. Make sure they're pulverized forever. Because if she doesn't have those things, she has nothing.

Dominic comes over. We play dress-up, with me in my maid's uniform. We have great sex pretty much everywhere in the house, including in the hanging egg chair on the top terrace. Now we're lying on the floor of the main living room staring at the clouds on ceiling, smoking a joint and I feel amazing, like everything is sparkling and new again. I take his hand in mine and squeeze it, losing myself in the clouds above and we're like Peter Pan and Wendy, flying through the sky.

"This is some place," he says, taking a drag. He pulls on the joint between his thumb and forefinger, but it's stuck on his bottom lip and it leaves a tiny shred of paper. I kiss it and lift it with my tongue. His lips taste of red wine.

He props himself up on his elbow and gently moves my hair away from my eyes. "Come with me tonight." He begins to fiddle with the buttons of my uniform. "I've got tickets to a party at the Guggenheim."

"Who has a party at the Guggenheim?"

"It's a marketing launch, a new soda brand."

"Soda? Sorry, I'm busy this evening. I'm washing my hair."

He laughs. "They've got an open bar."

"Count me in," I say.

But I have things to do first and the clock is ticking. Half an hour later, I send Dominic on his way with promises to catch up that evening. I'm like a giddy school-girl when I kiss him goodbye, standing on my toes. I'm dizzy and stoned and a little drunk, and I don't care anymore. Everything is going to be okay. After tonight I'll dump Hannah's stuff, her evidence, such as it is, then later I'll call her and arrange to meet somewhere, Dominic's house, maybe, and at last I'll finish what I came here to do.

I put everything back the way it was, more or less, then take a shower and get dressed into my casual clothes—jeans and a T-shirt. I leave the uniform crumpled on the floor. Knowing that I'll never wear it again is like shedding an old skin.

I pull out my suitcase from the shelf and drop it onto

the bed. I'm about to start shoving my few belongings into it when I think I hear voices upstairs. I wait a moment, then lean out the door and into the hallway and listen, my heart pounding behind my ears. Someone closes the front door, and I hear footsteps on the tiled floor.

THIRTY-TWO

Is she back? Already? I hear Mia gurgle and I run up the stairs, but it's Harvey standing on the landing, a suitcase by his feet, holding the car seat with Mia in it.

"Oh my God! Har—I mean, Mr. Carter! You're back so soon? What happened?"

He's about to say something, but his mouth just gapes, distorted and silent.

"What's wrong?"

"Hannah is in the hospital," he says at last. Then he looks down at Mia in the car seat, like he's forgotten she was there. He passes it to me. "I'm sorry, can you take her? Take her upstairs, please?"

So it has begun, whatever fucked-up plan she has in store for me. I didn't know what to expect, but not this, whatever *this* is. Harvey runs a hand back and forth over his bald head. "Look, Louise, I'm sorry, I know it's your day off, but would you…? Mia, just for a few hours. I'll make some calls."

"Of course, I'll stay, don't worry. I'll take her upstairs now."

He nods, his eyes red-rimmed and wet with tears.

The first thing I do is to take Mia out of her clothes and check her body for marks, rashes, cuts, anything that shouldn't be there. I check her temperature. I check the whites of her eyes and inside her mouth. I can't see anything abnormal and I let myself relax. I put her into clean clothes and hold her tight, breathing her in. "If you don't feel well, you just scream for me, okay?" I whisper. Then I wait until she falls asleep, make sure her breathing is normal, and only then do I leave the room.

I find Harvey sitting at the kitchen table with a bottle of white wine and two glasses in front of him.

"Sorry, I need this," he says, pouring himself a glass. "I'm going back to the hospital shortly, otherwise I'd make it a bourbon."

I sit down opposite, the monitor screen by my side. I push the other glass toward him. "May I?"

He nods, fills it up. "They think it's her heart," he says. There's a part of me—the awful part of me—that wants to blurt it out: *They're wrong. She doesn't have one.*

"We'd only just arrived at the beach house. I was parking the car. Hannah said she wasn't feeling well. She got out, complained about chest pains, and then she collapsed. My mother called an ambulance immediately." He closes his eyes, puts both hands over his face, just for a moment.

He takes another swig of wine. "Sorry."

"That's okay. You're doing great."

"They took her to the hospital in Southampton. I've just come from there. She's unconscious. I brought Mia home—I need to get some of her things in a bag and take them to her. Maybe you can help me with that?"

"Of course." I bring the glass to my lips, then change my mind and set it down again. I lean forward, like I'm going to whisper. "Are you positive she's unconscious? I mean, could she be faking it?"

Okay, too fast, definitely too fast. He jerks his head away, and he looks … afraid. He looks afraid of me.

"Look, this is going to be a lot to take in, Harvey—okay if I call you Harvey? Because I know a little about Hannah. No. Scrap that. I know a *lot* about Hannah. There are things you don't know. And I'm about to tell you, and it won't make any sense at first, I know that, but just bear with me, okay? This is really important. Okay? Please? Before we go on, how are you feeling? I mean, physically. Are you in any pain? Are you feeling anything out of the ordinary?" With my chin, I point to his hand around his glass. "I can see you're shaking a bit there. Are these tremors?"

"What the fuck are you talking about?"

I blink a few times and lean back. "Harvey, listen to me. What I'm about to say is going to shock you, but you have to trust me. She's lying."

He narrows his eyes at me. "What are you—"

I lift my hand up. "Whatever she's taken, she knows exactly what she's doing. It's a setup. She will recover, fully. She may even be faking it right now. It would be interesting to know what her vital signs are. I wonder if we could—"

His lips tremble. "Oh, God!"

"I'm afraid that you and Mia will get hurt." I glance at the video screen, quickly checking if she's all right and breathing.

He takes his glasses off and runs two fingers over his eyes.

I stand up quickly, sending the chair bouncing on the floor. "Wait here."

I return with the journal and open it to the first entry, the one about her wedding, the invitation still wedged between the pages. I set it flat on the table and push it under his nose.

"Look, Harvey." I jab a finger on the page. "This is her journal. I found it in her closet. See the ink? That color? That's from the Montblanc you gave her after Mia was born. Except this is about your wedding, and Mia wasn't born yet. And look, all the way through those pages, same thing." I fan through the pages. I'm breathless and I'm speaking too fast, but I'm desperate. I need to get a great deal out in a short time and the words tumble out in a mess. "Here. This is where the lies begin. The ones that I know of, anyway. I'm sure if you read it you'll find some more." I tell him about the tea I never made that makes her tired all the time, I show him the entry about the mythical doctor's appointments I'm supposed to have booked for her, the weird story she tells about me forbidding her coffee. "And it gets worse, wait for it." I lick my thumb and flip through pages until I find the right one. "There." I poke my finger at the page, like I'm trying to stab it. "She wants to tell her psychiatrist that she's afraid of me. I mean, really? She says I'm obsessed with Mia"—we both glance at the monitor—"and I'm going to hurt her or something. And then you, and her. Here, I'm going to hurt all of you apparently." I laugh. "It's all lies, Harvey! I swear to God, I would never, ever hurt Mia. Or anyone, for that matter."

He's looking down at the diary, slowly running his

finger over the page, then turning to another. A vein starts to throb on his temple.

"There's stuff about you, too. Check this out." I quickly flip through pages until I find the entry about putting Mia on solid foods. "She says here that I insisted. Makes no sense. But you know what she said to me that day? That it was *your* idea"—I jab my finger in his direction—"to put Mia on solid foods." I sit back in my chair. "I mean, really? What the fuck, right? It's you, it's me, but the whole time, of course, it's her. She is weaving this great big web of lies and laying down evidence like a trail of crumbs. We're all going to get trapped, Harvey. We're all going to get fucked."

I sit back, breathless, and take a big swig of my glass.

He reaches into his pocket and pulls out a handkerchief, shakes it open, and uses it to clean his glasses. We're both silent for a moment, and all you can hear is the sound of his breath through his nose. He runs his hand over his face.

"Oh, Claire."

THIRTY-THREE

There's a second where the room tilts around me then rights itself again. Harvey is back on the diary, slowly reading the entries.

Maybe I misunderstood. Maybe he didn't say my name. Maybe I'm hearing things that are not there. And who could blame me? I tell myself to breathe. He probably said *Louise*, and in my mind I heard *Claire* because I am all over the place. Still, a flutter of anxiety has settled in the pit of my stomach, and I push my chair back slowly. "I'll check on Mia." But as I walk past, he grabs my arm and digs his fingers into my flesh.

"Harvey! What are you doing?"

"Where did you find this?" He's working his jaw sideways, like he's very angry. Angrier than I've ever seen him.

"I told you. I found it in her closet. There's a compartment at the back, but you know that already. It clicks open when you push the panel. Sort of secret, I guess—can you let me go now?"

Just as I say that, he raises his other hand and hits me across the face. It's so hard, so violent, that it sends my head spinning, and for a blink of time, I black out. I am on the floor. I am on my hands and knees, spit dribbling out of my mouth. My phone has fallen out and is spinning on the tiles right next to my knee. I reach for it, my vision blurry as I desperately work both thumbs to unlock it, but he kicks my hands, sending the phone clattering across the floor. I think I yell out. I don't know. Maybe it's in my head. I look at my throbbing fingers, my shaking hands, and I don't know what to do. Then he grabs a fistful of hair and pulls. I cry out, my hands scrambling blindly to grab hold of his.

"Let me go, just stop doing that! Why are you doing this? Harvey, stop! Stop!"

He bends down, still clutching at my hair. "What's this?" He picks up my cell, studies it, then shows it to me.

The phone is unlocked, and the video I took earlier of Dominic and me is still loaded, although it's not playing. You can see from the frozen still that we're in the office, Harvey's bookshelf clearly visible in the background. If you didn't know better, you'd think it was Harvey in the shot, standing in front of his oak desk and leaning casually against it. You can't see his head, only up to his Adam's apple, but the blue-and-white-striped shirt from Barney's is definitely his, as are the silver square cufflinks.

I'm there, too. On my knees, although you can't see those because of the way the shot is framed. But my head is level with his waist, and I'm looking up at him.

"What the fuck is this?" he asks, sitting down again so that I am now crouched at his feet. He hasn't let go of my hair.

He kicks the chair next to him. "Sit down," he says, releasing me. I'm trying to breathe again. Great big gulps of air hiccupping out of me. I put my hand against my cheek and hoist myself up on the chair. He points an angry finger at my face. "Don't move."

"Why are you doing this to me?" I whine.

He ignores my question, presses the play button.

I don't want to, Mr. Carter. Please don't.

That's me talking. I don't need to see the screen to know that I'm looking up at my boss. My eyes are pleading. So is my voice. You can see clearly the buckle of his belt loosely hanging by the side of his hip—and it is his belt, from his collection—as he unzips his pants right in front of my face.

"Come on," he says—in the video, that is—and his voice is strange, low and hoarse. His other hand comes to rest on the top of my head, pushing it closer. I try to resist —*Please, Mr. Carter, I don't want to*—but he's a lot stronger than I am, and the glint of his gold band catches the light as he pulls my head toward his groin, then all you can hear is a low groan coming from his throat.

Harvey—the one sitting at the table, not the one in the video—is clutching my cellphone so tight that his knuckles have turned white.

"What the fuck is this?" he asks.

"It's—my friend," I say, wiping the snot with the back of my hand. The video is still playing in the background. *Yeah, baby, that's it! Oh yeah … keep going … baby…* Even with everything that's happening right now, it's making me cringe with embarrassment. I half stand to reach for it so I can turn it off, but Harvey slams the table with his hand, making me jump.

"I said, don't move! If you do that again I will hit you, do you understand?"

"Okay, yes, I understand."

"Now. Who is this man, and why is he in my house,

wearing my clothes? Why are you calling him by my name? Is this some kind of setup? You're going to black-mail me with this? You want money? Is that it?"

"No, I can explain—let me explain, okay? It was for Hannah. If I could get her to believe it was you—"

"Why?"

I'm trying to breathe. Trying to gather my thoughts. "I used to know Hannah, before I came here, I mean. She was my little brother's nanny, briefly."

"I know that. I know who you are, Claire Petersen."

"How do you know?"

"You work in my house, what do you think? I did my due diligence. Unlike my stupid wife. What does this have to do with me?"

Unlike my stupid wife. Up until this moment I thought maybe he'd believed everything in the diary. Maybe he thought I was some crazy person out to get his family. Then I thought maybe they're in this together, whatever *this* is, some crazy scam at my expense. But now? I don't know anything anymore.

"Do you know what Hannah did to my family?"

"I just said that!" he snaps. "I know everything there is to know about her, and about you. I'm asking again, what does this have to do with me!"

I take a breath, try to sift some coherent thoughts out of the panic that's engulfed me. "I was going to make a trade. I wanted her to admit it wasn't true, what she'd said about my father. In return I would delete the video."

"You expect me to believe that?"

Slowly, I retrieve a folded piece of paper from my pocket and with shaking hands, open it flat on the table. "I prepared her confession." I slide it across to him. He picks it up and begins to read.

"My name is Hannah Wilson and I am a liar." He turns to me. "What are you, twelve?" He shakes his head, then resumes reading. "Ten years ago, my father and I came up with a scam which worked like this: I would work as a nanny for a very wealthy family, then I would immediately accuse the father of sexual abuse. At this point I would demand to be sent home, and then I would threaten to sue in civil court for millions. We banked on the fact that the family would rather quietly settle out of court than face a scandal. Unfortunately, the Petersens, the family I chose as my target, didn't agree to my demands. Gerald Petersen died of a heart attack as a direct result of the legal and public ordeal, followed shortly after by the death of his wife, Amelia Petersen. Although I was young and under the influence of my father, I acknowledge I am directly responsible for both their deaths. Everything I said about Gerald Petersen's actions was a lie. He never touched me. I made it all up for financial gain."

He folds the piece of paper again and slips it in his shirt pocket.

"I think Hannah would have realized it's not me."

I half shrug. "I wasn't going to show it to anyone. Not even on social media." *I liked you too much to do that to you.* "But she didn't know that. Would she want to see it on YouTube? She'd have to tell the world that the man fucking your housekeeper in your office, wearing your clothes, your cufflinks, your wedding ring, is not you. How would she think your firm, your partners, your clients, would react to the scandal? Would people believe you both, if you swore it wasn't really you? It's pretty clear I'm being coerced—no one would expect you to admit to it. And how long before someone figured out who *she* is? That the wife of the man in the sex tape is none other than Hannah

Wilson, a woman who herself once inserted herself into a respected family, only to accuse the husband of sexual assault. Right in this neighborhood, in fact."

He raises an eyebrow and shakes his head slowly, like he's conceding me the point.

"Nobody gives a shit about your father, Claire. Move on. He was a dirty old man."

I slap my hand down hard on the table. "No, he wasn't! That's not true. He was a decent man, and she tricked him."

"For Christ's sake, grow up. Look it up, do your research. After Hannah's accusation became public, more young girls came forward. It's documented—talk to his lawyer. Your father was a pervert and he'd been fiddling with girls for years. Why do you think your mother killed herself?"

I feel like I'm moving sideways, like I'm going to fall. My mouth is open, but no words come out. I'm staring at him, trying to understand why he would say such a thing.

"It's a lie," I finally manage to say. "And how would you even know that? Did Hannah tell you that?"

"I married Hannah. Do you really think I wouldn't look into her background? Take a look around you. I'm a very rich man. I need to protect myself. I found out about the case and her role in it. Did that bother me? Not really. It has nothing to do with me. I wish she'd told me; I don't know why she would keep it a secret. But at this point it's water under the bridge, as far as I'm concerned." And then he hits me again. A backhander that sends me flying to the floor, my teeth rattling and my mouth filling with blood. "But you have a fucking nerve." He stands above me and bends down, his face inscrutable in a burst of light, and everything goes black.

THIRTY-FOUR

The pain in my head is shocking, blinding. I open my eyes, feel the coarse surface of a rug against my cheek. Light through the bottom of a door. It takes a second for the world to come into focus. I'm on the floor of my own room. My chest hurts as if I've held my breath for too long.

I sit up slowly, notice the blood on my T-shirt. I touch my mouth gingerly and feel the dried blood on my chin. I'm okay, I think. My heart is still hammering as I emerge from the dream I left behind. I was in a big crumbling house. I had Mia in my arms and the floor was full of holes. You could see through below in places, where slats were missing and bits of plaster had fallen off and lay crumbled below. Before taking a step, I'd check the floor with my toe and only move forward if it felt solid enough. But then suddenly my arms were empty and it was Hannah holding Mia. She had her back to me and was a few steps ahead, navigating her way around with the confidence of a tightrope walker. Then there was a loud crack and they fell through in a cloud of gray dust, and I screamed for help. I screamed and screamed but no one came.

The sound of Mia crying erupts through the monitor, and for a moment I think I'm still trapped in the nightmare. I hold on to the bed frame and pull myself up. The side of my waist aches, like I've been kicked. Harvey. Where's Harvey? How did I get in here? I just need to breathe. I try to remember, but all I get are snatches, like flash photographs. I'm on the floor in the kitchen. Harvey panting, dragging me. Pulling me by the arms, jerkily down the few steps that lead to this floor. My limbs too heavy. Then I'm in here, on the rug. I can't move. A loud noise in my brain, like a drill. Then nothing.

I put one hand against the wall to steady myself and look around for my cell, but then I remember. He has it. I try the door. It's locked. That makes no sense because there's no lock on my door, no keyhole, nothing. I put one eye against the gap between the door and the wall, where a sliver of light shines through. About eye level is a break, like a thick black line. Like a bolt that's been drawn across it. Except there is no bolt. Then I remember the drilling sound.

He has locked me up in my own room.

I pull hard on the handle, but it's no use. I slam my fists against the door and call out his name. I kick the door, and all the while Mia is wailing. I sit on the bed, shaking, take the baby monitor in my hands and speak into it, as if that's going to make a difference. *I'm here, sweetie, it's okay, I can hear you, I'll come as soon as I can.*

The sash window behind me opens onto an alleyway that runs between this house and the side of neighboring buildings, with a fire escape running up and down the facades. It has thick steel bars on the outside, but I open it anyway, and a warm gust blows in, bringing with it smells of cooking, curry, whatever—and it's making me even more nauseous. I try the bars and they don't budge. It goes without saying. I could scream for help, but what would that do? He's got all the cards. He'll claim he never knew who I really was, that Hannah hired me in good faith. That he found the diary, Hannah is in the hospital, and he locked me up while he got the cops. That's what I'd say in his position. Then I imagine what the real Louise Martin would say, considering I spent an hour with her, picking her brain. She'll pick me out of a lineup before I have time to say salted caramel mocha.

I pull the sash window back down and put my hands over my ears. I could just turn off the monitor, but I don't want to. Still, it's unbearable.

Two hours later, I'm sitting on my bed, my arms wrapped around my knees, when I hear the bolt being dragged open and Harvey appears at the door.

"How you feeling? You all right?" he asks, as if I had a headache and went to lie down. As if he didn't just punch the daylights out of me. So it's official. He's completely crazy. I stare at him under heavy eyelids.

"Don't just sit there. You can come out now," he says.

"Mia's crying," I say.

He sighs. "No kidding."

I can barely walk, my body sore and bruised. He holds the door of the elevator open for me, but there's no way I'm going in there with him.

"Don't worry, we're just going upstairs to Mia."

"Why? What have you done to her?" I ask, panic rising.

"I haven't done anything to her. I tried to calm her down, but she won't, and I've had enough. I want you to do it."

"Can I have my phone back?" I'm trying it on. A quid pro quo. Will soothe baby for cellphone.

"Don't be ridiculous. Get in, Claire, before I lose my temper again." Then he shoves me inside and walks in behind me. I wedge myself in the farthest corner, my arms crossed over my chest.

In the nursery I peer over the crib, my hand over my mouth because I'm terrified he's done something to her. But Mia sees me and her arms spring out like a wound-up toy that's been released. I pick her up, breathing with relief. I whisper in her ear. *Hey, you, you're very noisy today*. I take her to the changing table where the video monitor is—the transmitter part, with the camera. I pick it up, fiddle with it, make some room to put Mia down while Harvey watches me closely, eyes narrowed.

"How did you know? About me?" I ask.

"That your name isn't Louise Martin? When your work form was returned because of your Social Security number. I asked Hannah to sort it out. She said you asked to be paid in cash. That raised a flag for me. I called the employment agency the next day and they were, how shall I put it … puzzled. 'Mr. Carter, you didn't even interview Louise Martin.' Well! You can imagine my surprise. You must be mistaken, I said. Of course Louise Martin works here, she's my housekeeper. And she said, 'Mr. Carter, we didn't place anyone with you. Your wife told us you found a suitable employee and no longer required our services. Louise Martin never received an interview. She secured another position, but not with you.'"

My hands are red and swollen from where he kicked

me earlier, but I've finally managed to remove Mia's soiled diaper. He wrinkles his nose in disgust. "She stinks," he says. "She's disgusting."

"I'm changing her. It will only take a minute."

"She needs a bath."

I turn to him. "A bath? Now?"

"Look at her. She's filthy."

I lift her up, but I don't see anything unusual. She's not filthy, she just crapped in her diaper. That's what they do. But the way he has turned his head away, his mouth twisted, you'd think she'd been dunked in a bucket of rotting blue cheese.

"Did you hear what I just said?"

"Seriously?" But the looks he gives shows he is serious. "Can you hand me this towel, please? The one hanging on the corner of the crib. That's it."

Christ. I don't know what I'm doing. It's like I'm in one of those hostage movies, where the mailman comes to the door and the hostage has to pretend everything is normal while spelling out *H-E-L-P* with their toe but the mailman just leaves without ever looking down. Then I think, no, wait. This is exactly the situation that I'm in.

"I really thought my *wife*," he says, sneering on the word *wife*, "had engineered this. That for some unknown reason, she had brought an accomplice into my home under the pretense of hiring a housekeeper. Someone"— he looks at me up and down with a degree of contempt —"unvetted. Frankly, I thought you were slow, and a terrible worker. If you didn't improve soon, I would have told Hannah to fire you. But after talking to the agency, I realized there was a lot more to this. I needed to find out who you were, and why my wife had brought you in. Was that why she fired Diane? To make room for you?"

Is he asking me? Of course not. He just wants me to know how clever he is.

We're in the bathroom now; I've run the bath for Mia and I've settled her in it. Harvey puts a towel on the top of the toilet seat and sits down, watching us.

"I drowned a kitten once," he muses. "When I was ten years old. I found it on the terrace behind our summer house. I don't know how it got there. It was all wet and scraggly, and its eyes were shut and full of gunk. It made these little sounds like tiny squeaks. I put my finger under its throat and I could feel its little heart drumming. I took it to the fountain and I put it in the water. It tried to swim away, but it didn't even know how. I turned it around and put the tip of my finger on its pink belly and pressed down. Let's face it, it was going to die anyway. I just wanted to see how hard it was to kill it. Not hard, is the answer to that question, should anyone ask."

I close my eyes for a moment. "You're a very sick man, Harvey Carter."

"Right. Coming from you, that's quite a statement. Meanwhile, if I want your opinion, I'll ask for it." He crosses and uncrosses his legs. "I went to see Diane. She was terribly anxious at first, like a bird that had been caught, all nerves and flutter. She believed I'd come to accuse her of harassing Hannah. Now why would I do that? I asked, and I got the whole story out of her. My favorite bit was the part about Diane meeting a woman called Claire on the day she was fired, a strange woman who took her for a drink at the Pierre—"

"The Plaza."

"The Plaza. Good choice. I like the cocktail bar at the Plaza. Diane explained that said strange woman was now working as my housekeeper under the name of Louise.

When she became aware of that, she came here to warn Hannah about you. Funny Hannah never mentioned it to me, don't you think?"

It's not funny. It's because she's scared of you. I should have seen it before, her reluctance to tell him anything that might provoke a reaction. Hardly ever leaving the house. Not telling him about her past. How many times did she say, *please don't say anything to Harvey*? I put it down to her being a consummate liar. I'm a consummate liar. I recognize the signs. Or so I thought.

"I went to your room," he resumes and wags his finger at me. "You are quite the slob! If I didn't need you, I'd have fired you just for that! It took a while—you don't have any personal things, I noticed. But eventually I found a rent receipt in a pocket, with your real name and your address. I had my secretary make some calls. I already knew about my wife's background. I'm not a fool. But your story is interesting, too, more of the 'riches to rags' variety. Sad, really. It's no surprise you're mentally unstable. And you really have no friends, do you? Just a roommate and some guy who sees you as—what does your generation call it? A pity fuck?" He rubs his knuckles on the side of his chin. "I could kill you and no one would miss you." Then he slaps both hands on his knees like he's on the move, and I flinch.

"And that's when I realized, Hannah has no idea. She really thinks you're Louise Martin. You have some nerve, Claire Petersen. I'll give you that. You do realize I could have reported you for impersonating the real Louise Martin? You could be in jail right now."

"So why didn't you?"

"Because I need you. You're a gift. Straight from the heavens."

I'm about to ask him what he means by that when my cell phone rings with the sound of church bells. *Dominic.* Harvey taps his pocket and pulls it out, and before I have time to think I'm halfway across the bathroom floor, my hand outstretched.

He has his hand out to stop me and I grab it with both hands and bite it so hard I can taste his skin. He cries out in pain and snatches it back. The phone is still ringing, I'm desperately trying to get it when he draws his leg back and kicks me hard in the chest. I stumble backward and lose my balance. I hit my hip bone against the tile, but in my state it's not enough to break my fall and my head hits something hard.

"You're an animal," he hisses, cradling his hand. "I swear to God if you've given me a disease…" The phone stops ringing. I close my eyes, then snap them open again.

"Oh my God, Mia."

I scramble to get to her but he's already there. He snatches a towel from the rack and throws it at me. I hoist myself up on the side of the bathtub. She has her eyes open under the water and I scream her name as I pull her out. But she scrunches up her face, then laughs. I wrap her up, kissing the top of her head softly. I'm finding it hard to breathe.

Harvey is towering above me, still cradling his hand. "You shouldn't have done that, you—" He stops and stares at the floor. "What's this?"

My heart does a somersault. "Baby monitor! Okay?" I snap. I scoop it up. "Jesus, Harvey, what do you care?"

He narrows his eyes at it and for a moment I think he's going to take it from me. He's going to look closer.

"The other one is charging. This one is audio only," I add.

225

"For fuck's sake." He mutters. "Okay, fine. Put a clean diaper on her and put her to bed."

My legs are wobbly as I carry Mia to the changing table, the monitor safely in my hand. "Is Hannah really ill?" I ask. My mouth doesn't work properly and the words come out blurry.

"Hannah? Of course she is. She may even be dead by now." He chuckles. "You should know, you're the one who tried to kill her."

THIRTY-FIVE

He brings me back to my room, his fingers digging into my elbow, and I think he's going to leave me there and lock the door again, but instead he shoves me inside and crosses his arms over his chest.

"Put your uniform on, Claire."

He is standing at the open door. His body is in shadow with the light from the hallway behind him. It's dark outside. "I want my phone."

"Don't be stupid," he says. "I turned it off. Any more calls will go straight to voicemail. Now put on your uniform."

"Why?"

"Because the place is filthy, that's why. You've never done any cleaning, but you still took my money. You've taken me for a fool all this time. You think I wouldn't notice? Well, I did. Party's over. Put on your uniform and get to work."

For a moment I consider arguing because I have done some cleaning. Just lately, in fact. But he's very unstable, so the best thing for me right now is to play his game, one move at a time. I look around the room, finally spot my uniform on the floor in a bundle and pick it up. Harvey is standing at the door, watching me. No. Surely…

"I can't get changed if you're going to just stand there."

He closes the door, and I turn around, pull my T-shirt off over my head and, with some difficulty, put the uniform on. Only when I have buttoned it up do I take off my jeans. I look around the room for something I can use as a weapon, because it's occurred to me, right now, that the video on my phone may have aroused him, and he'd like a repeat performance.

He opens the door again. "Come on," he says. "Get your cleaning trolley and start with the foyer."

I push the cleaning trolley into the elevator. It's too tight for the both of us and the trolley, so he presses the button but doesn't come in with me. When the elevator opens one floor up, he's still walking up the stairs. My eyes fly to the console table where one of the house phones usually is, but it's not there. The wall socket is bare.

He's almost here now, and before he has reached the landing, I've opened the front door wide.

"I will kill her," he says calmly, behind me. "I will kill Mia and tell them it was you. They'll believe me, you know. It's unlikely Hannah will survive. The police will find the diary my wife wrote, they'll read all about her growing unease about you, her eventual conviction that you were a danger to her, to my child, my family. I think I was quite convincing, don't you?"

I close my eyes and ball my hands into tight fists. "You wrote it."

"Obviously."

"They'll know, they'll check it against her handwriting. They'll be able to tell."

"They won't check. Why would they? And if they do, they'll find it's the same. It might not withstand forensic examination, but they won't take it that far. It's more than close enough for our purposes." Then he adds, "It's a bit of a hobby of mine, calligraphy, have I told you? I find it very relaxing."

I am staring out to the street, where people are rushing past. It's dark, but not that late. I could scream right now, and ten people would hear me. I could run, shout, yell out for a cop.

Then his voice again, so close I can feel his breath on the back of my neck.

"The police will figure out all by themselves that your name is Claire Petersen, and that you have held a grudge against my wife for the past ten years. That you have tracked her down and inserted yourself into this house under false pretenses in order to hurt her. By the time I'm done, they'll bring back the electric chair, just for you."

I lower my head and close the door.

I am on my hands and knees polishing the tiles while Harvey watches from a side chair, a straight-backed walnut antique that looks unbelievably uncomfortable, so that's something. He's smoking a cigarette, which I find completely confusing, because it's Hannah who smokes, Hannah who says, *Don't tell Harvey, he'll kill me if he knew*, and yet here he is, picking up a speck of tobacco off the tip of his tongue and flicking ash straight onto the floor I've just cleaned. I'm so tired I could go to sleep right here on the shiny tiles, and we've only just started. But I need to keep him talking. That is the most important thing right now.

"Hannah didn't really have a heart attack, did she? What did you do to her?" I ask.

"You mean, what did *you* do to her."

I sit back on my heels. "Fuck you, Harvey! I didn't do anything to her, and you know it!"

He leans forward, elbows on his knees, hands clasped, and very calmly, he says, "Don't use that tone with me. I won't ask you again."

I'm still feeling the ring in my ears from earlier, and I grit my teeth.

He sits back. "Foxglove," he says, then takes a long drag, blows smoke toward the ceiling.

Foxglove. I know that word. I repeat it in my head, visualize it—*foxglove*. Of course. I read it in one of Hannah's—or should I say Harvey's—diary entries. Something about Hannah showing it to me or something. A very toxic plant, lethal. Except it wasn't me she pointed it out to. It was Harvey.

"You've lost weight," he says, tilting his head as if to see me better. I give him a sly look over my shoulder then go back to wiping the last of the tiles, sweat running down my neck.

"She told you about foxglove," I say.

"Quite amazing, really. It says something about mankind's survival instinct, that children can live happily among toxic poisonous plants such as that and instinctively know not to put it in their mouths. But, yes, you're right, she told me. It causes cardiac glycoside poisoning. It slows the heart right down until it stops completely. We stopped for a picnic on the way to East Hampton, very nice spot, near the golf course. I sent Hannah off to buy a bottle of water—I'd drunk it all you see, silly me—and while she was out of sight, I put the leaves in Hannah's sandwich, and in the tub of puree for Mia. I considered ingesting a little myself, not enough to make me very sick but enough to make it look like you were after all of us, but I'll be honest with you, Claire, I didn't have the courage." He sighs. "Unfortunately, Mia decided to have a tantrum and knocked her puree right out of my hand and onto the grass. Most of it fell out. I would have fed it to her anyway, but there were people nearby who noticed and laughed. Hannah didn't even finish her sandwich because of it. That's why she's still alive."

I stand up, take off my rubber gloves and wipe the sweat off my forehead with the back of my hand. My legs are wobbly, and I have to rest against the wall. "Why are you telling me all this? If I'm supposed to have done it? Aren't you worried I'll tell someone?"

He buries his cigarette butt in the potted green plant. "It doesn't matter. After this is all over, and I'm hoping it will be soon, you will kill yourself. Shall we go upstairs? The furniture needs polishing."

THIRTY-SIX

He's waiting for Hannah to die. That's what he said. And when she does, he'll smother Mia. He admits it like it's no big deal. Just stating the facts. He wishes she'd hurry up.

"What if she doesn't die?" I ask.

"Oh, she will. The only way she lives is if she gets the antidote."

"There's an antidote?"

"Unfortunately."

"But why do you want them dead?" I ask.

"She was going to leave me."

I wait for more, but there is none. I don't know what I expected, but it wasn't that. At the very least I thought his justification would involve some kind of blackmail attempt on Hannah's part.

"Nobody leaves me, Claire. Nobody." He says this forcefully, like it's a really important point and I better remember it. He goes to the bar, pours himself a drink. "I picked up that girl from nowhere and brought her here. I *chose* her. She should have been grateful. And she was, for a while. She was sweet, she adored me. You should have seen her in her tiny apartment baking a gourmet dinner for me…" He stops, like he's lost in his happy memories of Hannah circa 1950s.

Keep him talking.

"What about Mia?"

"What about her? I'm not going to be left with the child after Hannah dies. What would be the point of that? They both have to go."

I close my eyes. He's insane. A dangerous psychopath. There is no trace of emotion in his tone, except for some mild annoyance at the trouble he's being put through.

"You said before I was a gift. What did you mean?" I ask the question like I don't really care, like I'm just making conversation while concentrating on polishing a chest of drawers.

Apparently, until I showed up, his plan was to make it look like Hannah had killed her child, then herself. That was the purpose of the journal entries he wrote before I came along, the ones where she complains of postpartum depression, of confusion, of not coping. "I've been drugging her with Zolpidem."

Which were hidden in the back of my dresser. Nice touch. Then something comes to me, a dream I had, not long ago. I dreamed my father had come to see me; he was in my room and he was holding my hand. It was so strange that when I woke up, for a moment I thought it had really happened. God. I think it really did happen, but it wasn't my father—it was Harvey. I think he'd given me a sleeping pill or two, and he was pressing that bottle of Ambien into my hand so that my fingerprints would be on it.

"Anyone who knows Hannah would vouch for how depressed she'd been," he says now. "How paranoid, too. I made sure of that. I'd tell her I was going away overnight, then I'd come back through the garage and up the elevator, and I would hide out in one of the spare bedrooms on the third floor. She never goes in there. No one does."

"You turned on a lamp once," I say.

"She told you that? Yes, I did. Other things, too. Little things. Enough to make her feel like she was going crazy. I got the idea from an old classic movie: *Gaslight*. Have you seen it?"

I need a moment to process what he just said. He is asking me if I've seen some old movie called *Gaslight*. This is what we are doing now. Okay.

"I can't say that I have, no." *Have you seen Fight Club? Also a classic. Check it out if you haven't already.*

"Anyway," he resumes, "the point was that she'd tell Dr. Malone about these episodes of confusion, and Dr. Malone would testify later that Hannah was losing her mind, although not in those terms."

"So it was you, the night Mia was so ill—you came downstairs and stood outside my door."

"That's right. I did. You can move on from that now. Do the glass cabinet over here. So, yes, that was me, although I didn't *make* Mia ill, that just happened. But where was I? Hannah. Right. You can take an overdose of sleeping pills, you know. People think it doesn't work anymore, but that's not true. If you take enough and you're weak to begin with, you will die. But she'd also have to kill Mia, and that was the risky part. There would be extensive inquiries, as you can imagine. Still, I was prepared to take that risk. But then you came along, and I didn't need to. Once I found out who you were, I'd just have you kill them both."

Maybe it's the adrenaline, I don't know, but I feel some of my strength returning. It comes with a sliver of hope and I begin to think of all the ways I could kick him when he gets close to me again.

Keep him talking.

"I thought Hannah adored you. Why did she want to leave you?"

He sighs. "Who knows? She hadn't met anyone else, so it wasn't that. She simply announced it one day, not very long before you joined us. You should have seen her, she was like a little bird, shaking and frightened. I told her to give us some time, give our marriage a chance. For Mia." He chuckles, then sighs again. "But I suspect it's because... Well. Let's say I have certain tastes. They're not as unusual as one might think. I like to inflict pain. Hannah knew that, but then she turned out to be just like Serena. At first they say they're happy to experiment. They think it's exciting. But then they turn. Serena threatened to take out a restraining order against me. I don't know why I even married her. She never looked at me the way Hannah did. She was too ambitious, too selfish. I would have had to pay an awful lot of cash for her to keep her mouth shut. And I'm not sure she would have."

"So you sent her to London, and now you're paying her off. I found the credit card statements in your office."

He smirks. "Serena isn't in London. I just use her credit card online, or whenever I go there, to make it look like she is."

"What do you mean? Where is she?"

He takes his time, sips his drink, his eyes not leaving mine. Something about the way he's grinning is making my pulse race and my insides turn to water.

"Not far," he says.

I'm glad I did what I did.

Oh God. She's dead. I'm sure of it. He was going to

make it look like Hannah had something to do with it, but then he changed his mind and involved me. He must have forgotten that detail in the diary. *I'm glad I did what I did.* That was back when Hannah was guilty. The room spins around, I'm going to faint. I am on my knees, my head in my hands. Because now I know, without a shadow of a doubt, that I'm not getting out of here alive. And neither is Mia.

"You're insane," I whisper.

"Right. Nicely argued, Claire. Your early education is showing." He wants to say more, but he's interrupted by his cellphone ringing. My breath catches, and our eyes lock.

He raises a finger. "You say one word..." He lets the threat trail off and answers the call.

"Eryn, sweetheart!"

THIRTY-SEVEN

Sweetheart?

He has left the room and closed the door behind him. I turn my gaze to the French doors leading to the balcony. I could go out there, call out … and then what? We're too high up here anyway, and even if I did manage to catch someone's attention, what then?

I position myself behind the door and listen.

"I know, it's shocking…. No, I didn't know she had a heart condition, I'm not sure she did either…. No, don't do that, Eryn, there's no need, really…. I'd rather you didn't. … Of course, sweetheart. No, please don't…. You know I do…. All right…. Me too…. Give me half an hour…. All right, I'll see you then."

I'm back staring out the French doors when he returns, but not before I hear him swear under his breath. *Fuck.*

"Is Eryn in on this?"

"Of course not."

"Of course not," I repeat. "Does she know you beat up women? That you kill them?" I ask, then regret it immediately. But he just gives me a small smile, like we're in a conspiracy together.

"She'll be here in thirty minutes. Let's get you cleaned up," he says.

I am sitting at Hannah's dresser, looking at my face in the mirror. I have a large purple patch near my left cheekbone, like a stain. There's a cut on my bottom lip; it's swollen. My eyelids are puffy and there are dark circles under my eyes.

Harvey is sitting next to me and has me facing him. As he picks up a jar of foundation, he flicks his chin toward the baby monitor on top of the dresser. "You're really fond of Mia, aren't you? You always carry that thing with you, wherever you go. Keep still."

But I can't. I'm so close to him, it's making my body quiver uncontrollably. I couldn't stop if I tried. I can smell a whiff of bourbon on his breath. With a small sponge, he starts to apply the foundation on my face in small circles. I wince, but I keep still as much as I can and let him paint my face, because surely my best shot out of this is Eryn.

"How long has it been going on?" I ask.

"A while."

"Did Hannah tell you that I'd warned her about Eryn after the gala?"

"No, but she told Eryn, and Eryn told me."

He puts down the sponge on a small glass plate and chooses a makeup brush. He opens drawers, checks various items until he finds the face powder and brushes it on my cheeks. Then he selects a lipstick, pale pink, and puts it on my lips. He rubs some of it off with his thumb, and I close my eyes and try not to vomit.

"There was a photo on this dresser before, did you move it?" I don't know why I bother asking, since I already know the answer.

"I might have."

I don't tell him I found it. What would be the point? He'd only ask me to return it, then he'll hide it somewhere else.

"There," he says, taking my chin and admiring his handiwork. "That should do it." And just as he says that, the doorbell rings.

I expect Harvey to go downstairs and open the door, but he stands up and says, "Bring her upstairs to the main living room. I'll be watching you, Claire. If you say anything, anything at all, Mia dies. Do you understand me?" His gaze flicks to the monitor.

There's a narrow pane of thick glass squares on one side of the front door. Eryn has cupped her hands around her face and is looking through it. It makes her look distorted, like she's underwater. Then she rings the bell again.

When I open the door she barely looks at me. She hurries up the stairs and I follow. She wraps her arms around his neck. "Harvey, you all right?" I want to whisper a warning in her ear, *Don't. You'll be next.*

He holds her by the shoulders and smiles sadly. "I'm fine, thank you for coming. It's a terrible time."

She looks at me, then gives him a quick smile, as if to show she understands this is for my benefit, because let's face it, it's not a terrible time at all. It's a fantastic time. If only Hannah could die, then she'd really pull out the party hats.

But maybe Harvey's handiwork wasn't as good as he

thought, because she does a double take and says, "What on earth happened to you?"

"Cl—Louise was terribly upset by the news." He almost said *Claire*. The fact that he corrected himself suggests she doesn't know who I am. "It's been quite a shock for her," he says. "She hasn't stopped crying since she heard. Louise is very fond of Hannah, very protective, as you know. Aren't you, Louise?"

Eryn narrows her eyes at me.

"Would you like a drink?" he says. She nods, and for a moment I think he's going to ask me to do it, but instead he goes to the bar and pours something without asking what she wants.

He's got his back to us, and I'm thinking of whispering in her ear. *Call the police, as soon as you can, tell them he's poisoned his wife, he's going to kill his daughter, tell them to come here right away.* But I don't think she'd do it. She'd think I was crazy. She'd tell Harvey, and whatever plans he has for me, he'd move them forward.

She takes the glass from Harvey and grabs his wrist. "What's this?" She's looking over the bite mark on his hand. My teeth, nice and deep, the sight of which gives me a little jolt of satisfaction, so that's nice.

"What happened?" she asks.

"Nothing." He pulls it away from her and rubs his thumb over it. She doesn't look satisfied, though. She reaches for it again so he says, "Mia. She was just playing."

Eryn clearly thinks that makes no sense—and it doesn't, obviously. Mia has no teeth. Her mouth is the size of his thumbnail. Eryn jerks her head back and frowns. "Mia?" And then, right on cue, Mia begins to whimper. We all stop speaking and listen, but I know that sound, and it's just the beginning.

"She's hungry," I say.

"She'll be fine," Harvey snaps.

"She won't be if she doesn't get fed. There's a bottle ready in the nursery."

Eryn looks from him to me and back again. "So? Go and feed her!" she says. Harvey hesitates, but it would be too strange for him to say, *No, don't feed her. Let her starve.* Eryn would be confused. She'd ask questions, because that's what she's like. But Eryn's goal right now is to be alone with Harvey, and Mia needing to be fed is just the opportunity to do that.

Harvey glances at the monitor that isn't making any sound, then gives a small shake of the head. I am banking on him knowing nothing about what we do with Mia around here. He's never paid attention before, let's face it. He wouldn't know a baby monitor if I smacked him on the head real hard with one. I move to pick it up.

"Leave it. You don't need it," he says. I mumble something about the bottle and leave the room.

I scoop her up. She's a bit warm, but that's because she's got the blanket all wrapped up around her. I loosen it a little, then grab the bottle I prepared earlier and give it to her.

What are we going to do? I whisper. I can hear Eryn laughing one floor up. God, really? With her friend dying in the hospital? She may as well enjoy it, I suppose. She won't be laughing long if she ends up with this creep.

I walk over to the landing with Mia in my arms. I hear them talking, alternating between whispering, silence, then speaking at a normal level, which I suspect is for my benefit. I glance down the stairs and close my eyes. *Do it. Now.* I walk down quickly, silently. I glance at every spot along the way where there should be a phone, but each one has been removed. Mia is looking up at me, her eyes wide, but there's no fear in them.

I am on the second floor, where the kitchen is. The video monitor, the screen, is still on the table, next to the fake journal.

But I've already screwed up. I should have found a way to take the other monitor with me. It's my proof, my life-line, but it's too late now. There won't be another reason for me to be down here. I take the bottle out of Mia's grasp and her little mouth makes an O of surprise. I hold my breath for what comes next as I whisper *Sorry sorry sorry* over and over. She smacks her lips, and I almost laugh. I shove the bottle in the refrigerator and the monitor screen in the cutlery drawer. I snatch the journal from the table. I'm taking too long, but I feel like I've got bionic hearing and even from down here I can pick up the tone of their chatter. And hopefully hear any footsteps where they shouldn't be.

Then I silently hurry down that one last floor and open the front door, slip out, and pull it behind me, bracing against it so it's as quiet as possible, until I feel its gentle, satisfying click against my hip.

THIRTY-EIGHT

It's raining softly. I turn the corner onto Fifth Avenue, doing that walking-but-really-running thing, like a geisha on speed. My face is damp, and I pull the blanket over Mia's head.

This is bad, really bad. I didn't think it through, I just did it. But I don't have a phone, or my wallet, or money. Should I go to the police station? They won't believe me. They'll take me back to Harvey; he'll find a way to explain the bruises on my face. And he would have figured out by now that the audio monitor is in fact a video monitor. He'll know that it's recording everything he has said and done for the past three hours onto an SD card. He might be an absentee father, but he's not stupid.

I reach the bus shelter and look behind me. The M1 bus is almost here. I could plead with the driver. *I lost my wallet. My baby needs to get home. She's tired. Please, sir?* But I catch the glances of passersby. They start with a small smile (oh look, a baby) that immediately becomes suspicious. It's almost ten o'clock at night. My uniform is soiled from cleaning for the last two hours, and it's missing a button. My hands are red and swollen. I have a purple bruise on my knee and another on my forearm, and those are just the visible ones. Take the makeup off my face and I'll look like Mike Tyson on a bad day. I am carrying a baby in my arms, wrapped in a blanket. Underneath that, she's wearing a diaper and a white cotton singlet. That's it.

They're studying me. They're learning my face in case they're asked later for a witness statement. Baby abducted! Can you help with a composite sketch? *Ugly, crap skin, short messy hair the color of compost, uniform too big for her that looks like it could use a wash. I couldn't see the baby, she was wrapped up in a beige blanket.*

But they're not game enough to stop me yet. Mia is blinking and scrunching her eyes as the rain hits her face. I pull the blanket over her head again, but it's too much, too hard, and she starts to cry.

A voice behind me. "Are you all right?"

My heart bounces around in my chest like a pinball. I walk faster without turning around. Someone comes out of a taxi a few feet ahead. I hold Mia tighter and run up to it. I could go to April's. She can pay the driver when I get there. She'll help me figure out what to do next, but someone else goes for the taxi at the same time, a woman in an office suit with a bag over her shoulder and a cell in her hand and we're both at the door, our hands almost touching.

Please.

Her gaze shifts, and she stares at a spot behind me, just as I feel a hand on my elbow.

"Sweetheart. There you are."

I lock eyes with her, try to plead silently for her help. She doesn't know it, but I've wet myself. She looks back at me, then at Harvey. She's not sure, but she doesn't want to get involved. I try to think of all the things I could say to her in this moment, but all I can think of is, *Take the baby.* Then I lean close to her ear and whisper. "Call the hospital, Stony Brook Southampton. Hannah Carter. Tell them it's foxglove."

I wanted to say more. *Ask them to send the police to Hannah Carter's house.* But Harvey has already yanked me away. "Come home, sweetheart. We can discuss it there. You'll catch cold out here." He turns to the woman and with a small, resigned sigh he says, "I need to get her home…"

The woman is frowning at me, then she shakes her head and moves on. Like she couldn't care less. Like this is too hard, and all I can think is, *we are all going to die* and something inside me wonders if this is a song and how come I can't remember.

Harvey grabbed Mia from me and he's holding her roughly with one arm. With the other he pushes me inside and I trip on the tiles.

"What did you say to her?" he bellows over Mia's cries. The notebook falls to the floor and he scoops it up, holds it up, like he's trying to understand what it's doing there.

"I told you already," I wail. "I asked her to take Mia away!"

He yanks me up and drags me up the stairs to the next landing, where Eryn stands, arms crossed, her face a mixture of triumph and disgust. And I know, before she says it, that she's finally remembered.

"Her name is Claire Petersen!" she says. "She knows Hannah—" But I don't hear the rest because he hands Mia over to her and she disappears upstairs. I yell at her to keep her safe and Harvey drags me back into the living room.

"Shut up!" he hisses, his face inches from mine.

I nod and wipe the snot off my face with my sleeve. He throws the notebook on the coffee table. It slides off and lands on the floor. My eyes dart around for the baby monitor, but it's gone and I am overwhelmed with a wave of despair. It's all I had, and he found it. He figured it out, and now it's gone, and nobody will ever believe me. I have nothing. *We're all going to die.*

Then a loud noise. Someone is pounding the front door.

"Stay there," Harvey snaps, but you can already hear them running up the stairs. Eryn still has Mia in her arms as she leads them inside and points at me.

"There she is! Get her! Shoot her! Her name is Claire Petersen and she tried to steal the baby!"

Cops, guns drawn, and it's pandemonium. "Are you Claire Petersen?" someone shouts at me. Harvey is saying that I tried to kill Mia. I'm under arrest, someone tells me I have the right to remain silent, but I don't hear the rest because Harvey picks up the notebook from the floor and hands it to a policeman. "My wife's diary," he says, jabbing his finger on top of it. "Take it. It's all in there."

I'm yelling that it's a lie, that he wrote it all because he's trying to kill his wife, but I know it's hopeless and someone has put handcuffs on me and already I'm being dragged away. Mia is crying and my heart is breaking because surely, I will never see her again, never hold her, never console her. She is gone from my life and I don't even know if I kept her safe. I turn to Eryn, tears and snot streaming down my face. "Don't give Mia back to him, please. He will hurt her."

But as I'm being dragged past the coffee table I almost trip on something. The video monitor. It's on the floor; it must have fallen when Harvey pushed me down. I turn to the policewoman who is holding my arm and yell out. "Pick it up, now! I recorded everything! It's on the SD card!" And everyone stops talking except me. I'm yelling, telling them where the screen is, I'm begging them to go and get it so they can watch everything that's been happening for the last three hours. I say all this over and over and then Harvey is in my face, shouting that I'm a liar, that I have come here to hurt his wife and it's all in the diary, but I can see in his eyes that he's not sure what's happening. And I know, right then, he never guessed about the monitor. That thing has been with us all afternoon, silent as a fucking stone, and he never caught on, and suddenly someone has returned with the video screen.

"But why do you want them dead?"

"She was going to leave me. Nobody leaves me, Claire. Nobody."

Harvey's eyes are wild with panic, and he knows it's over. In an instant he has grabbed Mia from Eryn and hurled himself at the French doors leading to the terrace. He has hoisted himself onto the brick wall with Mia in his arms.

"Oh my God. Stop him, somebody stop him!"

The policewoman lets go and I run to the terrace. Harvey has turned around and I am on my knees in front of him, my hands, still in their handcuffs, outstretched to him. I'm so close I could touch his feet.

Harvey. Please, don't. I beg you.

All the cops have their guns out and trained on him, but they can't shoot, can they? If they kill him, he and Mia will fall. He looks around, then stares down at me with a look of pure hatred.

"Give her to me, please, Harvey."

"Fuck you." Then he holds up Mia under her arms and I watch his whole body begin to lean backwards.

"*No!*" And it's like watching the end of the world in slow motion. My scream is so loud, so piercing that I feel it slice my chest. I've leapt up and grabbed Mia's ankle with both hands just as his whole body loses its balance. There's a surprised look on his face for that split second when he still wants to hold on but it's too late, and there's panic in his eyes. He instinctively lets go and spreads his arms out, as if he could fly, as if he could undo it all.

THIRTY-NINE

I expected Hannah to be hooked up to machines and fed by tubes, but she's sitting up in bed idly watching TV, looking better than I've ever seen her, with Mia asleep in a crib by her bed.

She looks up and there's a moment where her eyes narrow, like she's angry with me, but then her features relax and I don't know if I've imagined it.

"Can I come in?"

She doesn't reply, just looks at me as if she's considering it, and I think this is a mistake. I shouldn't have come. But then she says, "Sure. Come in."

"So, how are you?" I ask after I've brought the chair closer to her. "You look well."

"I trusted you," she says, her eyes not leaving mine.

"I know. I'm sorry."

"I thought you were my friend."

I tilt my head at her. "Did you? Really?"

"Yes!" she snaps, then slaps the top of her bed with the palm of her hand, although since it's a soft cover, the effect is non-existent. But then a nurse appears at the door.

"Everything all right in here?"

"Yes," we reply in unison. The nurse leaves and I get up to close the door. When I return to my chair, I bring it even closer and lean forward.

"Look, I'm sorry. I really am. I lied to you, but you have to understand, I really did think you were…"

"What?"

"I don't know! Some kind of scheming, lying, a fraud, a con—"

She puts her hand up. "Seriously?"

"Yes, seriously. What do you think? Everything that happened back then, it ruined my life, Hannah!"

"But that's not my fault!"

We're both silent for a moment.

"I didn't lie, about your father," she says. Words that days earlier would have sent me into a fit of rage.

I shake my head. "I don't want to talk about that right now."

She gives me a quick nod. I want to tell her it's because I have a call still to make, I need to talk to my father's lawyer, but it's too soon for that conversation.

"I'm sorry, Hannah, that I went into your house like this. I'm sorry about all of it." Suddenly I can't stop talking. Maybe I want absolution, I don't know. But I tell her everything. About seeing her that day at the hair salon. How I stalked her and met Diane. I tell her about the rat, about the threatening calls. What I'd said to Diane when she stormed into the house, trying to warn Hannah about me. She's staring at her hands, which are picking at the blanket. Only when I get to the Instagram post does she look up.

"That was you?"

I nod. I tell her about Dominic and the lies I told him

to make him take the photo. I tell her about the dress, and when I run out of things to say, I tell her about finding the notebook.

"He really did play us both," she says. She tells me the police examined it for fingerprints. They found plenty of mine, lots and lots of Harvey's, but not a single print belonging to her.

Then she reaches for my hand. "I know what you did. I know I should be thanking you, not berating you. Sorry." She gives a small laugh, but her eyes have filled with tears and I take a deep breath.

As soon as the doctors realized it was a case of foxglove poisoning, or cardiac glycoside toxicity, they were able to save her. The woman I spoke to on the street, she did call the hospital, incredibly. And Hannah recovered fully, which frankly was nothing short of miraculous considering how sick she was.

We talk some more, about what Harvey was like, what he did to her. He liked to burn her breasts with cigarettes if he thought she'd been smoking. I remember the mark on her chest the day of the dress. I recall with burning shame how shaken she was the day of the Instagram post, when she asked me to go with her and Mia to the park. I think of all the things she wouldn't tell him, like the fact she'd been involved in a scandal years before.

"What will you do now?" I ask.

We both turn to look at Mia. "I haven't decided. My mother wants me to go back to Canada, but honestly, I don't think I could bear it." She sighs. "I can't go back to the house, obviously."

"No. Of course not." Then before I realize what I'm saying, it's too late. The words are already out.

"You could come and stay with me and April if you

like. You two could have my room, I can stay on the couch."

"Really?"

It's funny, but I have no regret about blurting it out. I only hope that she will say yes. The thought of having Mia around for days or even weeks fills me with a strange emotion. I don't dare name it out loud, so I whisper it to myself. *Joy*.

"Shouldn't you ask April first?"

I laugh. "Yes, you're right, I should. But she'll say yes. Trust me, April is something else. She's on the angelic end of the spectrum."

We talk some more about the events of the last few weeks, and then she asks, "What about you? What are your plans?"

I tell her I don't know yet. I have to deal with the fallout of all this. The cops want to interview me again. They're going to want to know how I came to be a house-keeper called Louise Martin if my name is Claire Petersen.

"I've managed to put that one off, for now, because I had to get a lawyer. April is going to help me out. Apparently impersonating someone is a criminal offense in some circumstances."

"I haven't told them anything," she says. "I mean, I haven't told them about hiring you or anything. We haven't gotten to that part yet. Maybe I could tell them I knew who you were?"

"What do you mean?"

"What if I said that we ran into each other? The day you saw me at the salon? I told you about Harvey. I'll say we concocted this subterfuge so you would go and work for me and see what could be done to help me."

I think about this, try to understand. "What about Louise Martin?" I ask.

"I'll say it was for Harvey's benefit. In case he checked you out. We only used Louise Martin's name to fool him. We'll have to apologize about that part, especially to the real Louise Martin."

I tilt my head at her. "You would do that for me? After everything I've done to you?"

She pulls herself up higher against the bedrest and stares at me like I've got two heads.

"You saved my child's life! I was angry with you, yes, because you have to understand, the whole time you were in that house with me, I thought you were going to help us. I could tell how much you loved Mia. I was building up to telling you what it was like, what Harvey was like. How frightened I was. Because I didn't know if he'd let us go and that's the truth. I needed a friend to confide in and I didn't think Eryn was it. But I thought you were. I thought you were going to save us."

I drop my head. I don't know if I can take another round of hearing how screwed up I am, but then she says, "And you did, save us. The police told me everything. Your bravery?" She shakes her head. "I don't even have the words. When I think of everything that went on in that house when you were alone with Harvey—you could have run away and saved yourself, but you stayed for Mia. And even right at the end—" She stops with a sharp intake of breath. "Mia would be dead without you," she says simply, then squeezes my hand. "As I would. You did save us, Claire. I owe you everything."

FORTY

I'm sitting on a chair. It's made of dark plastic supported by a steel frame. It's not very comfortable, but I don't mind. I'm at the back of the auditorium looking down at Professor Caldwell. The class is Ethics and Society, and she's talking about euthanasia and the idea of personal identity and persistence. "What does it take for a person to persist from one time to another—to continue existing rather than cease to exist?" she asks. Good fucking question, I think. I was in the shower the other day, and it dawned on me I hadn't thought of Harvey or my parents in literally days. Considering it's been close to a year and a half, and it used to be that I couldn't go for an hour without thinking about one or all of them—I count that moment in the shower as a revelation. It was like being on a raft and seeing land for the first time in years.

Harvey turned out to be an even bigger monster than we thought possible. When no one was able to locate Serena, the police feared he must have killed her. We all did. There was only one clue. *Not far.* That's what he said on the video when I asked where she was. The police asked

254

Hannah about the places Serena could be. Was there a house in the country, maybe? Somewhere with a garden where he could have buried her?

Hannah told me it was the words *buried her*, and also the fact that she'd disappeared not long before Hannah had moved into Harvey's house. She said she dropped her head into her hands because she was going to faint. She knew then. She'd figured it out.

"Harvey put in a gym downstairs. Just for me. There was even a new concrete floor poured in."

And that's where they found Serena, dead from a sharp blow to the head, wrapped in layers and layers of thick black plastic. Harvey had loosely laid a layer of timber over her, and a tradesman had come and poured concrete, not realizing what was beneath. Sometimes I think it's not just Hannah and Mia whose lives were saved when he died. It's all the other women he would have tortured and killed after that.

I don't know if I believed Harvey when he talked about my father and the other women who had come forward. But later I thought back on the day my father's lawyer came over to see my mother. My father had just died, and they locked themselves up in the living room and stayed there for hours. Shortly after, my mother instructed him to sell all our belongings and told us children that she had to pay out his clients because of some financial mess he'd gotten himself into.

I went to see that lawyer, and I asked him about that day. He sat with his hands clasped together on his desk and a look of pity in his eyes. It wasn't the clients that were paid off, he said. There was nothing wrong with my father's company or the way he administered his finances.

It was his other victims. They were the ones whose silence was purchased.

"What if they'd lied?" I asked. "Once a scandal like that happens, lots of other people want to cash in, surely."

But in a cruel twist of irony, he had filmed some of his victims with a small spy camera hidden in the office bathrooms. A secretary had found it, and she'd confronted him. When Hannah came forward and it looked like it was her word against his, and his was louder and more convincing, other victims, the secretary included, decided to speak up. But then he died. They still spoke up, only because they wanted to set the record straight, and they had proof. Video is what saved me and it's what incriminated him. I understand that in the end, my mother's offer was too good to refuse.

Then there's Eryn. I saw her once more since that terrible day. It was her who called the police after I walked out with Mia. She told me that when the two of them realized I'd gone and taken Mia with me, Harvey started shouting my name, accompanied by lots of swearing, obviously. Eryn clicked then. *Claire… Claire Petersen! Groton School!* Harvey had run out into the street looking for me and left Eryn behind. He didn't know she'd called the police, thinking that would be helpful. *There's a woman called Claire Petersen who stole a child, this is the address.* I honestly don't know what would have happened if she hadn't done that. I know that Hannah was already on the antidote at that point, but I'm not sure I would have lived long enough to see her recover.

Eryn and I had a drink at a bar, where we hugged awkwardly. I thanked her for calling the police, and she chuckled. "Honestly, Claire, when I realized it was you, I nearly died. I thought you were going to do something criminal and despicable. So just saying, I wasn't trying to help you." She smiled. Then she said something strange. She went back to that day at Philippa Davenport's birthday party.

"No, don't," I said, putting up my hand.

She took it, put it back down. "Listen," she said. Then she told me how awful it was for everyone that day. That she tried to find me, but I'd already left.

I cocked my head at her. "You were laughing, like all the others," I said. "Not that it matters anymore."

"Nobody laughed, Claire. But you left immediately with your mother and I never saw you again. But nobody laughed. I swear to God. Why would we?"

Did I even remember that day as it really happened? Or was it another construct of mine? I don't know anymore. Maybe she's telling the truth, maybe not. And it doesn't matter now anyway. We left with the same awkward embrace and promised to catch up soon, then she emailed me to say she and her fiancé, Carlos, were moving to Puerto Rico and she wished me well.

It was Dominic who suggested I enroll in college. I laughed. People like me don't go to college. We're too damaged, too stupid. Irretrievable. But he told me not to knock it—that's what he said, don't knock it—so I looked into it, the way you might through your fingers, because everyone deserves another chance. That's what my therapist said. Even me? I asked. Especially you, she replied. I wasn't sure about the *especially*.

So now I'm in my first year of Social and Public Policy at NYU. It might seem like an odd choice, but I hope that it will lead me to a law degree eventually. Because it's true that everyone deserves another chance. I've lived that truth. You wouldn't recognize me if you saw me today. I'm a different person—on the outside, anyway. And on the inside, too. I work out every day. I run every morning, two miles minimum. I'm fast, too. I love it. My body loves it. I'm strong, I'm fit. I'm happy, I think. Most of the time, anyway. And, hey, I try not to lie! I seem to be managing it. Lies were a tapestry for me to hide behind. The more lies, the better. When I said that to my therapist, she said, "Hide from what?"

Loneliness. Being abandoned. Knowing that you're unworthy, unlovable.

Why would you think that? she asked.

Because they left me. All of them. My family, my friends, everyone. My mother especially. Who does that? Dies like that? Gives up, knowing that she's leaving two children behind who'll never be right again? But if you're an awful person who lies and steals and hates the world and the world hates you back, well, then, it all makes sense. *Of course they left you, Claire! Look at you! You're a horrible person! What did you think would happen?*

I used to think that if Hannah suffered as much as I did, then it would go some way to right the wrong, as if the world was one massive ledger with credit and debit columns. But I've learned a lot since then about what illness does to people, and I understand a lot more about what my mother went through than I did then. She needed help, but no one could do it. It's finding the courage to help people that's the hard part.

Like Dominic. He has more courage in his little finger than I'll ever possess. I don't know why, but he stuck by me even after I told him the truth, that Hannah had no idea who I was. I really wanted to harm her. I think he helped me find the better part of myself that I'd buried away. We live together in a two-bedroom apartment in Greenwood, a lovely small neighborhood in Brooklyn. He's busier than ever with his photo work. Me, when I'm not studying, I work part-time in a childcare center as an office assistant. I volunteer also, at a place near here that supports youth at risk. My job is to help them with homework and writing. I've never been so busy in my life, ever.

Hannah was awarded a lot of money. She could live anywhere, but for now they still live with April. They even started a business together: One Petal at a Time. I told them, no, you can't. That's a terrible name. But they just laughed, and I guess they had every reason to because they're doing really well. It's a gardening center in the West Village with a focus on kids' education. I see Mia most days because, of course, she comes to the childcare center. Where else would she go? Hannah or April will drop her off and I will be there, waiting at the gate, always. I pick her up and I lift her in my arms and she laughs, her little hands opening and closing, her fingers grabbing my cheeks. I am in love with her and she is the purest joy of my life.

Dominic and I are having a baby, and April will be its godmother. Well, not right now; we've only just found out and we're not even telling anyone yet, although I did tell my brother. We speak often now, John and I. It wasn't easy to reconnect; we had to get to know each other again. He told me things I didn't even remember, like all the times I'd call him late at night, drunk, shouting like a lunatic. "I don't need to know, thanks all the same," I said. He lives in Colorado in a charming house, with his partner and their baby boy.

Dominic is going to be a wonderful father. He's already mapped out his schedule for the first two years of our child's existence, which made me laugh. He's starting to tell his clients he won't have much time then, because I'll be studying still and he'll need to take care of a very important person.

Professor Caldwell ends the class and I gather my books, but the question still remains. What does it take for a person to persist from one time to another—to continue existing rather than cease to exist? Once upon a time I would have said loathing. That's how you keep someone alive. You keep them in your head and you hate them till you can't stand it anymore and still you gnaw at them and watch them grow. But now I don't know, and I don't care. I'm done with all that. I'm blessed with the people I love. I'm one of the lucky ones.

ACKNOWLEDGMENTS

As always, there are a number of people who generously help me produce a better book, and this one is no exception.

Thank you to Traci Finlay, my wonderful editor whose brilliant suggestions always send me on the right track.

Thank you also to the very patient Mark Freyberg, for answering my many questions on all things legal.

Thank you to Eliza Dee for her fabulous proofreading.

Thank you to my wonderful friends and family who always cheer me on, and to my husband, who is always there for me and reads all my books and never blinks at how many husbands get killed off in them.

Thank you, dear reader, for getting this far, it means the world.

Made in United States
Troutdale, OR
09/14/2023